Jack P9-DGM-912

When Bond had struggled with the guard for possession of the Palm Pilot, he had deftly managed to activate the timer for the built-in explosive. The problem was that he didn't know exactly how long he had set it for. . . .

"I have yet to see how my mosquitoes will feed upon human beings," Aida said. "So far we have used only laboratory animals for testing purposes. This will be a treat." As a smile played upon his lips, Aida commanded, "Open the inner door."

The technician reached for the control, but at that moment, the Palm Pilot exploded . . .

ALSO BY RAYMOND BENSON

THE JAMES BOND BEDSIDE COMPANION

ZERO MINUS TEN

TOMORROW NEVER DIES
(based on the screenplay by Bruce Feirstein)

THE FACTS OF DEATH

HIGH TIME TO KILL

THE WORLD IS NOT ENOUGH
*(based on the screenplay by Neal Purvis,
Robert Wade and Bruce Feirstein)*

DOUBLESHOT

NEVER DREAM OF DYING

THE MAN WITH
THE RED TATTOO

Raymond Benson

JOVE BOOKS, NEW YORK

This is a work of fiction. Names, characters, places, and incidents either are the product of the author's imagination or are used fictitiously, and any resemblance to actual persons, living or dead, business establishments, events, or locales is entirely coincidental.

THE MAN WITH THE RED TATTOO

A Jove Book / published by arrangment with
Ian Fleming (Glidrose) Publications Ltd.

PRINTING HISTORY
G. P. Putnam's Sons hardcover edition / June 2002
Jove edition / May 2003

ISBN: 0-515-13563-1

A JOVE BOOK®
Jove Books are published by The Berkley Publishing Group,
a division of Penguin Group (USA) Inc.,
375 Hudson Street, New York, New York 10014.
JOVE and the "J" design
are trademarks belonging to Penguin Group (USA) Inc.

PRINTED IN THE UNITED STATES OF AMERICA

10 9 8 7 6 5 4 3 2 1

For Judy

Acknowledgments

The author and publishers would like to thank the following individuals and organisations for their help in the preparation of this book:

In the U.S. and Canada
Paul Baack
Claude Berman
Tom Colgan
Contra Costa Mosquito and Vector Control District (Concord, California): Steve Schutz
John Heaton
Imperial Hotel Tokyo (Chicago): Walter Hladko
Japan Airlines (Chicago): Yasuharu Noda, Toshinara Akita, and Otoya Yurugi
Japan National Tourist Organization (Chicago): Yasutake Tsukamoto, Masahiro Iwatsuki, Risa Sekiguchi, and John Ventrella
Lawrence Keller
Prince Hotels Japan (Chicago): Yasuko Machida-Chang
Doug Redenius
David Reinhardt
My wife, Randi, and my son, Max

In Japan

Hamaya, Kazuhiro Horiba, Masahiro Ichijo, Mitsugu
Tamai, and Hiroshi Inayama
Takanawa Prince Hotel/Sakura Tower (Tokyo):
Yusuke Watanabe, Kajiwara Satoshi, and Hiroshi
Moriyama
Tokyo Convention and Visitors Bureau: Naotaka
Odake, Yasuyuki Yabuki, Yuka Takahashi, and
Koichi Hagiwara
Yayoi Torikai
Akiko Wakabayashi

In the U.K.

Carolyn Caughey
Hillingdon and Uxbridge Coroner's Office: Bob
Greenwell
Ian Fleming (Glidrose) Publications Ltd.
And as always, the Heirs of Ian Lancaster Fleming

A special thank-you to the Japan National Tourist Organization for its generous contributions to the making of
this book, and to James McMahon for being my
"Richard Hughes" while in Japan.

Contents

1

Final Flight

What was that high-pitched buzz in her ear? she wondered as a wave of nausea swept over her once again.

An hour ago she had been fine. Now Kyoko McMahon felt weak and chilled, and she had an agonising headache that pounded through her skull.

The Japan Airlines flight had left Narita Airport two hours earlier and wouldn't reach London for another ten hours. Would she be able to stand it? She felt woozy and disoriented. All she wanted was to stop the world from spinning around her.

Kyoko dismissed the idea that the food Shizuka had served at their mother's birthday party was to blame. Her sister, like all her family, was meticulous in everything she did, and her careful preparation could be trusted. Come to think of it, her father had complained of a stomach ache at breakfast, and her mother had barely made it out of bed to say good-bye to her that morning. Perhaps they had drunk too much of the excellent Ginjo sake the night before.

Feeling ill on an aeroplane was never fun. The pretty twenty-two-year-old half-Japanese, half-Scottish woman was thankful that she was nearly alone on the upper-deck executive-class cabin of the aircraft. Not many travellers were aboard today. There was only the businessman sitting two rows in front of her, and the two other men were three rows behind her. Not that she needed more room. The business-class seats on JAL's 747 were luxurious: plenty of leg room, reclining and with a personal television monitor that provided a wide choice of movies. As a member of the successful McMahon family, Kyoko took business-class travel as her right whenever she made the long flight from London back home to Japan.

This trip had been for a special occasion—her mother Junko's fiftieth birthday. Her father had organised a party of the immediate family. Shizuka, the elder sister, had ensured that the banquet was appropriately elegant and delicious. It was a shame, thought the younger and more beautiful Kyoko, that Shizuka would probably never find a husband who would benefit from her accomplishments.

Kyoko had flown to Tokyo to surprise her mother. It had been a wonderful dinner party and a loving reunion. But in the middle of the family toasts and celebration, Junko could not forget her youngest child and said quietly, "I wish Mayumi was here." Nobody could speak and they all sat silent for a moment, remembering the lovely and vivacious girl who had disappeared from their lives.

"Are you feeling all right?" the young flight attendant asked her.

Kyoko moaned, "Not really. I don't know what's wrong. I feel ill."

The flight attendant felt Kyoko's forehead and said, "You're burning up. I'm not supposed to do this, but I'll give you some aspirin. All right?"

Kyoko closed her eyes and tried to smile in acknowledgement. The woman left her side, and Kyoko's mind drifted back to the previous evening's festivities.

Her father, Peter McMahon, had made a short, affectionate speech declaring his love for his wife, causing

Junko to blush. Kyoko had thought it was sweet. Even in manners-conscious Japan, her parents had never felt that they should hide their affection for each other. It was her father's devotion to her mother that had convinced him to move permanently to Japan, learn the language and raise a family there so many years ago. Even though he had always kept his British citizenship, Peter McMahon had wholeheartedly embraced Japanese culture and integrated himself into it. CureLab Inc., the company he ran, was hugely successful. He had rescued it from bankruptcy after Junko's father, the company's founder, had retired. With Peter McMahon at the helm, the struggling pharmaceutical company Fujimoto Lab Inc. became the front-running CureLab in just eight years. The McMahons had become wealthy as a result. The *gaijin* who had married into a long-established Japanese family had gained respect in a world where business was made up of inner circles and closed networks. Kyoko could appreciate the hardships her father had gone through as a foreigner. She knew what discrimination foreigners could face in Japan when they attempted to squeeze into society. There was an old adage that a foreigner in Japan was "a friend after five minutes but still an outsider after twenty years." For someone who was half-Japanese it was even worse. It was one reason why she had chosen to study business at Oxford, her father's alma mater. There she was treated as an exotic and mysterious Eurasian, not as a "half-breed." She hoped that she would someday be able to take over her family's interest in CureLab and gain great face in Japan.

The flight attendant brought Kyoko some aspirin and water. "Drink plenty of water. Try to sleep, all right?"

Kyoko took the pill, drank as much of the water as she could stand, and pulled the blanket around her body. She reclined the seat and closed her eyes.

Kyoko's tired and unhappy thoughts drifted to Mayumi. *Why had she gone?* Their parents' hearts were broken. The last they had heard about Mayumi was that she was living in Hokkaido, probably the girlfriend of a gangster. Mayumi had brought shame upon the family, though if she came home, Kyoko was sure that her younger sister would be forgiven. The furious fight Mayumi had had with their parents four years ago had ended with Mayumi walking out of the house at the age of sixteen, vowing never to return. At first their father had said that Mayumi would come home once she had "found herself." Junko had been distraught. None of them had liked Mayumi's boyfriend, who was nothing but a common street thug. Peter McMahon had chalked up Mayumi's actions to teenage rebellion and put his faith in the notion that one day Mayumi would return the prodigal daughter.

Kyoko vaguely remembered thinking that "teenage rebellion" was quite an understatement. Mayumi had been a rebellious child from the day she was born. She had been plagued with colic and proved to be a big problem for her mother. Her first word was "No," and it had continued to be a regular part of her vocabulary as she grew up. Her parents, especially her father, had fought her hard over the years. It had been a losing battle for them, for Mayumi's will was shockingly strong. What a waste, Kyoko thought. Mayumi was easily the prettiest and possibly also the most intelligent of the three girls.

Kyoko's limbs felt heavy, and she was struggling to think. The drone of the plane's engines reminded her of last night too and the annoying whine of the mosquitoes. They were usually bad in the summer months, but they had shown up in greater numbers this particular June. Kyoko remembered slapping at least three on her arm.

Another wave of nausea overtook her. Kyoko reached for the airsickness bag and vomited. The passenger two rows in front of her turned around to see what had happened.

Kyoko managed to close the bag and drop it on the floor before she fell back into her seat and drifted from consciousness.

The flight attendant came by and frowned before picking the bag up from the floor. She tucked the blanket snugly around Kyoko's shoulders. Thinking that the poor girl needed some sleep, the flight attendant elected to leave her alone for the next few hours. The other passengers on the upper deck were asleep as well, so there was no reason for her to do anything but walk through the cabin every now and then.

Four hours later, Kyoko was still asleep, but the blanket had been tossed aside. The poor girl was bathed in sweat. The flight attendant thought about waking her to see if she wanted water but decided against it. Best to let her sleep.

Two hours later, the call bell alerted the flight attendant to come into the cabin. The passenger in front of Kyoko had rung it. He pointed to the girl and said, "Something's wrong."

Kyoko McMahon was convulsing in her seat. The flight attendant ran downstairs and fetched the cabin officer. After he saw the writhing girl, he used the intercom to ask if there were a doctor aboard. A Japanese man in his fifties responded. The doctor came up from the main cabin, examined Kyoko, gently talked to her and held her still. Eventually she choked and coughed, gasping for air. The doctor gave her a sip of water. After a few minutes, she had settled down again and drifted back to sleep. The doctor told the cabin officer that the girl probably had the flu. "It might possibly be a form of malaria," he said, "but I suggest that we just let her sleep. It's the best thing for her right now. Keep an eye on her, though."

The pilot was informed of the situation. The plane had already flown over Siberia, Russia, and Finland. They could make an emergency landing in Copenhagen if necessary, but London was only three hours away.

"As long as she's sleeping, we'll continue," the pilot said. "At this point, it would be better to get her to her destination." He radioed ahead to make sure there would be no delay at the gate.

Everyone agreed.

The flight attendant looked in on Kyoko every half hour. At one point, the girl was struggling and mumbling as if she were having a bad dream. The flight attendant shook Kyoko gently until she calmed down and began breathing deeply again.

Two hours later, the flight attendant decided to wake Kyoko but couldn't rouse her. This time the girl felt cold and clammy.

When the doctor examined Kyoko again, he pronounced her dead.

Since they were so close to London, the flight crew agreed to keep it quiet and continue on.

Kyoko McMahon died alone, 39,000 feet above the earth. She never knew that her mother, father, and sister had also died at approximately the same time with identical symptoms in their opulent house in the Tokyo suburb of Saitama.

2

Assignment: Japan

Major Boothroyd cleared his throat and began.

"As you know, I asked you here this morning for a routine equipment briefing for all Double-Os and other field agents." He added, with sarcasm, "I see that we have the usual splendid turnout."

They were in the soundproofed shooting range in the basement of MI6 headquarters. Shooting Instructor Reinhardt stood at the back, genuinely concerned that the good major might accidentally cause a dreadful explosion inside his beloved range. 004 and 0010 were present and they sat near 007, close to the table that displayed the various items Boothroyd had brought to the meeting. Three lower-level field agents and several technicians also sat or stood near the major.

There never seemed to be more than three Double-Os around headquarters at any given time. Most of them, after all, were on assignments or stationed in other parts of the world. Or they were dead.

"Right," Boothroyd continued, his voice echoing in the stone room. "We have a few new pieces of hardware for you to review, and most of them involve explosives."

A tall, thin man with wavy, white hair, the major was

wearing a pair of workman's coveralls and a hard hat. A pair of safety goggles hung loosely around his neck. Bond had learned long ago to overlook his ridiculous appearance.

"Double-O Seven?"

"Yes, Major?"

He approached Bond and handed him a tubular cigar holder. "You're one of those who still indulge in the filthy habit of smoking. Might I interest you in a nice Cuban?"

Bond took it and noticed that it was slightly heavier than it should have been. "Thank you, Major. Now, what is it *really*?"

Boothroyd took it, popped off the cap and removed the cigar. He displayed it to the group and said, "It appears to be an ordinary cigar. But if you use your thumbnail to take off the end . . ." He did so and revealed that the cigar was not filled with tobacco. Boothroyd moved farther back into the room some thirty feet away, where a small iron safe sat on a laboratory table.

"Two-thirds of the cigar is filled with plastic explosive. You can dispense it by squeezing the cigar like a tube of toothpaste." He demonstrated by squirting a small amount of brown paste onto the combination knob of the safe.

"The cap from the holder is a timer. It is preset for ten seconds. You simply set it by pushing this tiny button and placing it in the plastic explosive." The major fiddled with the cap and displayed a tiny readout to the group, although they were too far away to see the numbers clearly. Boothroyd realised this and said, "It has already begun to count down."

Boothroyd thrust the timer into the paste-like substance and moved behind a lead shield that had been set up away from the table. The Double-Os looked at each other with concern, but the technicians seemed confident that the major knew what he was doing.

Seconds later, the explosive ignited and smoke filled

the room. The noise had been much louder than anyone had expected, but no one was harmed.

The front door of the safe hung on one hinge, grossly bent out of shape.

Boothroyd emerged from behind the screen and walked back to the group. "With practice, you should soon be able to estimate near enough how much explosive is needed. Note that the cigar can get through Customs with no problem and we have even given it the odour of tobacco. Now then."

He walked over to the near table and picked up a blister pack of a well-known brand of indigestion tablets.

"No business traveller should be without antacids, wouldn't you agree?" he asked. "These are now standard issue. The white tablets are real antacids. The pink ones, if you throw them, burst and produce a thick cloud of smoke." He nodded at a technician, who threw one against the far wall. There was a loud pop and a dark billow of smoke appeared.

"The red ones are a little more powerful," Boothroyd said. "One of them can blow a small hole in a wall, create a pothole in a pavement, knock a door off its hinges. It can also take your hand right off, so be very careful with them."

The major dropped the blister pack. His audience didn't have time to gasp before it hit the floor. "You need not be worried. You have to throw them with great force to explode them," he said. "The packaging is designed to withstand being dropped on the floor and even the jostling that occurs within airline baggage."

Boothroyd spent the next twenty minutes demonstrating a variety of other incendiary devices. Bond thought that thirty per cent of them were not very practical, fifty per cent were possibly useful, and twenty per cent were brilliantly conceived, if not quite perfected. Q Branch was capable of designing some ingenious stuff, but only some of the products had a life beyond the initial testing period.

The meeting broke up so that the technicians could familiarise the agents with the new equipment. Bond took a look at some of the other things on the table that Boothroyd hadn't presented.

"What's this, Major?" Bond asked, picking up a Palm Pilot V. Boothroyd beamed and said, "Ah. Our little electronic organiser. That's still in the testing stage, Double-O Seven. We haven't worked out all the bugs."

"What does it do?"

"Besides being a real Palm Pilot, a cross section is filled with a stronger plastic explosive than we've seen here today. It has the force of a stick of dynamite. You set it off simply by inputting the data into the Palm Pilot. It becomes its own detonator."

"Ingenious. How much memory does it need to do that?"

"You're being facetious, but actually that's the problem we're having with the device's other function. Not enough memory. Or rather, not enough of a power source to be truly effective."

"For what?" Bond asked.

Boothroyd turned on a small desk fan that sat on the table. As the blades spun and whirred, he held the Palm Pilot a few inches away from it and pressed something. The fan's power immediately shut off. The blades slowed to a stop.

"It's a fairly weak electromagnetic pulse," the major said. "We'd like it to be able to knock the power out of cars at a reasonable distance, but we can't figure out how to give it a large enough energy supply."

"What can it do now?" Bond asked.

"Oh, just what you saw. Small appliances. Televisions. Perhaps some security alarms. At extremely close range, mind you."

"May I have it now? I'll test it in the field for you."

Boothroyd thought for a moment and then nodded. "All right, Commander, I'll let you do that. I'll put it on your clearing slip for M. Just make sure that—"

A loud explosion made everyone in the room flinch. Someone shouted, "Whoa!" And there was laughter as Instructor Reinhardt cursed aloud.

"—you know how to operate it properly," Boothroyd sighed.

"I think it might have something to do with Japan," Nigel Smith said.

Bond winced. "Doesn't she realise that I'm doing everything I can about this Yoshida business? It's all that I've *been* doing since we beat the Union."

"You and me both," agreed Nigel, Bond's relatively new personal assistant, a clear-eyed young man who had been discharged from the Royal Navy due to an injury. Bond had originally bristled at being assigned a male assistant, but Nigel had shown that he was sharp and capable. He also possessed much of the same sardonic attitude towards the job as Bond. And while Nigel made it a point not to be overimpressed with Bond, it was obvious that he admired his boss. Taking a cue from the style with which Bond presented himself, it wasn't long before Nigel upgraded his own wardrobe by buying his shirts from Turnbull & Asser.

Bond appreciated Nigel's candour and honesty, especially when it came to intelligence matters. The young man had a knack for reading between the lines and interpreting oblique reports from the field. His opinions were blunt and often gelled with Bond's. In a very short time the young man had become an ally.

"It might be about the G8 summit conference," Nigel suggested.

"Lord, I hope not," Bond muttered. He had seen the

memo. An emergency session had been scheduled to take place in Japan in less than two weeks. "She probably wants me to baby-sit the PM."

"That's because you're the PM's best friend since that business in Gibraltar a couple of years ago," Nigel said, chuckling.

Bond glanced at the digital clock set into the wall, a standard feature in all outer offices. The working day was nearly over.

"How long ago did she ring?" Bond asked.

"Miss Moneypenny phoned me about a half hour before you arrived."

"All right," Bond said. "Surely she was aware of my appointment with Q Branch. Call Penny back and tell her I'm on my way."

"Right." Nigel picked up the phone as his boss turned around and left the office.

Bond cursed silently as he got into a lift. If it wasn't about the G8 conference, then it was certainly about Goro Yoshida. He was just as concerned about Yoshida as M was. After all, the exiled Japanese extremist had been the Union's client for the recent affair that ultimately proved the unmaking of that terrorist-for-hire organisation. It was Yoshida who had put up the money. It was Yoshida who was now at the top of the "most wanted" lists of Japan and nearly every country in the world.

Just before the lift stopped on M's floor, Bond gazed into his indistinct reflection on the silver panels of the lift doors. He ran his fingers through the coal-black hair, not bothering to push the comma that hung above his right eyebrow back in place.

He got out of the lift and strode down the hall toward Miss Moneypenny's outer office, continuing to run through the precious little new information that had been uncovered since Yoshida's last venture. All that MI6 and MI5 knew about the terrorist was that he was a wealthy businessman who had hooked up with criminal elements, probably the yakuza, and became a prominent nationalist. At first he was harmless, confining himself to travelling the streets of Tokyo in a green van, as most of the nationalists did and still do, announcing his views through a loudspeaker. He proclaimed that Japan had lost its traditional values and was being poisoned by the West. It was the same rhetoric that dozens of nationalists have spouted since before World War II. But shortly after Yoshida publicly declared "war" on the West, he mysteriously disappeared. He handed over his company to others to run, then left Japan just as several violent terrorist acts were instigated against Western countries. An embassy was bombed here; a fast food restaurant was obliterated there. Intelligence agencies speculated that Yoshida had been behind the incidents.

Yoshida, now wanted by the police in Japan for "treasonous views and acts" as well as terrorism, was believed to be hiding somewhere in a remote part of Russia with his own private army.

Miss Moneypenny was on the phone when Bond walked into the office, but her bright eyes held a greeting for him. Before she could mime a message, the door to M's inner office opened.

"Ah, there you are, Double-O Seven. I wanted to see you. Come inside."

M handed a folder to Moneypenny and walked back into her office, leaving the door open. Bond moved forward as Moneypenny gave him a wink and a little wave.

As soon as the door had closed behind them Bond said, "Ma'am, if this is about Goro Yoshida, I assure you that—"

"It's not about Goro Yoshida, Double-O Seven," M said as she moved around her desk. "Please sit down."

Bond did as he was told.

So what was the score? he wondered. *Something new?*

M, who was dressed in a sharply tailored charcoal grey Bella Freud suit, sat down and asked, "You've seen the memo about the emergency G8 summit conference?"

Here it comes, he thought. "Yes, I have."

"The Koan-Chosa-Cho is in charge of security, but every representative brings his or her own entourage. I'd like you there with our PM. Bodyguard duty. As a matter of fact, the PM requested you. You should be flattered."

Bond smiled to himself.

"Is something funny, Double-O Seven?"

"No, ma'am."

"The Japanese are a little worried about security in this day and age, as are we all. Potential threats to representatives of Western governments are a constant concern since the events of September 2001. The Japanese secret service want intelligence operatives from all of the participating governments to accompany the G8 members. I believe you are acquainted with the head of the Koan-Chosa-Cho."

"Indeed," Bond said. He had an old and dear friend who worked for the Japanese Secret Service.

"Mr. Tanaka was the one who initially put forth your name. The PM, after discussions with the U.S. president, has agreed and made the official request. The Japanese have received some information that suggests there could possibly be a danger to the summit conference. In light of this revelation, I suppose your earlier comment about Goro Yoshida might not be too far off the mark."

"What kinds of threats have been made?" Bond asked. "Do they involve Yoshida?"

"We don't know. Tanaka will have to brief you on that. Now." She reached across the desk, picked up a folder and handed it to him. "There is something else I want you to look into while you're in Japan. In fact, I'm sending you over ahead of the summit conference so that you can do so. We don't want your presence to arouse too many suspicions in Japan, or cause undue alarm, so you will ostensibly be in the country to investigate the suspicious deaths of a British citizen and his family."

Bond opened the folder and saw photos of a man named Peter McMahon.

M continued talking. "Two days ago, the Japanese-born daughter of that man died of a mysterious illness aboard a Japan Airlines flight from Tokyo to London. It just so happens that the girl's parents and older sister in Japan died around the same time that the plane was in flight. I'm waiting for the pathology results on the dead girl, but the examining doctor at Heathrow thought that she might have died from some fast-acting form of West Nile disease. He had never seen anything like it. From what news we can gather from an unhelpful Japan, it appears that the same thing killed the rest of the family."

"Had they been together recently?"

"Yes," M replied. "At the mother's birthday party the night before, in a suburb of Tokyo."

Bond quietly cleared his throat and asked, "What does this have to do with us?"

"Have you heard of Peter McMahon?"

"I don't think so."

"A shrewd businessman. Ran a pharmaceutical company called CureLab Inc. in Tokyo. He married the founder's daughter and pretty soon the old man gave him a job. McMahon turned the company, which was in the throes of bankruptcy, into a business worth millions of pounds. They're one of the leading firms in the pharmaceuticals industry. And he has important friends in this country."

Bond looked straight into M's cool, blue eyes.

"I see," Bond said.

"The Japanese police have yet to declare whether or not the McMahon family died of accidental or natural causes or if they were murdered."

"Murdered? You think this was an assassination?" Bond asked. "Why?"

"Apparently McMahon had a lot of enemies," M said. "His father-in-law, Hideo Fujimoto, died three years ago. Ownership of the company passed to Fujimoto's daughter, as his wife was already dead. I would imagine that in the case of the McMahons' deaths, ownership would have passed to their three daughters. One of those daughters died with her parents in Tokyo. Another one died on that aeroplane."

"Where is the third one?"

"We don't know. The Japanese bureaucracy is with-holding information about the McMahons. But you'll have the full cooperation of the Koan-Chosa-Cho, which seems to be taking a more aggressive view of the situation than the Tokyo police. We have a right to look into the mysterious death of a British citizen, and they know it. You can begin by going out to Uxbridge tonight to have a word with the coroner who is looking after Kyoko McMa-hon's body. His office has been alerted, and you are ex-pected at seven-thirty this evening."

Bond felt a flicker of fear. Even the thought of going back to Japan after all these years gave him reason to pause.

"It all sounds very interesting, but with all due respect, I'm really not qualified to be a crime-scene detective," Bond said truthfully.

M looked at him hard and said, "That may be true, but that's not the real reason you don't want to go."

Bond raised his eyebrows.

"I know you better than that, Double-O Seven," M said. "I am quite aware of your history with Japan. I un-derstand that you might have certain reservations about returning there."

Bond sighed inwardly. The old girl was perceptive. Bond had spent a significant amount of time in Japan, the victim of amnesia, after his pursuit of Ernst Stavro Blofeld. It had happened a lifetime ago, it seemed, but Bond didn't enjoy being reminded of those dark times.

"You might think of it as a holiday," she proposed with a wry smile.

"A holiday?"

"Your friend Tanaka is eager to see you."

Bond nodded. "It would be nice to see Tiger again. But still . . ."

"James," M said, uncharacteristically referring to him by his forename. "I need you there. You have the ability to see the wider picture. I want you to investigate CureLab itself. I want you to find out if Peter McMahon had an enemy who would be willing to assassinate him and his family. Was it really murder? And if so, who was responsible? And I want you to locate that missing daughter."

Bond remained silent. He knew that she was giving him an order, but the prospect of facing the ghosts that haunted his memories was daunting.

"That's all, Double-O Seven," she said. "And just to ease your mind, I'm not taking you *off* the Yoshida case. See what you can learn about him while you're there. If these threats to the summit conference concern him, well . . ."

"I understand."

"I know you hate baby-sitting jobs, Double-O Seven," she added. "Every Double-O has to do it every now and then."

Bond stood and raised his hand to stop her. "I'll get the details from Miss Moneypenny. You're right. It will be a change of scenery for me. And I certainly can't let down my old friend the PM."

M couldn't help but smile as he walked out of the office.

3

A Night at the Mortuary

The sun was on its way down as Bond drove west on the M4 out of London in the decommissioned Aston Martin that he had purchased from Q Branch a few years back. He had always enjoyed the DB5 and he drove it around London more often than his old much-loved Bentley.

Bond came off the motorway at the Heathrow exit, turned north, followed the signs to Uxbridge, found his way to Kingston Lane and pulled into Hillingdon Cemetery. The Hillingdon Public Mortuary was in a fifty-year-old single-storey T-shaped brick structure built on a corner of the cemetery, adjacent to a playing field. A Ford and a Range Rover were the only other two vehicles in the car park. Bond parked the Aston Martin next to them, got out and took in his surroundings. The gravestones in the cemetery were bathed in the dull glow of dusk as the sky was caught between dark navy blue and golden orange.

Bond entered the lobby through blue front doors. The building was silent and dark, save for a few lights on in the offices. The staff had gone home, and the place seemed deserted.

"Hello?" Bond called.

A man dressed in a white shirt with the sleeves rolled

up came into the room from an office on the right. He had the rugged look of someone who might once have been a police officer or perhaps served in the fire brigade.

"May I help you?" the man asked.

"The name's Bond. James Bond. I'm here to see Dr. Lodge."

"Oh, right. We've been expecting you. I'm Bob Greenwell, coroner's officer. This way, please."

Bond followed him into the office, where another man was looking intently at a laptop computer. The man looked up and stood.

"Mr. Bond? I'm Chris Lodge. I'm the pathologist assigned to this case." They shook hands. Lodge appeared to be in his mid-thirties, was soft-spoken and had a gentle grip.

"I hope it wasn't too inconvenient to see me tonight," Bond said. "I'm leaving for Japan tomorrow."

"I quite understand," the doctor said. Greenwell sat at another desk, picked up a paperback novel and began to read.

"The staff usually go home at night," Dr. Lodge said. "I come in when I'm called. Please sit down." The doctor gestured to an armchair on the other side of his desk.

Bond got to the point. "Can you tell me about Kyoko McMahon?"

Lodge shook his head with pity as he sat down. "An ugly and lonely death. We're still waiting for the toxicology results. We've sent all of our information to the Imperial College people at Charing Cross Hospital. There will have to be an inquest, I'm afraid. The coroner has yet to sign my postmortem report."

"So it's a suspicious death?" Bond asked.

"Downright baffling. We still don't know what killed the poor girl. To tell you the truth, it's one of the more interesting cases I've ever seen."

"Why don't you take me through the chain of events

that occurred after the plane landed at Heathrow. Then I'd like to see your report, if you don't mind."

The doctor frowned. "This is highly unusual, Mr. Bond, but as you're with the Ministry of Defence, I suppose it's all right. Postmortem information is normally kept confidential and is released only to the family . . . and to the police if the cause of death wasn't natural."

"I assure you that I'm not a reporter for the *Daily Express,*" Bond said dryly.

"Right. Anyway, the pilot radioed ahead to Heathrow, the normal procedure should a passenger die on board. Under international law, when a passenger dies in flight, the death is taken to have occurred at the destination airport. The authorities were waiting for the plane; the Port Health Authority doctor examined the girl and pronounced her dead. The body was removed from the aircraft by an Uxbridge funeral director that we use. A hearse brought her here, where she was identified and tagged. Finding next of kin was quite a performance. I understand her immediate family is in Japan, am I correct?"

"Yes."

"Anyway, after failing to reach her parents, we finally got hold of her great uncle." Lodge consulted his notes. "A Shinji Fujimoto. I must say that he was rather uncooperative. He didn't want us to touch her body at all—just wanted her sent back to Japan. He was informed that it was a matter of law that we do a postmortem in this country. Permission was granted, reluctantly. I was called in from Tooting yesterday morning, and I performed the postmortem yesterday afternoon."

"And what were your findings?"

"It is my opinion that the cause of death was a highly virulent form of West Nile disease. Do you know it?"

"No, but it sounds as if I'm about to become an expert."

"Pretty serious stuff. Victims normally experience

fever, headache, aching muscles, sometimes rashes or swollen lymph glands. Some individuals experience more severe symptoms like neurological damage, encephalitis and coma. In extreme cases, it can be fatal. When we heard about the outbreak of West Nile in New York City a couple of years ago, we were all a bit concerned. They actually think that the virus came into New York via Asian mosquitoes that had been brought into the country accidentally inside a shipment of tyres."

"I remember reading about that. Didn't someone die?"

"There were a couple of deaths, but in the majority of cases it just made people ill. West Nile doesn't do what happened to this girl. The symptoms were similar, but they were magnified ten-fold. The onset was apparently very rapid. As I understand it, she boarded the plane in good health and became ill during the flight. She was dead within twelve hours. That's very fast. Normally, West Nile would take days or weeks to go through that kind of cycle."

Bond whistled appreciatively. "Is there a cure?"

"Unfortunately not. Look here." The doctor gestured for Bond to step around the desk and look at the laptop. Lodge punched some buttons, and a cross section of brain tissue appeared on the screen. "The mechanism of death, that is, what actually killed her, was that her brain suffocated. The high fever caused the meninges, the membranes surrounding the brain, to swell from the inflammation. An abscess was formed and grew very quickly, cutting off oxygen and blood flow to the rest of the brain. See this?"

The doctor pointed to indistinct blobs as Bond said, "Mmm hmm."

"She went into a coma, which is why the flight attendant thought that she was sleeping. At some point her brain simply shut off, and she began to asphyxiate. The

cause of death? I suppose I would say 'natural' or 'accidental.' Depending on what the toxicology report says."

Bond sat down again and thought for a moment. "Were
there any unusual marks on her body? Needle marks?"

"No," Lodge said. "As far as I could see, there was no
evidence of drug taking. No herpes simplex virus, which
can be a cause of encephalitis. However, speaking of mosquitoes, she did have a fair number of insect bites and they
looked to me like mosquito bites. Mostly on her arms and
legs."

"Could that have been it?"

The man shrugged. "West Nile disease is normally carried by mosquitoes, and humans are infected with the
disease when they are bitten by them. And while the
symptoms are similar, whatever this was, it was certainly
not West Nile. I'm not ruling anything out, but in my experience a mosquito isn't capable of transmitting a disease
that has *this* kind of reaction."

The sound of a crash in the back of the building caused
all three men to turn toward it.

"What the hell was that?" Lodge asked.

"I'll go and see," Greenwell said as he stood and left
the room, still holding a mug of coffee.

Lodge grinned at Bond. "Our guests back there are restless, perhaps?"

Bond did not acknowledge the joke. Instinctively, he
rose and went to the door. There was a shout of surprise
from the back of the building.

Lodge looked alarmed. "Was that Bob?"

The Walther PPK was in Bond's hand; Lodge could
have sworn that the weapon had materialised from thin
air.

"Which is the way to the postmortem room?" Bond
asked.

Lodge replied, "Go through the lobby and into the
other office. There's a door at the back of the room that

opens into a corridor. Go right, and then left. You can't miss it."

"Stay here." Bond peered into the dark lobby and saw nothing. He darted across and into the empty office behind reception. The door to the corridor was ajar. Bond crept to it and listened.

Silence.

He went through the door and into the hallway, where he found Greenwell's broken coffee mug. He heard something—a noise, a scuffling—coming from the postmortem room. Bond moved slowly toward the door, which was also ajar. He carefully leaned in to look and felt a significant drop in temperature.

Greenwell was unconscious on the floor next to the postmortem table. Two men were bending over a nude corpse that was lying on one of the mobile metal carts. They were attempting to wrap it in a blanket. Bond could see twenty refrigerator doors lining the wall in rows behind them. Three were open. One had obviously contained the woman's body that they were wrapping. The other two cubicles were empty and were also open at both ends. The other side of the refrigerated cubicles opened into the body reception room, which was where bodies were delivered from the outside.

The two men were wearing surgical masks, and from where Bond was standing they appeared to be Asian.

One of the men must have sensed Bond's presence, for he suddenly whirled around, his pistol spraying fire at the door. Bond ducked back into the hall and crouched. He heard the men shout to each other in Japanese. Bond dared to look low around the open door and saw both men climb into the open refrigerated compartments so that they could escape through the body reception room.

Bond fired the Walther at one of the men, but the intruder pulled his legs in just in time to avoid being hit. As Bond got up to run into the room, a third man who had been hiding against the wall beside the open door kicked the Walther out of Bond's hand. Before Bond could register surprise, the attacker struck him with two lightning fast *tsuki* punches to the chest. Bond fell backwards and crashed into a metal table with a scale used for weighing dissected organs.

Then Bond was hit with a powerful blow to the solar plexus, knocking the breath out of him. He fell to his knees, gasping for air as his assailant stood back, ready to kick. The young man wore sunglasses and a surgical mask. His hairstyle was a "punch perm"—short and permed into tiny skull-hugging curls.

Acting quickly, Bond reached up to the metal table and grabbed the first thing he felt, which happened to be a metal tray covered with dissecting instruments. Bond flung the tray at the attacker just as the man's right foot left the ground for the kick. The tray bashed loudly into his boot, scattering the instruments over the tiled floor.

This gave Bond the time he needed to get to his feet, but not enough of an interval to defend himself against a perfectly executed *mawashi-geri,* or roundhouse kick, to the chin. Bond fell back again, this time knocking several metal trays off the postmortem table. He hit the floor next to Greenwell, who was moaning softly.

This boy is a professional! was the only thing Bond was capable of thinking.

When he looked up, the "boy" had slithered through a refrigerated cubicle and escaped with his friends.

Bond got up and went to Greenwell. "Are you all right?"

The man nodded and put a hand to the back of his head. "Who's the corpse?"

"It's the McMahon girl," Greenwell answered.

Without hesitation, Bond retrieved his handgun, dived into one of the refrigerated cubicles after the men and crawled to the other end. He unlatched the door, then jumped down into the body reception room. The door to the car park was just closing. Bond hugged the wall and looked outside.

The back of the building was adjacent to a driveway where hearses and ambulances could pull up to drop off bodies. Beyond that were bushes, hedges and trees lining the edge of the cemetery. A black Toyota was pulling out of the driveway into Kingston Lane. The man he had fought was just jumping into the backseat as the tyres squealed. The light had diminished greatly, but Bond could still see well enough to take a shot at the driver. He held the gun with both hands, assumed a modified Weaver firing stance, aimed carefully and squeezed the trigger. The Walther recoiled with a satisfying jolt.

The Toyota swerved out into the street and crashed into a telephone pole. The horn blared.

The two remaining men jumped out of the car and fired in Bond's direction. The bullets flew around him. Bond leaped for the pavement and rolled behind a tree that would shield him from the gunfire.

"Mr. Bond?" Dr. Lodge called from the body reception room.

"Call the police!" Bond shouted. "And get back inside!"

Bullets sprayed around the tree, then at the open door of the building. Lodge disappeared from view.

Bond was pinned down. He was safe but he couldn't move to either side of the tree for fear of taking a bullet. He knew that the thugs wouldn't wait forever; they would have to move eventually. He just had to be patient.

When a siren could be heard approaching, the two men decided to go for it. Bond heard their footsteps as they ran off across Kingston Lane and into the cemetery, which was growing darker by the second.

Bond swung out from behind the tree and fired. One of the men jerked, cried out, and fell to the ground. The other man leapt to the side, taking cover behind a large grave-stone. Bond began to run towards him, but the man reached around and fired his handgun, forcing Bond to take cover behind another tree.

As the police cars pulled into the front car park with sirens blaring, the gunfire ceased. After a few seconds, Bond carefully looked around the tree and could faintly see the man running. Bond raised the Walther to shoot, but at this light and distance, hitting him was unlikely. He let him go.

Bond sprinted to the man who was down and examined him. It was the same man he had fought in the postmortem room. The bullet had caught him in the upper chest, a direct hit. Bond pulled off the surgical mask. He was a young Japanese, probably in his early twenties. Bond searched his clothing and pulled out a Dutch passport and a Colt 1911 A1 semiautomatic from underneath a light jacket.

Lodge came running outside with a torch. "Mr. Bond, are you all right?"

"I'm over here. There were three of them. One's in the car. The third one got away."

Lodge crept warily up to the body and directed the torch on it. "Who is he?"

"I don't know. Shine your torch on his passport here."

Lodge took it and read it. "Somebody Hito. He lives in Amsterdam. Lived. What did they want?"

"It looked to me like they were trying to take Ms. McMahon's body."

"But why?"

"That's a very good question."

Then Bond noticed something unusual on the dead man's neck. "Shine that torch over here."

The light illuminated something sinister and extraordinary. Bond carefully unbuttoned the man's shirt and opened it. The dead man's entire upper torso was decorated in an elaborate, colourful tattoo depicting dragons and waterfalls.

It was a signature of the Japanese mafia, the dreaded yakuza.

4
Yami Shogun

The MBB-Kawasaki BK-117 Eurocopter left behind the land mass of Hokkaido, the northernmost island of the cluster that makes up Japan. It flew northeast towards the Kuril Islands, the so-called "Northern Territories" that Japan and Russia have been in dispute over since 1945. The Sea of Okhotsk stretched to the horizon ahead of them, while Russia lay hundreds of kilometres to the left and the Pacific Ocean expanded endlessly to the right.

Yasutake Tsukamoto shifted uncomfortably in his seat. He was not usually a nervous man. He was one of the most feared and respected men in Japan, the reigning *oyabun*, or father, of the Ryujin-kai. As *kaicho*, or boss, he had hundreds of men under his thumb, all willing to do his bidding. They were prepared to die for him. And, as the Ryujin-kai was one of the strongest and most powerful yakuza organisations in the country, with tentacles that reached into Japanese communities worldwide, Tsukamoto had no reason to be afraid. He was superior to every man in his organisation—except one.

He always felt uneasy going to see the *Yami Shogun*. Even after all these years . . .

Tsukamoto didn't enjoy the flight across the sea to

Russian territory. He hated the fact that Russia had occupied the islands since the 1945 Yalta Conference because they rightfully belonged to Japan. He hated doing business with Russia at all, but circumstances with the *Yami Shogun* dictated that it must be so. After all, the master was exiled from Japan and could not set foot in the country without being arrested. The deal the master had made with the Russian Organizatsiya ensured that he would have a safe haven where he could live with his private army, train them and prepare them for the battle yet to come. The *Yami Shogun* hated the Russians as much as Tsukamoto did, but business was business. Tsukamoto thought that one day the time would come when business partners would have to change.

The Kuril Islands were an ideal spot for the *Yami Shogun* to hide. They are considered a mysterious no-man's-land by both Japan and Russia. While they are governed as part of Sakhalin Oblast, in many ways they are still culturally tied to Japan. The islands are heavily forested and contain many active volcanoes. Hunting, fishing and sulphur mining are the principal occupations of the inhabitants, among them the Ainu, an ancient race believed to be indigenous to the area.

Eventually the helicopter approached the island called Etorofu by the Japanese and Iturup by the Russians. The helipad was on private property hidden amongst the trees. The property owner was associated with a mining operation that worked a nearby quarry; if anyone at the firm were questioned, they would have no knowledge of who that owner might be. If someone dug deep enough, they might discover that the owner was a Japanese corporation called Yonai Enterprises. It was a legitimate diversified company, involved mostly in chemical engineering.

It was also a front for one of the biggest yakuza gangs in Japan.

It was not unusual these days for yakuza to infiltrate

"Big Business" in Japan. It was an unspoken and accepted part of the way society worked. Many *kaicho* and *oyabun* were heads of or sat on the boards of directors of large, influential companies. Any formidable yakuza gang in Japan had to flaunt its wealth and management skills.

Yasutake Tsukamoto was on the board of directors of Yonai Enterprises, which was one of the many reasons that he had no reason to complain about his life. He was successful. He was very wealthy. He was powerful. Two bodyguards travelled with him wherever he went. They sat across from him there in the helicopter, two burly men with punch perms and sunglasses. He saw them more than he saw his wife.

So why did he always feel like a child in the presence of the master?

Like the *Yami Shogun,* Tsukamoto was a nationalist. The type of yakuza he headed was *Uyoku,* which roughly meant "political right." It was ironic, Tsukamoto thought, that when *Uyoku* groups first came into fashion, Big Business was one of the enemies along with communists, anything from the West and anyone who suggested a deviation from a traditional monarchy. Today, however, Big Business was indeed big business. Yonai Enterprises was a megacorp, soon to become a major player in Japan and abroad. Today's *Uyoku* might still hate the Russians and the Americans and the British and the Chinese, but they didn't have a problem with taking their money.

Just as the helicopter landed in a square patch of flat land surrounded by tall trees, Tsukamoto suddenly understood why he was nervous about seeing the *Yami Shogun.* It had nothing to do with pleasing one's master. The ideological direction in which the master wished to go was what troubled him. For he, of all people, knew that the master was deadly serious about the upcoming project.

Tsukamoto knew the *Yami Shogun* better than anyone else.

• • •

He had first met Goro Yoshida when they were both children. They had gone to the same school when Goro was nine and Tsukamoto was eight. It was during the Occupation, when the United States dominated everything in Japan. Tsukamoto could remember the anti-American propaganda that circulated underground, the impassioned speeches of nationalists who deplored America and what it stood for. Even then, Goro Yoshida was emotional in his beliefs. He had embraced the rhetoric profoundly and it hardened into a fundamental principle as Goro grew into his teens.

Goro's family owned a consortium of small industrial and chemical engineering firms that later consolidated into what was now Yonai Enterprises. He had been born in 1943, just in time for the climax of the war and the Occupation. His only sibling, Yukiko, came along a year later. Despite his family's prosperity, Goro had had a troubled childhood. As a teenager, he had turned to street gangs for a place to fit in. Wayward teenagers were prime recruitment material for the yakuza, so by the time Goro was thirteen he was involved in various levels of a Tokyo yakuza called Ryujin-kai. So was his friend Tsukamoto.

During this early period, Goro despised his family. Tsukamoto remembered the horrible things Goro would say about his father. His father represented big business, and this was a Western thing. He was doing business with Western companies, many of them American, some British.

It wasn't until Goro was sixteen that he changed his mind about his father, who had secretly joined the Red Guard, a volatile nationalist group that was often blamed for terrorist incidents. And, to the amazement of young Goro, his father's name was ultimately attached to several bombings around the globe and he became a wanted man. Japan forced Goro's father into exile, so he went to live in

Europe — in the West that he detested. He travelled around, working for various militant groups and was in London when a series of explosions rocked that city. Informants talked and Goro's father was identified as being a suspect.

The official word was that Goro's father died resisting arrest.

Yasutake Tsukamoto was with Goro Yoshida when the news came. They had just celebrated Goro's twentieth birthday. The sake had been flowing, and Goro was very drunk. They had been talking about the latest work by Yukio Mishima, the writer who had become the most controversial and honoured Japanese author of his time. They both admired the nationalist themes that ran through Mishima's works and hoped that they could meet him someday.

To his great surprise, Goro inherited his father's fortune. It was Goro who eventually consolidated Yonai Enterprises to focus on future technology. In the 1960s, Yonai became the leader in chemical engineering and it was entirely attributable to Goro's leadership.

His friends at the Ryujin-kai were very pleased with the situation. Goro invited the yakuza to insinuate itself into the running of the company, and it wasn't long before Yonai Enterprises had tentacles reaching into many facets of organised crime in Japan. With the future of the company secure, Goro began to concentrate more on his other interests, namely the philosophies of nationalism, attending kendo and karate classes, and honing his body.

As time went on, Tsukamoto watched his friend Goro further withdraw from society. Goro spoke of nothing but his militaristic dreams. For a while he was a member of Yukio Mishima's private army known as the Shield Society. But disagreements over Yoshida's connections with the yakuza led to his discharge from the society before that fateful day in 1970 when Yukio Mishima committed public *seppuku.*

Even though they had had their disagreements, Yoshida was greatly moved by Mishima's act of defiance. Partly in tribute to the writer's act, Yoshida liquidated his private assets and hid his money in a network of front companies, bank accounts and foundations. He formed his own private army of nationalists, modelled after Mishima's Shield Society. Using some of his father's Red Guard connections, he made arms deals first with the Soviets and later with the Russian mafia and supplied *his* private army with weapons.

Eventually Goro Yoshida became the shadow *kaicho* of the Ryujin-kai. While Tsukamoto had by that time become a rising yakuza enforcer—first as a *wakashu,* a "child," then as a *shatei,* a "brother," and eventually acting *kaicho* of the Ryujin-kai itself—in reality Yoshida always pulled the strings. And Tsukamoto was honoured to work for him. Tsukamoto thought of Yoshida as his *sensei,* his master or mentor, but because of their lifelong friendship, Tsukamoto never called him that to his face. Even so, Yoshida had become something larger than life. He had a mystique among the yakuza as a man with a persuasive charisma and a tangible inner strength that seemed to transcend the earthly plain of existence. In essence, he became the spiritual leader of the Ryujin-kai, a position created specially for such a unique individual. Tsukamoto could not deny that Yoshida possessed an enlightened intelligence. He had seen it in action. And it should be said that Yoshida poured money into the yakuza and that didn't hurt his stature in the organisation either. There was no question that Goro Yoshida should be *Yami Shogun,* the Dark Lord, of the Ryujin-kai.

By that time, their relationship had changed. Yoshida respected and trusted Tsukamoto as his lifelong friend and loyal colleague, but there were times when Tsukamoto was the victim of Yoshida's volatile nature. Tsukamoto would never forget the shame he had felt when he had bungled a business arrangement with a rival yakuza. Yoshida had slapped him across the face, a gesture that left no doubt about who ran the organisation.

Nevertheless, Tsukamoto continued to support and serve the *Yami Shogun,* even when Yoshida went off the deep end in the 1980s with what he called the "New Offensive." The targets were all over the world: Western companies whose businesses had a detrimental effect on Japanese traditions were bombed. The countries hit the hardest were the United States and Great Britain. The bombings started in Japan and then they spread to neighbouring countries. When the terror reached the big cities in the U.S. and Britain, the authorities knew that something had to be done.

The intelligence communities of the world gathered information and compared notes. Like his father before him, Goro Yoshida became a wanted man. He fled Japan, but since he rarely made an appearance anyway, no one really knew if he was in Japan or not. What was certain was that he and nearly one hundred followers mysteriously disappeared. He was thirty-eight years old.

Yasutake Tsukamoto was one of the few men outside of Yoshida's camp who knew where he was. Most of their dealings were conducted by telephone and the Internet, but Tsukamoto had to fly to Etorofu once a month to meet with the *Yami Shogun.* He would then come back to Sapporo with Yoshida's advice and guidance on Ryujin-kai business. In 1993, Yonai Enterprises moved its base of operations from Tokyo to Sapporo so that the headquarters of the Ryujin-kai would be closer to their spiritual leader. A cover story was created to pacify the authorities: Goro Yoshida had sold Yonai Enterprises and others were now running it. In reality, Yoshida was still the owner, operating Yonai from afar through a puppet president.

The ensuing years were exciting and profitable.

Yoshida masterminded several satisfying ventures, with only one notable failure—and if it hadn't been for the incompetence of the Union, a terrorist-for-hire organisation, that would not have been the case.

Now the *Yami Shogun* was about to embark on a plan that frightened the hell out of Tsukamoto.

Today Goro Yoshida was fifty-nine years old, but he still had the vitality of a twenty-four-year-old. Yasutake Tsukamoto was fifty-eight and felt the weight of the world on his shoulders.

After the helicopter had landed, two uniformed soldiers escorted Tsukamoto to a bunker. He had been through the routine dozens of times before. Steps led down to a dugout that had been completely furnished in the style of a traditional Japanese home. Tsukamoto removed his shoes and stepped up onto the *shikidai*. A guard opened the *fusuma*, the sliding door made by stretching thick decorative paper over both sides of a wooden frame—a distinctive component of a Japanese home or inn. The room was covered in eight *tatami* mats. *Shoji*, translucent screens of thin paper stretched over frames of crossed laths, lined one wall and allowed light to come into the room. A *tokonoma*, another traditional element, adorned a side of the room. This was a recessed alcove in the wall where a scroll was hung, and, in this case, an exquisite spray of orchids was displayed. One single unfinished vertical wooden post, the *tokobashira*, helped to support the *tokonoma*.

In the middle of the room was a low table. Tsukamoto sat on one of the *zaisu*, cushioned chairs with backs but no legs, and waited for his friend and mentor.

He could hear the hum of the power generators through the walls. It was an impressive complex—barracks for a hundred men, a mess hall, training facilities, arms storage—in fact a small army base, mostly located underground. It had taken Yoshida more than a year to have it constructed. It was a monumental achievement.

After a moment, the *fusuma* at the back of the room slid open, and Goro Yoshida stepped in. Tsukamoto remained in his seat but bowed as low as he could. Yoshida bowed less deeply and then sat down across from Tsukamoto.

The *fusuma* slid open again, and a woman in a kimono, on her knees, looked in. She greeted the guest, placed a tray inside the room, then stood and came inside. She knelt at the table and served green tea to both men, then left the room in the same manner.

"You are looking well," Tsukamoto said.

Yoshida shook his head. "I am looking old."

"No, you are not. I look much older than you." It was true. Yoshida appeared to be a man in his late forties or early fifties, certainly not someone who was pushing sixty. He was a small but solid, man. His bodybuilding had paid off, and even at his age his muscles appeared still toned and bulky through the black and white silk kimono that he wore. His hair was short, cut in the style of his idol, Yukio Mishima. A portrait of the author sat on a low table against a wall, next to portraits of Yoshida's mother and sister.

"How proceeds our latest venture?" Yoshida asked.

"Very well. It is just a matter of time before Yonai Enterprises will completely control our rival. We will no longer have to rely on a CureLab pawn to provide us with their latest technology."

"This has taken much longer than you had anticipated."

"I know, Yoshida. I apologise."

"You sound like a woman," Yoshida spat. "Sometimes I wonder if you are competent."

Tsukamoto nearly gasped. The *Yami Shogun* had never spoken to him quite so harshly before.

"Yoshida," he said, "I am very loyal to you. Why do you insult me? Without me running things in Japan—"

Yoshida slapped the table hard, startling Tsukamoto. "Do you forget who you're talking to? Would you even be where you are without my leadership?"

Tsukamoto shuddered inside. "My mistake," he said, bowing. Even though they were childhood friends, the relationship between them could be turbulent. Tsukamoto never knew how Yoshida would react to anything. This was the main reason why Tsukamoto both respected and feared his master.

After a pause, Yoshida asked, "When do you expect the final phase of the merger to take place?"

"Very soon. Within the week. With the, uhm, unfortunate death of CureLab's CEO and chairman, the family's stock has passed to the only remaining daughter. And as you know, she is under the thumb of the Ryujin-kai, making good money for us!"

"Good. Another strike against the Western barbarians. Of course, the girl must be eliminated now."

Tsukamoto was surprised. "Eliminated?"

"We cannot keep her alive, Tsukamoto. Surely you know that."

Tsukamoto cleared his throat. "Yes, of course. Pardon me."

"And the product? Have our people been working on it?" Yoshida asked.

"Yes. The strain that killed the McMahons is being perfected. That one was too slow and took too long to take effect. The next version will be much better and will work faster. We are also almost ready with a new version of the transmitters."

Yoshida rubbed his chin. "I trust it will work. Our people have been working on them at the laboratory in Hokkaido for some time. The first version was a most impressive attempt, but it wasn't perfect. At this late stage, will we have enough time? You know the target date."

"Our engineers swear that they are ready. They hope to complete the work in forty-eight hours or less. After what was already supplied to us from the CureLab traitor, it shouldn't be too difficult to make the necessary adjustments."

"I hope you're right, Tsukamoto. Have all materials moved from Hokkaido to the distribution centre in Tokyo. We have to be ready by the end of the week."

"Yes, *sensei*." As soon as he said it, Tsukamoto realised that he had made a slip.

Yoshida shook his head slightly. "Tsukamoto, you know that you do not have to call me *sensei*. We have known each other since we were children."

"I know. I apol— er, my mistake. It's just that you *are* the master. I cannot help but think of you in this way."

"I appreciate your loyalty and respect, Tsukamoto-san. Let us leave it at that. And now, my friend, let's have lunch."

Yoshida smiled and Tsukamoto felt relieved for the first time in days.

It was later the same day. Goro Yoshida took a wet cloth and laid it across his forehead. The only time he felt at peace with himself was when he put his head back against the large cypress tub and closed his eyes. The hot water stimulated his skin, reminding him of the sensations he had experienced when he had received the exquisite red tattoo that covered eighty per cent of his body. The intricate tattoo, depicting an ancient battle between samurai and dragons, decorated his skin from the base of the neck, down his back and arms, across his chest and stomach, and down his legs to his calves. Its red colour dominated the design, with only hints of black outlining figures and creatures, a few touches of yellow for highlights, and a little orange tinting. But mostly it was various shades of red. Dark red, crimson red, fiery red, pink red, blood red . . . it was totally unique. Many yakuza adorned their bodies with tattoos, but none had quite the impact of Yoshida's. It was at once marvellous, beautiful and terrifying. He had gone through many hours of pain for the tattoo, one hundred for the back alone. The technique of traditional *irezumi* tattooing was painful. It was done slowly and manually, without the use of electric devices.

Tsukamoto was in another part of the complex. He would be leaving for the mainland in an hour, but Yoshida wanted him to see something first. In the interim, Yoshida had spent an hour in the gym practising kendo, lifting weights and participating in *kenjutsu,* Japanese swordsmanship. He had become one of the finest swordsmen in the Far East and was considered a master. Yoshida had first picked up a samurai sword when he was eight. By the time he was fourteen, it was a part of him.

Yoshida used a *shinai,* a bamboo sword used for practise, but his opponent always used a *bokken,* a wooden sword that had the potential to be deadly. So far, no opponent had ever been able to strike him. For a while, Yoshida thought that his opponents might be holding back simply because he was the *Yami Shogun* and no one dared to hit him with a real weapon. He told the students that he could tell if they were trying their best or not. If they did not attempt their best, then he would have them killed. From then on, Yoshida noted a discernible difference in the attitudes of his opponents.

Yoshida removed the cloth from his face and opened his eyes. The bath had been relaxing and the ritual soaking in the *o-furo* hot tub had been invigorating, but now it was time to act. He was ready to launch the project that he had prepared himself for since the death of his father.

• • •

Dressed in a *yukata* and *tanzen*, Yoshida strode through the corridors of his compound until he came to the gymnasium. The workout equipment had been cleared, and Tsukamoto and several guards were standing at attention. They all bowed when he entered the room.

"My friend, Tsukamoto, you shall now see the real beginning of our venture. We have been preparing for it for a long time and finally we have the great pleasure of watching it commence."

"I am honoured, Yoshida," Tsukamoto said, bowing again.

Yoshida clapped his hands and a *fusuma* slid open. Twenty men dressed in civilian clothes marched in quickly and formed two lines of ten. Once they were in place, they bowed to Yoshida in unison. Yoshida walked around the group once, inspecting them. Finally, he addressed his long-time friend.

"Twenty men," he said. "Not a bad luck number for us, eh, Tsukamoto?"

Tsukamoto knew what Yoshida meant. The name "yakuza" came from the combination of three numbers— 8, 9 and 3. This referred to an ancient Japanese gambling game called Oicho-Kabu, in which the number 19 was the strongest hand to possess. A 20, the sum of 8, 9, and 3, was completely useless and considered bad luck. In the old days, the yakuza were known as the "useless hands" of society. The name stuck and their lucky number became 20.

Yoshida continued, "Twenty men. Twenty messages. You men will be our carriers. Like the kamikaze pilots during the honourable war with the Americans, you are willing to end your lives to accomplish the mission. For that I bow to you."

With that, Yoshida bowed as low as Tsukamoto had ever seen him do. As there was a definite hierarchy of superiority that determined the degree of bowing in Japanese society, it was shocking to see the *Yami Shogun* bow so low.

Yoshida rose and said, "You will fly to Sapporo tonight for a couple of days of rest and relaxation. You will be the guests of Tsukamoto. Then you will fly to Tokyo for the final preparations. By the middle of next week, you will each be on a journey to deliver our messages to the West. Go swiftly and silently. Be diligent always, and never falter from your path. You and your families have been rewarded handsomely. If by some quirk of fate some of you do not return, then know that you will be rewarded more handsomely in heaven."

The men shouted, *"Hai!"* and bowed again.

5

Yes, Tokyo!

Bond had mixed feelings about returning to Japan.

Sitting in the executive-class cabin of the daily JAL flight from London to Tokyo's Narita Airport, Bond had plenty of time to consider the situation. On the one hand, a reunion with his friend Tiger Tanaka, the head of the Koan-Chosa-Cho, was very appealing. Bond genuinely enjoyed Japan; he appreciated the attention to detail and cleanliness that was so important to the Japanese people. He was impressed that the population had the consideration to cover their noses and mouths with surgical masks and wear them in public when they had colds. He admired their efficiency and good manners, their dedication to tradition and their generosity. He found the scenery beautiful. He enjoyed sake and Japanese beer. He thought that a lot of the food was unique and delicious, but he avoided raw fish whenever possible.

And he considered Japanese women to be arguably the most beautiful in the world. Besides possessing classically pretty, nearly perfect facial features, Japanese women held a poise and grace not found in other societies, as well as a certain delicateness that was endearing and attractive. He had once facetiously told the Governor of the Bahamas that he would only marry a Japanese girl or an airline hostess. And, considering the JAL hostesses on today's flight, it was still a half-serious proclamation.

The other side of the coin was an unknown. He had begun his first mission to Japan as a nervous and physical wreck due to his grief over the death of his only bride. By happenstance, Bond had discovered that Ernst Stavro Blofeld was hiding on a remote island in the south of Japan. The subsequent battle between the adversaries left Blofeld dead and Bond emotionally and physically scarred. He lived for months with an Ama girl, the lovely Kissy Suzuki, on a nearby island. Bond became a fisherman and boatman, with Kissy as his wife, until he was compelled to leave his simple existence as Taro Todoroki and search for his true identity in the Soviet Union.

When he had finally regained his memory, Bond retained everything that had happened on that island with Kissy. He had learned to speak Japanese (and could still do so, although he was very rusty) and had mastered the ability to read and write the script known as *kana.* He was less successful in learning *kanji,* the Japanese written language that was based on symbolic Chinese characters, but he had adopted many Japanese customs and manners and had practised them until they were second nature. It had taken him weeks to rid himself of a compulsion to remove his shoes before entering a house.

How would all this affect him upon his return to Japan? The ghosts of those he had loved or hated might be around to haunt him: Kissy and the son Bond had never had a chance to know, Blofeld, Henderson, even the phantom of Taro Todoroki . . .

What the hell is wrong with you? Bond scolded himself. The assignment was a breeze. Compared to that first mission to Japan many years ago, a task that had been considered "impossible," this one would be a holiday.

Enjoy yourself! he commanded. Drink a lot of sake with

Tiger and play that silly children's game, Scissors Paper Stone. Eat a lot of fish. Meet a Japanese girl or two. Have a traditional Japanese bath, a pleasure made in heaven. Here was a chance to delight in an assignment for a change.

"May I take that away, sir?" the pretty flight attendant asked.

"Yes, please."

She took the tray that had contained a fine Japanese meal consisting of a prawn sushi and an egg roll with crabmeat appetisers, sweet-simmered whitebait in soy sauce, boiled shrimp with fish roe, a piece of fried chicken in ginger starch sauce, miso soup, Japanese pickles and steamed rice. She left another bottle of Ginjo sake, his third but not his last, and cleared away the empty. It was a slightly sweet sake that came from the Kyoto Prefecture, and Bond thought it did nicely as an after-dinner drink. He had to admit that the service aboard Japan Airlines was in keeping with the first-class attention to detail that all things seemed to receive in Japan. The twelve-hour flight would be a pleasant one.

Bond settled back and gradually felt less melancholic and more optimistic about his stay in Japan. Perhaps it was the nice smile the Japanese flight attendant gave him every time she walked by, but eventually Bond stopped worrying. There was now no doubt that he should throw himself into the assignment and have a good time in Japan.

Bond wondered if Tiger had changed. It had been a long time since they had communicated, and it was Bond who had broken off the contact, embarrassed by what had happened to him in Japan. Tiger had always said that Bond had saved great face and would be regarded as a hero if it weren't for the classified nature of his deeds, but Bond had never bought into that rubbish.

It was time to reestablish the connection with his old friend.

• • •

At Immigration, Bond presented his passport, and the officer made a quick call to Bond's contact who came to greet him.

"Mr. Bond?" she asked. "I'm Reiko Tamura. I'm with the Public Security Investigation Agency." She bowed.

At first Bond didn't know what to say. He hadn't expected a woman.

"Konnichi-wa," Bond said, bowing slightly.

"Oh, you speak Japanese?" she asked with a look of disbelief.

"Iie, iie. Mada heta desu." Bond adapted the very Japanese way of being self-effacing when presented with a compliment.

"Well I don't think so. Your pronunciation is very good."

He shrugged. *"Arigato."*

She smiled warmly. Bond thought she was stunning. She seemed to be in her mid-twenties, but with Japanese women it was always difficult to tell because they appeared to stay young forever. She was dressed in a sharp, dark grey pinstriped Armani trouser suit. It was very modern and flattering, with a tapered waist that accentuated her curves splendidly. She had a classic, pretty Japanese face with a warm smile and terrific brown eyes. Her shoulder-length black hair was shaped around her head and tucked behind her ears. One couldn't help but notice the black pearl at her neck. It had a unique pigment, like a peacock's feather, and this suited her colouring. But what made her *sexy,* Bond thought, were her glasses. He didn't know why. She looked very corporate, trying hard to look right in a man's world, but at the same time Reiko Tamura exhibited an intelligence that put Bond at ease. This woman was a class act. Tiger would not have sent someone incompetent. The fact that he had sent a woman simply had to do with Tiger knowing Bond all too well.

She presented him with a business card. Bestowing *meishi* had become a very sacred and necessary ritual in Japanese society. A person without a business card was no one. It was customary for the receiver to take the card with both hands and make a point of actually reading it before putting it carefully in a pocket. Reiko's was a company-issued card with her name, the name and address of her organisation and phone and fax numbers. The front was written in *kanji* and the back was in English.

Bond had come prepared. The service had given him cards that read, very simply, "James Bond—Ministry of Defence" along with the public mailing address and phone numbers. His were written in *katakana* on one side and in English on the other.

"Hajime mashite," Bond said. She laughed and repeated the phrase. They were pleased to meet each other and shook hands.

"You have your luggage? Let's collect your handgun over here," she said. "You do understand that you cannot use it except in a case of extreme emergency."

She led him to the Customs officer and spoke some rapid Japanese that made Bond realise how out of practise he was. He hadn't understood a word she had said. The officer bowed to Bond and said something equally fast, then went and fetched a canvas bag with the airline logo on it. Bond had to sign some official papers to be able to carry his gun in the country, and then they were ready.

Reiko had brought a small Honda Life that she had left in the car park. Looking at the way the Japanese utilised space, Bond was amazed that they could design a world to live in that was like the way they made electronics—compact and neat. The cars were created specifically for a society that lived in a very small, crowded space. The Honda Life was one of those tall, cube-like cars, but it appeared highly efficient. The Japanese concept of car parks was just as unique. Their philosophy of trying to put as many things as possible into the tiniest conceivable space certainly applied in these locations.

They left Narita Airport and embarked on the one-hour journey to the sprawling city of Tokyo. At midday, traffic was heavy as it flowed along the major arteries. Once again, the city's immense proportions bombarded Bond. There were sounds and sights and smells that attacked the senses from every direction. Even more so than in other major cities of the world—London, New York, Paris— Tokyo was bursting with energy. Bond could feel it in the air here much more intensely than he could elsewhere. The people of Tokyo *worked,* and they worked long hours. The city was a constant hustle and bustle; it never slept and the lights were always bright. It all came back to Bond: how Tokyo was a megalopolis, in reality several smaller cities connected by Japan Rail's Yamanote commuter train loop. Each of these smaller cities had its own distinct character: the Ginza was the elite shopping area, the equivalent of New York's Fifth Avenue; Shinjuku was ultramodern, with towering skyscrapers and endless department stores; Akihabara was known for electronics; and Ueno was a hip older section of the city.

"Tanaka-san is waiting for you," Reiko said. "I will take you to meet him first."

"Thank you."

"He has invited you to his home where you can relax and talk for the rest of the day. He knows that you are probably tired after the long flight."

"I'm all right, but that's very kind of him. Thank you."

"I will take your luggage and check you in at your hotel, is that all right?"

"You don't have to do that."

"It is my pleasure, Mr. Bond."

"Tiger calls me Bondo-san. Please, call me James."

"James?" She smiled, saying it a few times to herself

as if to see if she liked the sound of it. "All right, I will call you James. James-san. I like it."

"Your English is very good," Bond said.

"Thank you, but no it isn't. I mix it up a lot. Especially when I write it."

"Your pronunciation sounds American."

"Could be. I studied the language in America. Although we have ten years of English in our public school system, it is impossible to learn to speak it well within Japanese education. You really have to go to America or England. My parents sent me to San Francisco to a private high school." She looked at him and smiled.

"Reiko is a nice name."

"It's very common in Japan. The way of writing 'Reiko' means 'a polite or well-mannered girl,' which my parents wished me to become when I was born. Well, I am not sure if my parents are so proud of me lately . . ." She giggled.

"How long have you been with the service? Are you in Tiger's outfit? The Koan-Chosa-Cho?"

"Yes, I am special agent. I mostly work abroad, but I am to remain in Japan for the G8 summit conference. I understand you will be attending?"

"Yes."

"That pleases me. We shall see a lot of each other in the next several days," she said brightly. She gave him a sideways glance through her glasses that possibly held more meaning. Was she flirting with him?

She drove fast and with skill, skirting off the expressway and into Shibuya. She navigated corners and intersections with the fervour of a race car driver until she finally pulled over near a JR rail station.

"Do you see that statue of the dog?" Reiko asked, pointing. Bond looked and indeed saw a brown statue of an alert, sitting Akita. It was erected on the little square outside the station. Masses of people were going in and out of the building.

"Yes."

"That's Hachiko. Everyone meets in front of Hachiko."

"Do they?"

"Tanaka-san will meet you there in a few minutes. I will see you later, James-san."

"I look forward to it," Bond said. He got out of the car and stood amongst the swarm of people. He had once heard a friend refer to the Japanese as "designer humans." They were all so attractive—the women, the young girls, the men, the teenagers, the children. Everyone seemed young. School-age children were just being let out for the day. Young "salarymen" and "office ladies" were going to and fro. A group of tourists all wore T-shirts that proclaimed, "Yes, Tokyo!" This was Shibuya, the young person's celebration of capitalism. It was not the superchic Ginza, nor was it the techno-pop Shinjuku. It was simply a fashionable place where a lot of young people came to shop, work and have a good time.

Bond approached the statue and stood beside it. "Hachiko" was sitting on a large stone cube.

"He was a very loyal dog." It was a voice that Bond would know anywhere. He turned and there he was, appearing out of the throngs of people. One second earlier and he hadn't been there; the next he was.

"Tiger," Bond said warmly.

"Bondo-san."

The two men embraced like brothers. When they parted, Tiger said, "Welcome to Japan, Mr. Bond."

Bond smiled. "It's good to see you again, Tiger."

"And you as well."

He looked thinner. That was the first thing that struck Bond. And he looked tired. But he was still the same man with the glowing almond eyes and smiling brown face. He was dressed casually, as if he lived in the neighbourhood and had just gone out to the shops.

"How are you, Tiger?"

"I am fine. Come, let us walk, and I shall tell you," he gestured. "But first let me tell you about this faithful dog, Hachiko."

"By all means."

"In the 1920s, a university professor living in this area kept an Akita dog. Every morning and evening this dog would come to the station to see off or meet his master. Even after the master's death in 1925, Hachiko continued to come to Shibuya Station for eleven years to wait for a master who would never return. Isn't that admirable? The Japanese treasure loyalty. Come, we shall walk. Are you not too tired?"

"I feel fine," Bond said. "I slept a little on the plane."

"Good. We will go to one of my private residences. It's in Yoyogi Park. We shall spend the rest of the day there. We can brief each other and eat an early dinner. Then you will be taken to your hotel for a good sleep. Tomorrow we begin. All right?"

"You're the boss, Tiger," Bond said.

They crossed the busy intersection when the light indicated that they could do so. Bond heard the sound of a bird chirping.

"That's the audio signal to alert blind people that they can cross the street," Tiger explained.

The two men walked up a street and then turned toward the block of Parco department stores.

"I walk everywhere now; it's for my health," Tiger said. "I am about to tell you something that many people do not know. I am no longer head of the Koan-Chosa-Cho. I have given up the position to my successor, Nakayama. He is looking forward to meeting you. You see, Bondo-san, I had a heart attack not long ago."

It was not easy for Bond to see weakness in men he respected, but he looked with sympathy at his old friend.

"What happened?"

"They cut me open, they operated. Triple bypass. So, you see, I had to step back a little. I still work for the service, and I retain authority. But I suppose you could say that I enjoy the 'street beat' now because my doctor told me I should walk a lot. I still have complete access to the service's facilities and work as a special advisor on just about everything."

"It sounds to me as if you're really still in charge."

"Only in the background. I pull strings. Much like the ancient feudal lords, the *daimyo,* who when they retired would shave their heads and join the priesthood—but in fact they gave orders from the background and still had much power."

"I had no idea, Tiger."

"No one does. That's still classified information. We don't want our enemies to know that I've retired yet, for security reasons."

"I understand."

They walked along the quiet and peaceful path. The sun was bright, and the day was warm. Bond enjoyed the stroll past the gnarled cherry trees, the blossoms of which had disappeared for the year. They would return the following spring, but for now, only the twisted trees remained.

A swarm of schoolgirls walked past them. Bond observed that the plaid skirts of their school uniforms were daringly high. The girls were also wearing their bulky white knee socks bunched down around their ankles. Tiger noticed Bond looking at them and said "Those are our *ko-gyaru,* or 'ko-gals.' At school they wear the skirts properly, just above the knees, and their socks all the way up their legs. As soon as they leave the school, they roll up the skirts and wear them short, and they pull down their socks. All to show off their pretty legs. You like?"

"Too young for me," Bond said, shaking his head.

Tiger laughed. "You look good, Bondo-san. Are you happy?"

"As happy as a civil servant can be, Tiger."

They approached the Meiji Jinju, the famous Shinto shrine that attracted more than two million people on one New Year's Day in the 1980s. It was originally built in 1920, but it had to be reconstructed after the bombing of Tokyo during the war.

"Do you mind if we go into the shrine for a moment?" Tiger asked.

"Not at all," Bond said.

They went through the huge wooden *Torii,* the archway that is the symbol of a Shinto shrine. The gate represents the division between the everyday world and the divine world.

Bond followed Tiger to the small pavilion where visitors purified their hands before entering the main courtyard of the shrine. Tiger took the wooden ladle and poured water over one hand and then the other. He took a drink, swished it around in his mouth and spat it out. Then he allowed water from the ladle to pour down the handle, cleansing where he had touched it. Bond took a ladle and followed suit.

They went inside the courtyard. The main sanctuary was built in the Nagaré-zukuri style of architecture. The corners of its green roof sloped out and upward. Several *miko,* the young female assistants to the priests, ran stalls along the sides of the courtyard that sold souvenirs and good luck charms. Bond inspected them and saw that there were talismans for good health, for scholarship, for love and even one for traffic safety.

Bond turned and saw Tiger tossing a coin into a collection box. Tiger bowed his head twice, clapped his hands twice and bowed once again. After a moment he returned to Bond and said, "I am finished. Do you care to pray before we leave, Bondo-san?"

"That's all right, Tiger," Bond said. "The gods don't have much use for me."

Tiger shook his head as they left the grounds. "I know that you have a spiritual side, Bondo-san. We all do. A man finds it when he is ready. You just haven't found yours yet."

"Some don't find it until the day they die, Tiger," Bond said.

They walked north through the park toward Shinjuku until Tiger went off the main path and stepped over a chain and a sign stating "Private — Keep Out" in English and Japanese. Bond followed him down a smaller path through the tall trees until they came to what appeared to be an ordinary garden shed. Tiger pulled a key from his pocket and unlocked the door. He held it open and Bond went inside.

It *was* a tool shed. The place was stocked with park maintenance equipment. One corner of the room was empty and had a metal floor.

Tiger shut the door and locked it from the inside. He led Bond to the metal floor and pressed a button. The floor began to descend to another level.

Bond couldn't help but laugh. "Tiger, what are you doing with a residence in Yoyogi Park?"

"I have several residences around the country, Bondo-san. You knew that. This is one that the government owns. It was built inside a natural cave. There is even a stream that flows nearby. I will have to move out eventually. It is completely underground, so I do not spend too much time here. It is only, how do you say, an 'oasis'?"

They walked down a stone corridor to a metal door. Tiger pushed another button and it slid open, revealing a beautifully furnished Japanese home. Bond removed his shoes as he stepped up onto the *tatami,* admiring the *tokonoma* and the welcome sight of the low table, the legless chairs and what would probably be green tea.

Four lovely women in kimonos were waiting for them.

"Irrashaimase!" they greeted the men in unison, then they bowed.

6

Briefing Below Ground

"Would you prefer cold sake or warm sake?" Tiger asked.

"I'll leave that decision to you," Bond said, diplomatically.

Tiger barked some quick Japanese to one of the women, who bowed and left the room.

"Please sit," he said to Bond, and they took places on either side of the low table. "It is so good to see you again, Bondo-san. It has been too long."

The woman entered the room on her knees, bowed, then stood and brought two *tokkuri*—small flasks of warm sake—to the table. She placed a small flat cup, a *choko,* in front of each man. Two other women knelt beside the men; their sole purpose was to pour sake into the *choko* when the cups were empty.

"Kampai," Tiger said, lifting the drink.

"Cheers," Bond said, doing the same, and then they drank. The sake was warm and not too dry.

There was a small package on the table in front of Bond. Tiger gestured to it and said, "That is something you may find useful during your stay in Japan. Please open it."

"Gifts, Tiger?" Bond raised an eyebrow in surprise.

"Please."

Bond opened it and found a DoCoMo mobile phone.

"My personal number is programmed into it. When-ever you need to reach me, punch 'memory' and the num-ber seven. There is also a homing device inside. We'll always know where you are as long as you carry it."

"Thank you, Tiger," Bond said, admiring the compact apparatus. "They make them so small in this country."

"It's a small country, Bondo-san."

Bond put it in his pocket. "So what's the score, Tiger? What can you tell me about the summit conference? You've had some threats?"

"Nothing we can corroborate. Some of the Japanese nationalists are using their usual rhetoric about us cooper-ating with the West. Some violence was threatened. We thought it best that each nation brought their best people. That means you, Bondo-san."

"I'm flattered. Now what about this McMahon busi-ness?"

Tiger sucked in air through his teeth. Bond noted that the Japanese had a way of doing that before delivering bad news or replying in a negative manner. It was a way of softening what they had to say. Other times they might in-hale through their teeth and then say, *"Saaaa . . ."*

Tiger reflected a moment, then said, "I am afraid that this McMahon business, as you call it, is mixed up with the business of the *sono-suji.*"

"The what?"

"The 'people in *that* world,' or the 'people in *that* busi-ness.' The *Boryoku-dan.*"

"The yakuza?"

"Yes, although in law enforcement agencies today, we do not call them that. It's too nice a name for them. We call them *Boryoku-dan*, which literally means 'crime or-ganisation' or 'violent mob.' However, old habits die hard. I still refer to them as yakuza. Ironically, they call themselves *gokudoh,* which means a man who has mastered the way of life."

"You must tell me more."

"I will. But please, let us first enjoy the delicious *kaiseki* meal that my chef has prepared for us."

They didn't talk about business during dinner. Instead, they each talked about their lives, as old friends, catching up after a long time.

The women began to bring in the first of several courses of a traditional *kaiseki* meal, the pinnacle of Japanese cuisine. Bond knew that it was a great honour to be provided such a feast. *Kaiseki* is served in several small courses, giving one the opportunity to admire the plates and bowls that are carefully chosen to complement the food, the region and the relevant season. The ingredients, preparation, setting and presentation are the most important aspects of *kaiseki,* not the food itself.

The first course was a small bowl of clear soup. Inside was a star-shaped cake of green tofu. Next was a bowl of warm soup containing a baby bamboo shoot and some kind of green jelly in the shape of a cube that Bond couldn't identify. A small square tray was placed in front of him for the third course. It held an arrangement of dainty titbits that had been arranged like a work of art. Bond didn't like eating raw food and found some of the items in *kaiseki* difficult to cope with. He did his best, though. Sashimi was next, followed by a serving of finely minced daikon radish and fish that was grilled on a tiny charcoal cooker sitting on the table. A dish of boiled fish, vegetables and other ingredients, cooked in soy sauce and sweet rice wine with sugar, came next. Another course contained steamed egg, vegetables, fish and meat. After three more courses of varying delights, rice, miso soup and pickles were served to round off the meal. The entire dinner took nearly two hours.

"How do you feel now, Bondo-san? Tired?" Tiger asked.

"No, just excruciatingly relaxed."

Tiger laughed and said, "It is impolite to fall asleep when someone is talking to you, Bondo-san."

"So, Tiger, you've fed me and you've got me drunk, now will you tell me what the hell this case is about?"

"Certainly. How much do you know about yakuza, Bondo-san?"

Bond shrugged. "What all of us know. They're a highly organised mafia-like group of criminals. A lot like the Chinese Triads. They have powerful right-wing support, and they operate vast syndicates with interests in everything from guns to property. Many of their businesses are completely legitimate. They are a widely tolerated component of Japanese society. Am I right?"

Tiger sighed. "You are very right, Bondo-san. And you are wondering why they are tolerated so. You see, many yakuza see themselves as custodians of honour and chivalry, traditional values that have all but vanished in modern-day Japan. The country's ultranationalist right—which also looks for a return to 'traditional values'—enjoys yakuza support. In the ancient days, the yakuza began as street traders and gamblers. They eventually organised into gangs, and while they developed their criminal activities, they insinuated themselves into business society. Many companies, many *successful* companies, have ties to the yakuza. It is a fact of life in Japan, and there is not much that can be done to change it."

"I wasn't aware that murder and extortion had been added to the list of essential qualities for honour and chivalry," Bond said.

"I know, I am fully aware of the irony too," Tiger said. "I have no respect for these people, the *sono-suji*. The law enforcement agencies try to arrest them when they can and when they can charge them with something that will stick. But they are very clever, some of these yakuza, Bondo-san. They are so accustomed to being an accepted part of society that the big ones now all have offices. Right in the open. The one we are concerned about in this case is the Ryujin-kai. They are based in Sapporo, up north on the island of Hokkaido. They used to be based in Tokyo, but they moved a little less than ten years ago. Sapporo is a busy yakuza centre. The town attracts Russian tourists, and it's a fairly large black market trading post. The leader of the Ryujin-kai is a man named Yasutake Tsukamoto. They call their leader the *kaicho* or *oyabun*. The members are his 'children,' or *wakashu*. Higher-ranking children are called *shatei,* or 'younger brother.' Each yakuza is broken down into smaller gangs, each with their own *kaicho,* but they all report up the chain to the main boss."

"Go on."

"Tsukamoto is in his late fifties. Wealthy. In the chemical engineering business. He is also on the board of directors of a company called Yonai Enterprises, do you know it?"

Bond nearly choked on a sip of sake. "My God, Tiger, that was Goro Yoshida's company, wasn't it?"

"Yes, it was. He sold it before he disappeared. Now it is run by others."

"What do they do?"

"It's a conglomerate, mostly in the chemical engineering field. They have wanted to acquire CureLab Inc. for a long time. CureLab, as you know, is known as a successful pharmaceutical firm. It was once called Fujimoto Lab Inc. and was owned by Hideo Fujimoto. When he died ownership went to his daughter Junko, who was married to Peter McMahon. McMahon was not well liked in Japan, Bondo-san. I realise that he is a fellow countryman of yours, but he did not play the business game fairly, at least by Japanese standards. We are only just beginning to learn things about him."

"What do you mean?"

"Only that some of his employees said he was very ruthless in his business dealings."

"Interesting."

"At any rate, it is no secret that Yonai Enterprises made a very good offer to McMahon to buy CureLab. McMahon refused to sell, of course. This was a few months ago."

"What makes CureLab so attractive to them?" Bond asked.

"CureLab's main business is drug manufacturing, but recently they have made strides in the medical community with the study of diseases and the discovery of cures. They are especially interested in what you might call 'exotic' Asian diseases—malaria, yellow fever, and the like."

"And you think Yonai Enterprises had the yakuza assassinate McMahon and his family? Wipe out the entire clan at once so that they could take over the company?"

"It's what I think, but I am having difficulty convincing anyone at my firm that that is what happened. If it was an assassination, I still am not sure how it was accomplished. The police do have on record a report of alleged threats made to McMahon by the Ryujin-kai. The police even advised that he should have extra protection for a while, but McMahon refused their help."

"Is it possible that Goro Yoshida is involved? Does anyone know where he is?"

Tiger looked to the ceiling as if hoping for divine intervention. "No one knows, but we suspect he's hiding in Russia, possibly the Northern Territories. It is quite possible that Yoshida keeps contact with the Ryujin-kai. He was a member for a very long time."

"Are there any other McMahon family members around? On the Fujimoto side?"

"Yes. Hideo Fujimoto had a younger brother, Shinji Fujimoto. He is currently vice president of CureLab."

"Next in line for ownership of the company?"

"Perhaps."

"What do you know about him?"

"Shinji Fujimoto has monsters in his wardrobe."

"Excuse me?" Bond asked.

"How do you say it? 'Monsters in the wardrobe?' "

"Oh, you mean 'skeletons in his closet.' He has secrets."

"Yes, that is what I meant. I apologise. I have not spoken English in some time."

"We can switch to Japanese if you like, but I'm finding that my Japanese isn't as good as I thought it would be."

"No, I would like the practise, Bondo-san," Tiger said. "Shinji Fujimoto is a puzzle. He is in his sixties now, not in very good health. He has always had income tax problems, a financial scandal or two. So far, though, he seems clean as far as the yakuza are concerned."

"Is he the sort of man who would kill his niece and her family?"

"I don't think so, no. However, as you imply, he has much to gain by their deaths. I will be interested in your opinion of him. You will meet him tomorrow. We have arranged for a car to take us to Saitama, where the McMahon family lived. He is to meet us there."

"Have you located the youngest daughter? Mayumi?"

Tiger took another sharp intake of breath. "*Saaaaa . . .* no, Bondo-san. That is difficult, but we have a lead. You see, Mayumi apparently ran away from home at the age of sixteen. She is twenty now. She has not seen her parents or her sisters for four years."

"Do we know why she ran away?" Bond asked. He picked up the girl's photo from a spread that Tiger had displayed on the table.

"She is very beautiful, is she not?" Tiger asked.

"Yes indeed."

"Mayumi McMahon was a very rebellious child. She got in with the wrong crowd, got into trouble. When she was fourteen, she got a boyfriend in the *bosozoku*."

"What's that?"

"Teenager motorcycle gangs. Juvenile delinquents who ride around on motorbikes looking for trouble. They are a prime recruiting ground for the yakuza."

"What's the boy's name?"

"Kenji Umeki. He is, as they say, a 'piece of work.' He has been arrested for a number of petty offences, once for assault, but he never served much time. He's at the age where the yakuza had better take him soon or he will end up riding a motorcycle forever or end up dead. It is surprising that he has lasted this long, with those gangs always trying to kill each other."

"I take it that her parents didn't exactly welcome him into the home with open arms."

"No, and in fact they had huge, terrible fights with the girl. Her great uncle told us that this went on for two years, and finally, at the age of sixteen, she just left with her boyfriend. She lived with him here in Tokyo. At any rate, we happen to know Kenji Umeki's older cousin, a fellow by the name of Takuya Abo. He used to be in the *bosozoku* until he was badly injured in a gun battle with police. He served three years in prison, got out and now he's straight. Today he works at the Tsukiji Fish Market. Very few people can walk away from the gangs but Abo did it. So, after the deaths of the McMahons, the authorities went to Takuya Abo in an effort to find Umeki with the hope that he knew where the girl was. Abo has told us that he would try and get a message to his cousin, but it has been four days."

"Did Abo know anything about the girl?"

"He said that according to Umeki, she had left him two

years ago and 'went north,' most probably to Sapporo. He told police that she accompanied some high-ranking yakuza and that she is now probably the girlfriend of one of them."

"I'd like to meet Abo," Bond said.

"It will be arranged."

"So it's possible that Mayumi McMahon doesn't know that her parents are dead."

"If she has not read the newspapers or seen the television, then yes, it is quite possible."

"What have your pathologists learned about the disease that killed the McMahons?"

"I will show you the postmortem reports. It was an unknown virus, something similar to West Nile disease, only many times more powerful and fast acting."

"That's what they said about the daughter who died on the flight to England. I hope the bodies haven't been cremated yet?"

Again, Tiger inhaled through his teeth. "I am sorry, Bondo-san, but last night something happened. Very curious. And suspicious. There was a fire at the morgue where the McMahons' bodies were being kept. Everything was destroyed. Not only their bodies but many others."

"Arson?"

"That's what it looks like. Not only that, but the tissue and fluid samples that were taken from the bodies during the postmortem—they have mysteriously disappeared as well."

"Well, I have a story for you too. The night before my flight, I went to see Kyoko McMahon's body at a mortuary near Heathrow. While I was there, three yakuza hoodlums were caught trying to steal her body. One was killed, one got away, and one was arrested. That one's not talking, either. All the police know was that they had ties to the London-based branches of the yakuza. There are several in England. Now why would anyone want to take her body?"

"Maybe they wanted to do the same thing as they did here? They wanted to destroy the body. Perhaps they thought it would be easier to take the body and destroy it rather than burn up your morgue. I have no idea."

"All right, so we have some corpses of people who died of a mysterious, unknown virus that they could have been deliberately infected with. Then after they are dead, the bodies are obliterated. Why?"

"To get rid of evidence, perhaps?"

"Or . . ." Bond thought for a moment. "What if whoever did this didn't want us studying that virus. They don't want us to find a cure."

"That is good thinking, Bondo-san."

"Luckily for us, we still *have* Kyoko McMahon's tissue and fluid samples in England, as far as I know."

Tiger gestured for Bond to join him on reclining chairs at one end of the room. There, two young women were waiting to wash and massage their feet.

Bond lay back and allowed the girl to work his pressure points. After a moment of bliss, he asked, "Tiger, do you have a mosquito problem in Japan?"

Tiger stared at Bond and then slowly smiled. "You are reading my mind, Bondo-san. How did you know about the mosquitoes?"

"Kyoko had bites all over her, but the pathologist didn't think she got the virus from them."

"Our bodies had mosquito bites too. The police report mentions that a few dead mosquitoes were seen in the McMahon home the day that the bodies were found. The crime scene squad probably didn't think anything of it. We sometimes have mosquitoes pretty bad in the summer months. It's all the water in our gardens, you see. Unfortunately, the investigators didn't think to bring any of the dead mosquitoes back to the lab, and now . . . we cannot find any more."

"The yakuza couldn't be sophisticated enough to create designer viruses and find a way to distribute them, could they?" Bond asked.

"It is not possible," Tiger said. "But CureLab has the means to do it. They do virus research. There is an interesting side story to that, which may have some bearing. A young molecular biologist by the name of Fujio Aida used to work for CureLab until a few months ago. He was touted as being a genius, a man who could manipulate the structure of viruses. CureLab had employed him to create cures for certain diseases."

"He *used* to work for CureLab?"

"Right. Six months ago, Aida was accused of industrial espionage, or rather, stealing trade secrets from CureLab. He was dismissed from the company in a messy case that actually made the newspapers. After it was announced that he had been fired, he simply disappeared. Vanished. No one knows what happened to him."

"Do you think he was killed?"

Tiger shrugged. "Possibly, but why? I have left the details and a photo of him in the packet of material I have for you. You can study it at your leisure. It also contains files on Tsukamoto and other characters who may have a bearing on this case, as well as the relevant McMahon crime scene documents."

"Thanks. You say that Yonai Enterprises is located in Sapporo?"

"Yes."

"I've never been that far north in Japan," Bond hinted.

"A trip has been arranged. But first you will spend a few days with us here in Tokyo. Tomorrow you'll see the McMahon home. You can have access to anyone at Cure-Lab Inc. We will try to locate that boy, Umeki. There are plenty of things to do here before you go to Sapporo."

After a moment of quiet contentment, Bond asked, "And the girl who picked me up at the airport . . . Reiko?"

"Miss Tamura, yes, very able-bodied. Very smart girl. She is one of the rare persons who pass our National Official Exams for entering the ministries and therefore never graduated from Tokyo University."

" 'Never graduated' is a distinction?" Bond asked.

"If you are in a top university in the first place, you are a very smart person already. The National Official Exams are given before the university graduation exams. If someone passes the National Official Exams, they do not have to take the graduation exams. They are allowed to walk away from the university and go right into the Ministry of Foreign Affairs. There is great status to be able to say you passed the official exam and never graduated from a top university."

The masseuses finished and the men savoured a few more moments of quiet comfort before they finally stood.

"As much as I hate to mention it, Bondo-san," Tiger said, "it is late. You are tired and need to be refreshed. My assistant will take you to your hotel. Everything has been done for you; just pick up your key at the desk. I will see you tomorrow morning."

Tanaka gave Bond the folder full of various reports and photographs. Bond thanked him and they embraced again. Then Tanaka walked Bond up through the complex, out of the park and to the waiting car, a black Toyota Majesta. The men said good night, and Bond was spirited away.

Night had fallen, and Tokyo was ablaze with life. The neon was blinding, the billboards were bright and colourful, the traffic was still dense and the noise and clamour bombarded the senses.

It was a mesmerising spectacle, but Bond couldn't wait to fall into bed.

7

Scene of a Crime?

"While we were getting drunk last night, Bondo-san, my staff heard from the old boyfriend, Kenji Umeki," Tiger said as they rode northwest out of Tokyo to Saitama through a vast network of suburbs that seemed to go on forever. "His cousin found him for us. We're going to talk to him later this afternoon in Shinjuku. He says that he knows where Mayumi McMahon is. He wants a hundred thousand yen for the information."

"Are you going to pay him?"

"I think yes, Bondo-san. The question is whether or not we can trust him to tell us the truth."

"Is he connected with the Ryujin-kai?"

"Yes. His motorcycle gang is called Route 66. The Route 66 work for them sometimes, I believe. Miss Tamura will know more about that. We will see her this afternoon."

Bond settled back and looked out the window. The roads were jammed with traffic, the trains sped along the tracks taking passengers from one end of the isles to the other, and everywhere one looked there were people. Here in Japan, he couldn't help but stand out in a crowd.

The advantage was that the Japanese tended to be extremely tolerant of any lack of etiquette that a *gaijin* might have. If the foreigner forgot to remove shoes before stepping up from the *genkan,* or entrance hall, into a house, the Japanese simply shook their head, rolled their eyes and muttered, *"Gaijin . . ."*

After travelling for an hour, the Majesta's driver brought Tiger and Bond to a pretty street that jutted off from a small park. Bare cherry trees were in abundance, but more impressive were the three large houses that occupied the land.

The McMahons owned the middle one. It was a two-storey mansion that was a unique mix of Japanese and Western styles of architectures. The interior was mostly Japanese with *tatami, fusuma* and *shoji*. Scattered through the rooms, though, were pieces of Western furniture: a dining table, chairs, a sofa, china cabinets and book-shelves.

Two police officers, introduced as Detectives Gunji and Sugahara, were waiting inside. They greeted Tiger as if they had known him for years, then they guardedly presented their business cards to Bond, bowed and shook his hand.

Another man moved forward from the middle of the living room. He had white hair and glasses and appeared to be in his sixties. He was wearing a jacket and tie and seemed to be very nervous.

Tanaka introduced him as Shinji Fujimoto, vice president of CureLab Inc. Fujimoto bowed and presented his *meishi* to Bond, and Bond did likewise. The man knew little English, so Bond attempted to converse with him in Japanese.

"My condolences for your loss," Bond said.

Fujimoto closed his eyes and nodded. "I appreciate your words. I have been full of grief. Thank you for coming all this way to find out what happened to my niece and her family."

The man indeed looked as if he were under a lot of strain. His eyes were bloodshot and his face was puffy. He wasn't getting much sleep and was probably drinking too much.

"Why don't you have a seat, Fujimoto-san," Bond said. "I'm going to have a look around the house, and then we'll talk, all right?"

Fujimoto nodded, then reached for a glass of something that he had been nursing.

The two police detectives took Bond and Tanaka on a tour of the house, pointing out exactly where each body was found and what its condition was. Peter McMahon and his wife had been in the master bedroom, lying on the futon together. They speculated that the couple had felt ill, gone to lie down and died there on the bed. The daughter Shizuka was in the bathroom, having collapsed on the floor.

As they went through the home, Bond noted the abundance of plants that populated the place. There were tall palms in the living room, while the bedrooms had smaller decorations such as *ikebana* flower arrangements.

"Every vase and pot was examined, Bondo-san," Tiger said. "Nothing out of the ordinary was found."

Bond slid open a *fusuma* that led to a respectably large garden.

"It's a *Tsukiyama*-style garden," Tiger said. "It is arranged to show nature in miniature, with hills, ponds and streams." Bond could see that the landscaping featured a pond with stones serving as a walkway to a teahouse on the other side of the garden. Plants were plentiful here too, and there were a number of mosquitoes buzzing near the water.

"Here's your mosquito population," Bond said.

"Ordinary mosquitoes, Bondo-san," Tiger said. "We have already checked. Unfortunately, in this season and with this much standing water about, they will breed easily."

"Can they get inside the house?"

Tiger shrugged. "I suppose if you leave the *fusuma* open, as you are doing!"

Bond nodded and slid it closed. "That might explain all the mosquito bites on the bodies. We'll have to think about alternative ways the virus could have been administered."

One of the detectives spoke rapidly to Tanaka, too fast for Bond to understand. Tiger realised this and translated. "He says that they are not treating this case as homicide. They have no evidence that it was so. The family simply got sick and died."

Bond said, "Tell him that until he can convince me otherwise, I'm not ruling anything out."

They continued to go through the house. Bond examined the screens in each room, looking for an opening. As they came into the central hallway that led back into the living room, Bond noticed a small electric-powered bonsai waterfall fountain on a table. It was about two and a half feet high and a foot and a half wide, and it was beautifully sculpted out of porous granite. The bonsai grew out of the top and an aquarium pump kept the water recycling continuously through the fountain, providing the constant sound of running water. At the moment, the motor was turned off. Bond looked inside it and saw that there was still water in the basin. He reached behind the contraption and found the switch. He turned it on, but nothing happened.

"That was a birthday gift for my niece," Shinji Fujimoto said. He had walked into the hallway behind them. "I delivered it myself a little over a week ago. When we plugged it in and turned it on, it wouldn't work. It was faulty. It made me very angry. I had promised to replace it but never found the time. But now, of course . . ."

Bond unplugged the device and said to Tanaka, "Have it analysed. Take it apart."

Tiger nodded and barked an order to one of the detectives. He proceeded to pick up the fountain, and Bond said, "Don't spill any of the water. Whatever is in there should be looked at."

The man said, *"Hai!"*

Bond turned to Fujimoto and said, "Let's go back in the other room and talk, shall we?"

Fujimoto nodded. The men went and sat down on cushions around the table.

"Fujimoto-san, my government has asked me to find out what happened to your niece and her family. I am also supposed to try to locate your great niece. I know that you have answered many questions that the police have asked you, and that my colleague Tanaka-san has asked you, but I need to ask them as well. Is there anything that you can tell me about CureLab that might have a bearing on the case? Did Peter McMahon have any enemies?"

"He had many enemies," Fujimoto said with a sigh. "McMahon-san was a very good businessman. One goes hand in hand."

"Can you give me an example of what you mean?"

Fujimoto thought a moment. "About three years ago, there was a Japanese company that sold digital microscopes. They were based in Tokyo. McMahon-san had wooed them, making them think that he was going to buy a great number of them. It would have been a hundred-million-yen contract. At the last minute, before the sale, McMahon-san met with some Swiss manufacturers of the same type of product. He got a better deal, cancelled the order with the Japanese company and bought the Swiss models. And while you might say it was simply a business arrangement — he had found a less expensive product — it was dishonourable to cancel the contract he had already made with the Japanese firm. He was criticised in the business community for this."

"How did the business community feel about a British citizen running a Japanese company?"

Fujimoto sucked in air through his teeth. "Difficult to say. I think he was respected because he was good at his job. But he was resented for being a *gaijin*. You see, in Japan, there are clearly defined, invisible circles of influence in the business world. If you work for one company, then that is your inner circle. Your colleagues are also your friends. You go out drinking with them every evening. You develop a second family with them. Say, for instance, you accept a job at another company. You cannot then socialise with your old friends at the old company. You are now out of that circle. It would not be appropriate. I think Tanaka-san would agree with me that in our world, these circles of influence are very important. You stay within your circle, whatever that place is in society. You might be invited to visit another circle, you might be a guest and be entertained by the members of another circle, for business purposes, but you will never be a part *of* that circle. Do you understand what I mean?"

"I think so."

"McMahon-san was a man who ignored the boundaries of these circles. He stepped over the lines many times. He played the game his way."

Bond studied the man's face. Fujimoto's eyes were sincere, but Bond could detect a faint hint of animosity. "What is your function as vice president?" he asked.

"I am in charge of administrative duties," he said. "I also run the research division."

"Doing what?"

"We are working on new techniques of controlling the spread of various diseases and looking for cures."

"Do you work with mosquitoes?"

Again, Fujimoto inhaled through his teeth. "Not really.

We study them, of course, but only for reasons of learning how diseases are transmitted."

"When was the last time you saw your niece or any members of her family?"

Fujimoto was clearly irritated at being questioned, especially by a *gaijin*. "Like I said, I brought the bonsai waterfall over last Wednesday. A little over a week ago. Only Junko and Shizuka were here. Peter was at the office."

"Do you have any idea where Mayumi is?"

Fujimoto sucked in air through his teeth again. "*Saaa* . . . I wish to God that I did. There is no telling what kind of trouble she is in. She was always a mischievous girl. A problem child. Reckless and wild. I hope that the police will locate her soon. I am very worried about her."

"I'd like to find her too," Bond said. "I want to ask her a few things. After all, she's the sole inheritor of the family's shares in CureLab, isn't she?"

Fujimoto nodded. "Yes, but I am sure she had nothing to do with this. My niece had not spoken to Mayumi in four years. This has caused my niece much pain. Peter too."

"What kind of relationship did they have when Mayumi was younger?"

"It seemed to be always bad. Mayumi is a very smart girl, but she was not a good student in school; she rebelled at an early age. She always fought with her parents and sisters. As long as I can remember. I hate to say this now, but when she ran away from home four years ago, I told my niece that she was better off without her."

"How did your niece react to that?"

"She was very upset. She made me apologise."

Bond shifted on the cushion. "What will happen to the company now?"

"The shareholders will decide the company's fate," Fujimoto said with conviction. "If and when Mayumi is found, she will have to deal with selling her share of the stock, I suppose. She knows nothing about the company itself. I can't imagine that she would want to remain involved. Peter and Junko owned sixty per cent of the stock. I own twenty per cent, so CureLab has always been controlled by the family. The other twenty per cent is owned privately."

"Who owns the other twenty per cent?" Bond asked.

Fujimoto shrugged. "Different private individuals. I suppose I can find out and get you the names."

Tanaka asked, "Did not Yonai attempt to buy Cure-Lab?"

"Yes, they are our biggest rival. Yonai Enterprises has made several bids for a takeover, but Peter always refused to sell. Yonai will want to buy Mayumi's shares, and that concerns me. I would hate to see CureLab under their thumb."

"Why is that?" Bond asked.

"They use . . . questionable business practices."

"And if Mayumi can't be found? What will happen?"

Fujimoto shrugged. "As I am the only other relative and I hold a letter from Mayumi's parents giving me power of attorney to act in the event of their deaths, I suppose I will continue to run the company. The board has already voted that I will be acting president for now."

"And would you sell your stock?"

Fujimoto reached for his glass of liquor, took a sip and began to cough violently.

"Did it go down the wrong pipe?" Tanaka asked.

Fujimoto nodded as he set down the glass and made an attempt to control his cough. He wiped his damp forehead with a handkerchief and stammered, "Excuse me. Now, what were you asking?"

"I asked if you would sell your stock," Bond repeated.

"My brother built the company from the ground, and I would not want to see it leave the family. Assuming she reappears, what Mayumi decides to do with her sixty per cent will have a major impact on what happens to us in the future. If she cannot be found, then I will use the power of attorney to hold on to her stock in the family name. I do not understand why you are asking me all these questions. My niece's family is dead due to a tragic accident. Why does all this about the company concern you?"

"Fujimoto-san, we are simply trying to cover all angles," Tanaka said.

Bond thought it was time to ask the man the crucial question. "Tell me, why did your brother not leave the company to you? You were with him at the start-up. Why did he leave it to his only daughter?"

Fujimoto frowned. He didn't like that inquiry. "As my brother is no longer with us, I cannot speak for him."

Tiger's mobile rang. He answered it, spoke some quick words and then rang off.

"That was Miss Tamura," he said. "She is in Shinjuku. It's Mayumi's old boyfriend, Umeki. He's dead. Looks like a homicide. We should go."

Fujimoto gasped. "How did it happen?"

"I do not know yet," Tiger said. He turned to Bond and said, "What did I tell you about that boy?"

Bond stood and thanked Fujimoto for his time.

"Please feel free to contact me at any time, day or night," Fujimoto said. "I would like to help with your investigation as much as possible."

Bond thanked him and said, "We'll be in touch. In the meantime if Mayumi contacts you or you are successful in reaching her, please let us know."

"I will."

They said their good-byes, bowed and left the house. As they got back into the Majesta, Tiger remarked, "I think I know why Hideo Fujimoto left the company to his daughter and not to his brother."

"Why is that?" Bond asked.

"Because Shinji Fujimoto is not a leader. You can see

that. He was very nervous, very unsure of himself. He probably drinks too much. It is fairly obvious that his brother had no faith in him."

Bond asked Tiger, "You want to know what I think?"

"What is that, Bondo-san?"

"I think that Shinji Fujimoto hated his niece's husband."

8
Yakuza Territory

Shinjuku is a massive commercial and entertainment centre that surpasses Times Square, Piccadilly, Sunset Strip and Las Vegas. One would not have to go much farther than here to find nearly everything that makes Tokyo tick. With the highest concentration of skyscrapers in Japan, the country's busiest rail station, government offices, high-class department stores, discount shopping arcades, theatres, pachinko parlours, restaurants, stand-up noodle bars, hostess clubs, strip clubs, hidden shrines and crowds upon crowds of people, Shinjuku is the place to see and be seen.

It was late afternoon when the Majesta got stuck in traffic right near the famous Studio Alta video screen. Fashion clips, information and commercials were broadcast nonstop from the large video billboard on the side of a building.

"Let's walk," Tiger said.

They got out after Tiger issued some instructions to the driver. Then he led Bond to the pavement and began to push through the mass of humanity.

"We're going to Kabuki-cho," he said. "It's still daylight now, but watch your step. This is yakuza territory."

They walked north, passing all sorts of colourful and noisy characters. Bond knew about Kabuki-cho. It was a notorious red-light district, containing strip clubs, peep shows and pornography shops as well as bars, restaurants and the uniquely Japanese "love hotels." These were places where an amorous couple could rent a room for a few hours during the day to get away from the relative nonprivacy they might have at home. Since families usually lived together in houses made with thin walls, couples often found it difficult to make love there. Love hotels did a booming business and were designed around themes — a fairy tale castle, a pirate lair, 1970s disco, 1950s Americana and other fantasy dreamlands. They were also completely discreet: a couple checking in never saw the staff. The exchange of money and keys was done through little windows the size of a hand. Obviously, the love hotels were popular among couples having illicit affairs.

"This place *really* comes alive at night," Tiger said.

"It's not exactly sleeping now," Bond replied, his senses overloaded.

There were signs advertising all kinds of sex for sale — one didn't need a translation to get the gist. Through distorted sound systems, high-pitched female voices called out invitations to enter their establishments. Rough-looking young men and women stood on the street handing out flyers. Some hawkers were aggressive, following the men for a half-block until Tanaka turned abruptly and shouted at them. One hawker wouldn't take "no" for an answer and kept on their heels. Finally, Tiger pulled out a badge and shoved it into the man's face. His eyes widened; he apologised profusely and bowed rapidly.

"It is not much farther, Bondo-san," Tiger said. "There, I see Miss Tamura now."

A police car and motorcycle with lights flashing were parked in the middle of a small side street. Reiko, still dressed in a suit, was speaking to several uniformed officers. She saw them out of the corner of her eye and waved.

As they approached, she bowed to them. "Tanaka-san, James-san, please come this way."

She led them into an empty noodle shop. The chef, a skinny old man, was sitting at a table smoking a cigarette. He looked shaken. A woman, presumably his wife, sat with him.

"The owners of this restaurant found him in the back. Come and look," Reiko said.

She took them into the back alley where the rubbish was piled in bags and boxes. Police tape had been strung around it. Several plainclothed and uniformed officers stood taking notes and photographs.

Falling out of the heap of rubbish was the body of a young man in his twenties. He was covered in dried blood and bent at a grotesque angle. The corpse was dressed in black leather and his long mop-top haircut was dyed red.

"Kenji Umeki," Reiko said. "The detectives are still examining the crime scene, but it looks like he was killed last night. Stabbed to death and dumped here. Look—"

She bent under the tape and pointed to the dead man's hand. Bond saw that all of the fingers had been chopped off, leaving bloody stubs.

"So desu ka," Tiger muttered. "He was killed by yakuza," he said to Bond. "The removal of all the fingers on the hand is a signature of the Ryujin-kai."

"Don't some of them cut their own fingers off?" Bond asked.

"Yes, but that is a penance to an *oyabun.* Something they do to make amends for a wrong that they might have committed."

"But didn't he work for the Ryujin-kai?"

"The relationship between *bosozoku* and parent yakuza are not always harmonious, Bondo-san," Reiko said.

"When did you say he contacted you for our meeting today?"

"Yesterday," Tiger replied.

"Is it just a coincidence that he was killed a few hours later?"

"You are thinking the same thing as I am, Bondo-san. Was he murdered for the information he was going to give us?"

"Perhaps his cousin, Abo—maybe he knows something," Reiko said.

"Let's talk to him," Bond said.

One of the detectives said something to Reiko and showed her a bag full of small gold-coloured, metal plates. She nodded and turned back to Bond and Tiger.

"Pachinko winnings," she said. "They give you those metal plates in exchange for the balls when you win. Then, you exchange those plates for money at an exchange shop in a different location. He had a bag with him, not worth a lot, but he might have just come from one of the parlours around here when he was killed."

"Perhaps we should visit a few of them and ask if our friend was seen," Bond suggested.

"That is police work, Bondo-san," Tiger said. "You would not enjoy it."

"What are you talking about, Tiger?" Bond said. "I'm here in your country to do police work. What else would you call it? Come on, let's take a look around. Besides, this area fascinates me. It's alive with electricity."

Tanaka's mobile rang. He answered it, *"Moshi moshi."* He listened, then spoke a few words.

"I must go to headquarters," he said. "Miss Tamura, if our British friend really wants to tour Kabuki-cho and stick his *gaijin* nose into the business of the yakuza, by all means, we should allow him to do so. But would you please accompany him and make sure that he gets into no trouble?"

"It would be my pleasure, Tanaka-san," Reiko said, bowing.

Tiger shook Bond's hand. "You will be in good company. I will speak to you later."

"Absolutely," Bond said. Tiger turned and walked back the way they had come.

"Come on, James-san," Reiko said. "Our tour of Sin City begins here."

They walked away from the crime scene and turned the corner. A placard that displayed the word "SOAP" and featured the faces of four lovely young Japanese girls stood on the middle of the pavement.

"Soaplands," Reiko said. "You know about them?"

"Only a little. Massage parlours, aren't they?"

"Much more than that," she explained. "Soaplands are the highest level of prostitution in this country. Technically, prostitution is illegal, but it's been an accepted part of our society since the beginning of time. When the Occupation outlawed the 'water trade,' as it's called, the yakuza took it over and it still thrives today. It's a wink-wink enterprise now. No one talks about it but everyone knows it's there. Supposedly you are going in to have a bath and massage, but you have sex too."

"Why are they called soaplands?"

"I was afraid that you would ask me that. It's because they rub you down with soap. The girl uses her body to lather you up. It is very elaborate, from what I understand. Of course, I have no experience in these things!"

"Of course not!"

She laughed, perhaps to conceal her embarrassment at discussing these matters with an attractive man. Or perhaps not. Bond couldn't tell. Reiko continued, "Actually they used to be called 'Turkish baths,' but the Turkish embassy complained about it some years ago. So the name was changed. Soaplands are very expensive. Sometimes soapland girls become very rich and marry someone of importance. Just the other day, there was an article in the newspaper. One of the Diet members announced his marriage to a former soapland girl and no one thought anything of it. The girls often marry celebrities or politicians. On one hand, the girls are considered prostitutes and lower-class citizens; on the other hand, they are admired and respected because to be a soapland girl you have to be the best. And usually soaplands do not take foreigners. Japanese only. There are some exceptions, if you are interested."

"No thanks."

"Oh," she said, "you don't find Japanese women attractive?"

"I didn't say that." Bond glanced at her and she smiled flirtatiously.

They passed a stand-up food stall and she asked, "Are you hungry?"

"Quite."

"Let's have some noodles."

They both ordered bowls of fresh *udon*, thick white noodles made from kneaded wheat flour. They were served in a hot broth mixed with fried soybean curd and with spices such as red pepper that could be shaken into the bowl according to taste. Bond found the meal delicious and ordered two cans of cold Kirin beer to go with it.

Bond noticed that the chef and another man at the stall were staring at Reiko.

"Don't pay any attention to them," Reiko said as she slurped her soup. "Most young women are probably afraid to go to a stand-up noodle stall. It's usually for elderly salarymen. But you know what? I don't care. About four years ago I made up my mind that I wanted to eat at one of these stalls and so I did. I have ever since."

"Reiko-san," Bond began, "if the soaplands are at the top of the water trade, what is below them?"

Reiko sucked a noodle into her mouth like spaghetti. "Mmm, *gomennasai*. Well, then you have the regular massage parlours, the so-called 'health clubs,' the strip clubs, the 'image clubs,' hostess bars, and everything else you can imagine. The lower you go, the worse the conditions. That's where you'll find imported Thai or Korean girls, or Filipinos, brought into this country illegally and forced to work for the yakuza. They believe they are going to Japan to work in a nice job as a hostess somewhere, but they end up being enslaved."

"That happens a lot in other countries as well," Bond said.

"Yes. But never mind about all of that. How are your noodles?"

"Delicious." He pulled out a wallet, but she stopped him.

"No, no, you are our guest," she said. "I will pay."

Bond thought that her formality was appealing. *"Arigato,"* he said.

"You're welcome. Come on."

They headed toward the nearest pachinko parlour, just down the street. A big business in Japan and mostly yakuza-controlled, pachinko was the equivalent of Western slot machines and the parlours were similar to game arcades. The establishments were hugely popular, and they were almost always crowded.

They went inside and were greeted by two thugs wearing money belts. One of them asked Reiko if she needed change, but she shook her head.

The noise was worse than in the casinos of Las Vegas. A pachinko machine resembles a vertical pinball table that uses dozens of tiny metal balls. Colourful designs adorn the front, behind the glass, where the balls fall through pins. This particular parlour charged a 2,000-yen minimum to play. Coins were dropped into the slot and a mass of balls emptied into a tray at the bottom of the machine.

They were then fed automatically into the machine when the player depressed a handle. The balls shot up to the top and fell down through the pins, dropping into slots that were worth points. The player could control the speed and force of the balls with a throttle knob. The skill apparently came from knowing how much speed and force to use. If the balls fell into a specific catcher, then three wheels containing numbers and pictures would spin, like on a slot machine. The goal was to finish with more balls than one started with. They could then be exchanged for prizes.

"It's gambling," Reiko said, "but not really. You can't exchange the balls for money. Gambling is illegal. You exchange them for things like cigarettes, biscuits and other prizes. But as I said earlier, you can exchange those gold plates at other places for money. More yakuza-controlled business."

"Do you have Umeki's photograph?" Bond asked.

"Yes, I have it here." She pulled it out. It showed two arrest shots, full front and profile. "This was taken a year ago when he was picked up for gang fighting. Let's ask these boys if they saw him last night."

She showed one of them the photograph and spoke to him rapidly. The kid barely looked at it and shook his head. He called over his friend, who also gave it a cursory glance and shrugged.

"I don't think we will get anywhere here," she said.

"Shall we try another place?"

They left the building and walked across the street to another parlour that was multilevel. Bright neon described it as "Pachinko Heaven."

Once again, they were regarded with suspicion by the staff. One boy, who had a scar on his face and three gold teeth, took the photo for a closer look. Bond noticed that the first joint on the little finger of his left hand was missing. The fellow smiled and said something to Reiko. She asked him more questions, but he shook his head.

After he walked away, she said to Bond, "He knew Umeki. Said that he used to come in here a lot. I asked if Umeki was in here last night, and he said that he didn't know. But he said something odd."

"What's that?"

"That Umeki finally got what was coming to him. I asked him how did he know that, and he replied that the word on the street travels fast."

"Did you see his little finger?" Bond asked.

"Yes. He is definitely yakuza. Or *bosozoku,* more likely. He is young."

"Tiger said that he must have made a mistake or something for him to do that."

"That's right. The ritual cutting off of the fingers is called *yubitsume.* When one of them does something wrong, they have to do the cutting themselves. They start with the first joint of the little finger, cut it off with a sharp knife, and they give the piece of finger to the *kaicho* as an apology. If they make more mistakes, the next joint goes and so on. Sometimes we see yakuza who are missing several fingers!"

"And what we saw on Umeki? What did that signify?"

"That he had done something *very* bad. His fingers were removed by his killer or killers to make a statement."

"Come on, let's try another place."

As they left the building, the thug who had identified Umeki pulled out a mobile phone and made a quick call.

It was growing darker. Now the Kabuki-cho neon was blinding. The buildings were solid walls of illuminated *kanji, kana,* and masses of bright colours that flashed and demanded attention.

A Mercedes with dark windows drove past them on the street.

"Yakuza," Reiko said. "A Mercedes is one of their status symbols."

The atmosphere in the area had changed markedly.

Nightfall had brought out even more touts, hoods and riffraff. Mixed in with these picturesque characters were members of Japan's working force: the salarymen. They were still dressed in the suits they had worn all day at the office, walking in groups of three or four, and they were already beginning the evening's debauchery. By nine p.m. they would be completely drunk.

"One of the products of our fierce Japanese work ethic," Reiko explained when one salaryman accidentally bumped into Bond. He apologised, slurring his speech, bowed and walked on. "We are encouraged to work ten hours a day or more. The men especially. Then they are pressured to go out drinking with their colleagues after the day is over. They don't get home to their families until late at night. The pressures of playing the corporate game are tremendous. No wonder they all drink so much."

"And the women?"

"Women in the work force are called 'office ladies,' and they can't hope to progress in a corporation like the men do. Housewives have to put up with never seeing their husbands except on the weekends. That's family time. I only saw my father on Sundays, never during the week. It is the wife who holds the purse strings. The husband brings home the pay cheque and immediately hands it over to his wife. She then gives him an allowance and manages the household herself. I am lucky. I have a man's job. That's a different situation."

The explosive sound of a motorcycle interrupted their conversation. A black Kawasaki ZRX blasted down the street, zipping around cars until it nearly sideswiped Bond and Reiko.

"Look out!" Bond shouted, pulling Reiko out of the way just in time. They fell on the pavement but were unharmed.

The rider turned back to them and raised his middle

finger. He was dressed in black leather and wore a yellow scarf to mask his face.

Bond stood and helped her up. Reiko said, "Creep. He was a Route 66—*bosozoku*—and that was no accident. They sometimes do things like that to intimidate someone. I would bet that one of the punks we have spoken to in the last couple of hours has put the word out that we are asking questions."

"I hear more bikes."

Bond was right. They could hear motorcycles revving their engines not far away.

"James-san, I think we have outstayed our welcome in Kabuki-cho. Let's go."

They started to walk fast against the flow of pedestrian traffic, back past the touts who had solicited them once already. The noise of the bikes drew closer, so Reiko grabbed Bond's hand and picked up her pace. She navigated through the crowd quickly but as soon as they got to the corner, three bikes zoomed around to face them.

The ZRX was back, and a Suzuki Inazuma and a Kawasaki Zephyr had joined it. They had four-stroke, four-cylinder engines and no fairings—what were generally called "naked" bikes. The mufflers had been cut off so that they were outrageously loud.

All three riders wore black leather. Unlike most yakuza, their black hair was long, and it blew in the breeze. Their eyes bore down on them from above the yellow scarves.

"Route 66," she whispered.

She did an about face and pulled Bond with her. As they ran back the way they came, the cycles revved and two of them shot forward. Pedestrians jumped out of the way and some screamed. The Zephyr rode onto the pavement behind Bond and Reiko and increased its speed. The couple was forced to break hands as the bike sliced between them. Reiko fell against a soaplands placard and grunted. Bond reached for her hand and helped her up.

The Zephyr and the ZRX met again in front of them, and this time they were obstructing traffic. A Honda Beat attempted to go around them but the biker nearest to it shouted obscenities at the driver.

Bond looked back. The Inazuma was still there, blocking that way. They were trapped.

The three bikers revved their engines and sat there menacingly.

"Reiko-san, I believe we have encountered an extreme emergency." He reached for his gun but she grabbed his arm.

"No, James-san, do not draw your weapon. They are teenagers. They are probably unarmed. Maybe they have knives, but I doubt they have guns. Let's walk calmly back the other way."

They turned and walked towards the Inazuma but the bikers continued to blast their engines. Then the ZRX burst forward violently, curved around a taxi and pulled up beside them. The rider shouted something at Reiko. Bond picked up the words "do not come back." Before the biker sped away, he noted that the kid had blue eyes and blond eyebrows.

"Come on," Reiko said, walking ahead.

"What did he say?"

"That we should get our asses out of here and never come back."

The three cycles followed them onto the street and began to ride up and down the block, back and forth.

"Good of them to take the trouble of escorting us out," Bond remarked.

They crossed at the intersection and walked into the next block. The other pedestrians seemed oblivious to what was going on, although some stopped to stare at the noisy motorcycles.

The ZRX pulled to the side of the curb behind them, then it leapt forward to sideswipe the couple. Bond quickly grabbed a soaplands placard and swung it at the biker. The wooden sign smashed into the kid, causing the bike to skid on the road several metres ahead of them until it crashed into the back of a van. The biker rolled off and then got up fairly easily. The loose scarf hung around his neck, and the blue eyes and blond eyebrows seemed to glow in the neon. He strode toward Bond and unwrapped a chain from around his waist. He was ready for a fight.

Bond took a defensive stance and was prepared when the boy swung. Bond ducked as the chain cut the air a few inches above his head. By the time the thug had control of his weapon again, Bond had parleyed back. He stepped forward once again, this time swinging the chain above his head like a lasso.

"Ki o tsukete!" Reiko shouted as she pulled a Glock M26 out of her handbag and pointed it at the hoodlum.

The biker stopped swinging the chain.

Reiko barked more words at him, and he slowly backed away. Finally, he went to his fallen bike, picked it up, mounted and kicked the starter. The engine roared. Again, he pointed his third finger at them, then sped away.

"I take it that the situation evolved into an emergency," Bond said.

"Shippai shita wa," she said, holstering her gun. "I was mistaken earlier. Besides he looked much older than a teenager, don't you think?"

"More like twenty-one, perhaps."

"I know him," she said, pulling Bond onward and putting her handgun back in her bag. "His name escapes me, but he is a well-known hoodlum. One of the *bosozoku* leaders. I can look it up at headquarters."

As the couple crossed the last intersection and walked out of Kabuki-cho, the other bikers took off after their boss, making as much noise as possible.

9
Morning Mayhem

The effects of jet lag notwithstanding, Bond could have languished in bed since his suite in the Imperial Hotel was among the most luxurious he had experienced. Bond had the perk of staying at first-class hotels because his cover sometimes necessitated it. On occasion he had to play the part of a rich playboy businessman who was accustomed to nothing less than the best. Miss Moneypenny had booked him into the Imperial without discussion.

Bond liked hotels with unique histories. Not only was the Imperial originally built at the behest of Japan's imperial family in 1890, but it was also one of the first hotels in the country to serve pork and beef dishes in its restaurant. The first building was designed to impress powerful international guests with the level of Japan's modernisation after three centuries of isolation, and it boasted the newest in Western luxury. Frank Lloyd Wright designed a second incarnation of the hotel, and when it opened in 1923, it became Tokyo's social centre for both foreign residents and tourists. There was a well-known story of how, one evening in the 1930s, the ultranationalist Black Dragon Society invaded a posh dinner dance at the hotel and with drawn, razor-sharp samurai swords began harassing the well-heeled collection of frightened foreigners. The guests were held hostage for four days until the rebels finally surrendered to the military forces outside.

The current building replaced Wright's fanciful hotel in 1970, and in 1983 the handsome thirty-one-storey Imperial Tower was added. Bond's corner suite was on the thirtieth floor of the tower, and it had a spectacular view of the city on two sides.

Bond finally swung his legs out of the comfortable king-sized bed, stood and stretched. He opened the curtains and gazed out of the window.

Tokyo lay before him, a sprawling, metropolitan machine.

He and Reiko had agreed to meet early for breakfast, and then she would take him to Tsukiji Fish Market for a chat with Kenji Umeki's cousin. "Dress casually," she had told him.

Bond did his morning callisthenics, showered with first hot and then cold water, shaved, and dressed in a navy blue short-sleeved polo shirt, pale khaki trousers and a linen jacket. When he was ready, he went downstairs to find Reiko Tamura waiting for him in the lobby, right on time.

She was dressed more casually than before, in a short-sleeved white blouse and vest, black Capri pants and a baseball cap. She looked years younger and the glasses made her look even more like a student.

"*Ohayo gozaimasu,* James-san," she said.

"Good morning to you too, Reiko-san."

"Come on, let's go. It's a twenty-minute walk to the fish market. We can have breakfast there."

"All right."

They walked out of the hotel, turned toward the Ginza and headed southeast toward the water. It was a beautiful day.

"I have some news," she said. "I identified that char-

acter on the motorbike. Remember I said that I knew his
face? His name is Noburo Ichihara. He is *socho* of the
bosozoku that Kenji Umeki was in. *Socho* means 'leader,'
the same as *kaicho* or *oyabun* in the yakuza. Ichihara has
been arrested three times, served some time for assault.
Wears contact lenses, that's why his eyes are blue. And
guess what?"

"What?"

"His *bosozoku* gang works for the Ryujin-kai branch
here in Tokyo."

"Tiger told me about them. What does Ichihara do for
them?"

"Well, we have evidence that links him and several of
his gang to a drug bust that occurred in Kabuki-cho a few
months ago. It was the Ryujin-kai that was behind the operation, importing drugs into Tokyo and shipping them
north to Sapporo and then points beyond. They use the
bosozoku as carriers sometimes."

"Interesting. And what about our dead friend Kenji
Umeki?"

"Word on the street is that he was killed over some
grievance between him and his gang bosses."

"Could this Ichihara character be Umeki's killer?"

"Possibly, although the finger cutting indicates that it
was yakuza who did the killing. Sometimes members of a
bosozoku have to commit a murder like that as an initia-
tion to get into the parent yakuza. It's usually not done to
one of their own members unless he has done something
really bad. It is a mystery. Hopefully the cousin, Abo, will
know something."

They crossed Chuo Ichiba and entered the Tsukiji Fish
Market, a huge wholesale market. Most of it was laid out
under a roof that ran along the dock, where fishermen delivered the early morning catch to wholesalers, who then
sold the product to fish shop owners and restaurant cooks
who gathered there at the crack of dawn. The big tuna auc-

tion usually occurred at around five o'clock in the morning, but there was still a lot of action going on as Bond and Reiko arrived.

The concrete floor was soaked in water and muck. Workers wore big rubber boots, some wore slickers over their torsos and they all had tools called *tekagi* that looked like gaffers' hooks—wooden handles about a foot long, with nasty two-pronged hooks on the ends for picking up fish carcasses. Rows of tables lined the interior, and all manner of sea creatures from exotic corners of the Far East were displayed, raw and, in some cases, still alive. Octopus, tuna, shellfish, salmon, shrimp and the more exotic catches such as eel, squid, fugu and shark were all available. The pathways between the rows were extremely narrow, just large enough for *ta-ray,* mini-motorised trucks with steering wheels in the centre, much like forklifts, to move through.

Bond and Reiko dodged a *ta-ray* that shot past them, forcing them to squeeze against a table, front to front. Their eyes met in a moment of intimacy, but the couple pulled away from each other without saying a word.

The market was a beehive of activity. The place was utter chaos, but in that uniquely Japanese way, there was an efficient order to the madness. Workers shouted back and forth to their colleagues, the *ta-ray* and forklifts zipped around carrying cartons of goods, men loaded delivery vehicles with produce, areas were sprayed down with hoses to wash away the offal and vendors hawked their stuff to anyone who walked by their stalls.

The smell was particularly memorable.

Bond dodged a forklift as Reiko led him through the thicket of workers into the inner bowels of the market. They walked past a group of men using their *tekagi* hooks on the biggest tuna carcasses Bond had ever seen. The heads and tails had already been removed and the white, barrel-shaped cadavers were being tossed from man to man as if they weighed as little as a rugby ball instead of hundreds of pounds each.

Reiko led him through a maze of vendors to an area where several *ta-ray* were carrying cartons from a vendor to a delivery truck parked on the dock. She pointed at a rough-looking man in his thirties who was driving one of them.

"That's Takuya Abo," she said.

"Does he know you?"

"Yes, I've talked with him before. Sometimes we use him as an informant."

The man glanced at them as they walked towards him. She waved and he glared for a moment, then pulled the *ta-ray* over to where they were standing.

"What are you doing here?" he demanded. He wasn't happy.

"We need to speak with you," she said. "This is Commander Bondo-san from England."

"I can't talk now! Are you crazy? This is the busiest time of the day for me!" he said, irritated.

"When can we talk? It's important!"

Abo looked pained. Then, with a sullen look, he asked softly, "Is it about Kenji?"

She nodded. "I'm sorry about your cousin."

Abo inhaled loudly then nodded his head. Only then did he turn to Bond and bow slightly. He said in English, "Pleased to meet you. I am Takuya Abo."

Bond bowed and then shook his hand, which was rough and coarse. He couldn't help but notice that Abo was missing his entire little finger.

"Pleased to meet you."

Abo turned to Reiko and said, "Look, come back in a couple of hours. Go get something to eat. I can talk then."

"All right," she said. "We'll be back."

She led Bond back through the busy market until they

came to an outlying area that featured a few fresh sushi restaurants in rows of one-storey, barrack-like buildings.

"Let's have a sushi breakfast," she suggested.

They went into the narrow place, which was about ten feet wide, and sat at the counter with several workers, still clad in rubber boots. Reiko ordered several pieces of tuna, salmon, and fish roe for them to share, along with a *tekka-maki,* a tuna roll wrapped in seaweed cut into six portions, and a *kappa-maki,* a roll stuffed with cucumber. Bond ordered extra wasabi to mix with the soy sauce, as he was not fond of raw fish. But he was willing to give it a go.

"That's a very Western thing to do," Reiko said.

"I know," Bond admitted. "But I like the feeling of the wasabi going up the back of my nose. Opens the sinuses." He quickly changed the subject. "I noticed Abo's missing finger."

"That's how he was able to leave the gangs," she replied. "After he had been in prison for three years, he asked the leader of Route 66 to let him go straight. He was told that if he offered his finger then they would let him walk away. Abo performed *yubitsume* and gave his whole finger to the leader. He gained great face doing that. Now Abo is *katagi,* the yakuza word for a straight citizen. It means 'a person who walks in the sun,' as opposed to the yakuza, who are men of the dark."

"Is this Ichihara fellow the leader who has Abo's finger?"

"Possibly. I am not sure how long Ichihara has been leader, but that is a good assumption."

They killed a little time after breakfast by strolling through the market. Bond watched her as she examined and commented on the colourful varieties of seafood. Her intelligence combined with her vitality and good looks made her extremely attractive.

When they walked out of the market and along the

dock, she asked him, "Do you have a girlfriend, James-san?"

He shook his head. "No. It makes life too complicated," he said, surprising himself with the truth.

"I know what you mean," she said. "I can never keep a boyfriend longer than a couple of months. They get tired of my having to work all the time."

"Do you work out of the country?"

"Most of the time. I am here now because of the upcoming G8 conference. Otherwise, I'd probably be in Korea, China, Thailand or somewhere. Lovers won't wait. I found that out the hard way."

Bond shrugged and said, "Tangential encounters are more practical for people in our profession than they are for the rest of the population."

She glanced at him sideways and smiled seductively. "You think so?"

He wanted to kiss her but the Japanese frowned upon public displays of affection. She read his mind though.

"Go ahead, if you want," she said.

He leaned in and pressed his mouth lightly against hers. Her lips were soft and tasted a bit salty from the breakfast. She was delicious.

When their mouths separated, he continued to stare into her almond eyes.

"Sugoi!" she whispered. It was the Japanese equivalent of saying, "Wow." Then she smiled and said, "We had better get back to Abo."

They walked back through the market, which by noon had calmed down considerably. The vendors were still selling their wares furiously, but the loading, the unloading and the truck traffic had diminished.

Abo was sitting on his truck eating a sandwich and drinking cola, looking out over the dock and the waterway that snaked out of Tokyo to the ocean.

"Abo-san," Reiko said, "we are back. Now is a good time?"

"As good as any," he said.

"My condolences for the loss of your cousin," Bond said.

"Thank you. But Kenji was asking for trouble. It wasn't going to be long before something bad happened. I had tried to get him out of that business, but he never listened to me."

"Abo-san," Bond said, "your cousin told us that he had information pertaining to Mayumi McMahon's whereabouts. Do you know anything about this?"

The man sucked air through his teeth and said, "All that Kenji told me was that she was in Sapporo, working in the water trade."

"She's a prostitute?" Bond asked.

"Soaplands girl," Abo corrected. There was a difference, apparently.

"Do you know why the Ryujin-kai would have Umeki-san killed?"

Abo stuffed the sandwich wrapper into a paper bag and wiped his mouth with the outside of the bag. "The Ryujin-kai didn't kill my cousin."

"Oh? Who did?"

"A kappa killed him."

Reiko said, "You are not serious."

Abo shrugged.

Reiko explained. "A kappa is a mythical creature that appears in Japanese folklore. It's a type of vampire, I guess. It lives in ponds or rivers and is said to resemble a cross between a human and a turtle or a frog. They can be remorseless killers. Their heads are misshapen—their skulls have a depression in the top that holds a little water. They say that if that water spills, then the kappa will lose its powers. They supposedly have a strong sense of loyalty to anyone who does them a good turn. Spare the life of a kappa, and he'll be your friend forever. And they like to eat cucumbers. One of the rolls we had for breakfast is called a *kappa-maki* because it has cucumber in it."

Bond narrowed his eyes. This was nonsense, of course, but an instinct warned him not to ignore Abo. He turned back to the man and asked, "What makes you think that a kappa killed Kenji?"

"Because Kenji told me that a kappa was stalking him. Apparently he saw him a couple of times. Listen, I could get in very big trouble if I am seen talking to you."

"This is important, Abo-san," Reiko said.

"So is my life," Abo said. "When I got out of the *bosozoku,* I made a vow not to talk to the authorities—about anything! I have already acted as informant on two occasions for you people. Route 66 are becoming suspicious. I was sent a warning the last time. Why don't you go away now?"

"Please, just a couple more questions, Abo-san, and we'll leave you alone," Bond said. "Have you heard anything about the Ryujin-kai being involved with the deaths of the McMahons? You know about that, right?"

"Yes, I read the newspapers. It is no secret that McMahon-san was an enemy of the Ryujin-kai. I do not know any more about that, but I do know that the Ryujin-kai is working on something big."

"What do you mean?" Reiko asked.

"Something top secret. I have my sources. I don't know what it is, but they are preparing something with that nationalist, Goro Yoshida."

At last! An important piece of the puzzle. "Yoshida? Are you sure?"

"Yoshida is the *Yami Shogun* of the Ryujin-kai. The dark master."

"Do you know where Yoshida is located?"

"No, not exactly. No one does," Abo said. "He is somewhere in the—"

But before he could finish his sentence, there was the sound of a gunshot and Abo's head jerked back violently. Blood splattered against a post behind him.

Bond and Reiko instinctively ducked and turned to see Noburo Ichihara fifteen feet away, holding what appeared to be a Heckler & Koch VP70. He fired again and the bullets sliced the air over Bond's head.

Years of training prevented both Bond and Reiko from being killed. Reiko rolled to the side and took hold of the single front tyre on Abo's truck. Using that for leverage, she performed a neat flip over to the other side of the vehicle. Bond spun the opposite way and positioned himself behind a thick concrete post. But by that time, Ichihara had run.

Bond drew the Walther and shot in the assailant's direction. The bullet missed, ricocheting off the back fender on a forklift. Ichihara ran straight into the vendor area of the fish market.

Bond leapt to his feet and chased him, shouting for civilians to get out of the way. Reiko had to take a moment to catch her breath before she could get up. She thought that she might have twisted her body badly when she had performed that manoeuvre, for there was a burning pain in her side.

There were too many people about for Bond to shoot again. It was just too risky. He managed to holster the gun as he ran, jumping over a dolly full of tuna.

Ichihara turned and fired in Bond's direction. A woman screamed from behind a food stall. Workers jumped back and tried to avoid the hoodlum, but he ran right into a big stallholder. The men collided with a crash and fell. Ichihara's pistol slid across the concrete and under a table laden with shellfish. Bond ran and leaped to tackle Ichihara before he could get up. The two men crashed into the table, knocking the slippery raw fish to the floor. Ichihara grabbed a handful of sea scallops and thrust them into

Bond's face as they wrestled in front of stunned onlookers. Reiko caught up to the scene just as Ichihara kicked Bond off of him and got to his feet. The killer seized a hook from a frightened worker. He turned to Bond and swung it quickly, back and forth. The hook whistled as it cut through the space in front of him. Bond dodged it repeatedly in the confined space between rows of tables. Ichihara advanced, coming closer to Bond until Reiko picked up a ten-pound octopus and flung it at the attacker. The wet, slippery invertebrate slapped Ichihara in the face and chest, taking him by surprise. He ripped it off his body, threw it at Bond, and turned to run again.

"Are you all right?" Reiko asked Bond, helping him pull off the slimy creature.

"Yes!" Bond spat. He started to take off in pursuit again when he noticed the blood on Reiko's blouse. She followed his eyes, looked down and saw that her side and stomach were soaked in blood.

"Oh!" she gasped, completely unaware that she was injured. She panicked as she pulled up her blouse. Bond's hands went to her abdomen, assessing the damage.

"You're not hit badly," he said. "The bullet grazed your side."

"I didn't feel it when it happened, James-san! Now it hurts like hell," she gasped.

"Stay here. You have your mobile?"

"Yes."

"Call Tiger and he'll get an ambulance faster than anyone. Do it now! I'm going to catch a fish."

Bond kissed her on the forehead, then gave chase.

Outside the fish market, Ichihara ran onto busy Chuo Ichiba. Horns blared as several cars screeched to a halt to avoid hitting the thug. A taxicab barely stopped in time but still collided with him. Ichihara fell over the car's bonnet and rolled over to the other side. He landed on his feet and continued running toward the Ginza with Bond not far behind.

Ichihara sped onto Showa Dori Street, a boulevard full of high-priced shops and restaurants. The killer ran past a huge crowd of waiting theatregoers queuing in front of the Kabuki-za Theatre and then disappeared around the corner of the building.

Bond had no choice but to follow him.

10

Kabuki Matinee

Bond sprinted down the side street and saw that Ichihara had ducked into the theatre's employee entrance. He acknowledged this smart move with a muttered oath. No *gaijin* could simply walk into the stage door of Japan's most famous Kabuki theatre.

He peered in the open doorway and saw a foyer lined with pigeonholes for storing shoes. Slots were designated for every theatre employee and most of them were full. An elderly man who sat on a chair beside the shoe shelves appeared agitated. Apparently his job was to help employees with their shoes as they came in, but it was obvious that the last person who had come through had upset him. The corridor went past the man through double doors and into the backstage areas of the building.

Bond acted quickly. He walked in, kicked off his shoes and stepped up to the caretaker. The old man looked up at him, confused.

"*Konnichi wa,*" Bond said as he put his feet in a pair of slippers that were sitting on the platform. Then he walked purposefully through the double doors before the aide could stop him.

The corridor was empty. Bond moved forward into an

area full of bulletin boards that displayed call sheets and other information for the employees. The administrative offices were here, apparently, so Bond walked quickly past them. The last thing he needed was someone authoritative to confront him.

He went around a corner and found a door with a *noren,* or half curtain, hanging over it. Bond carefully inched an edge of the curtain to the side and looked in.

It was a costume room. Men sitting on *tatami* mats were working with the fabrics. Traditional kabuki costumes hung on racks behind them.

Bond went on and into a corridor that contained the actors' dressing rooms. Each of the star actors had his own room, with his name written on the curtain over the doorway. Bond peered into each one, finding some actors meditating in costume or in the act of dressing; some of the rooms were empty. No sign of Ichihara.

Bond wasn't very familiar with Kabuki. He did know that it was a traditional form of Japanese theatre, like Noh and Kyogen. It was noted for its stylised acting, gorgeous period costumes, beautiful scenery and stories on an epic scale. He knew that the actors were all male, even the ones playing female roles, and that the famous ones were descendants of the original Kabuki acting families. Best not to bother any of them.

He left the dressing room area and moved along the main corridor until he came to a stairwell. He took the steps two at a time to the second floor, where he saw Ichihara creeping along and looking for a place to hide. Their eyes met. The killer froze in shock but after a second, he darted down the hall, which opened on to a metal fire escape. Bond dashed after him, kicking off the slippers as he went.

Ichihara clambered up the fire escape and into the third-floor entrance. Bond looked down briefly and saw that the metal stairs hung over the stage door by which he had first come in at street level. He climbed the stairs and entered the building again.

The hallway on the third floor was full of people — actors, stagehands and other staff. The dressing rooms for the supporting actors and musicians were up here, as well as other technical offices. One man shouted at Bond, commanding him to halt. Bond drew his Walther and ran past, ignoring him. His presence must have been imposing enough to quiet the man.

Bond looked into a room and found more technicians sitting on *tatami* and making wigs. Ichihara was standing inside the archway and surprised Bond with a series of lightning-fast *tsuki* blows, which made Bond drop his weapon and retreat as Ichihara jumped into the hall, swinging and kicking with great speed. Bond fell back into a wheeled rack of costumes. Ichihara turned and ran.

Bond looked frantically for his Walther, didn't see it, and decided to continue the chase rather than waste time searching for it. He got up and pursued his prey down two flights of stairs back to the first floor. This stairway emptied into a quiet corridor with a swinging door. Bond pushed through them and found himself in the stage wings.

The sound of a strange recitation flooded his ears. A *shamisen*'s strings were being plucked and the voice continued the eerie chanting that was typical of a Kabuki performance.

My God, the matinee had begun!

Bond ignored the stagehands looking at him in confusion.

Where had Ichihara gone?

Bond swept around the black curtains at the side of the stage and sprinted behind the cyclorama that spread across the back of the scenery. He got a glimpse of the audience as he passed beside a small slit in the curtains. It was a full house. There were two actors on stage. One was the *aragoto,* the type of character known for the style of acting that expressed anger in a highly stylised manner. This character was usually tragically sent to the next world to become a supernatural being and returned to this world for revenge. His makeup was fierce and demonic.

The other man was the *oyama,* the actor who played a woman. His appearance was totally convincing; his costume and makeup were elaborate and breathtakingly beautiful, which added to the illusion that he was a female.

Both actors were seated on the stage and speaking in a slow, flowing language that Bond couldn't understand at all.

He saw a movement out of the corner of his eye. Someone moved between the curtains on the other side of the stage. Bond looked across the scenery from stage left to stage right and saw Ichihara. Bond turned to scan the area around him and found a prop table upon which sat a large *odachi,* a samurai broadsword more than two metres long. Bond took it and began to move behind the cyclorama again to the other side of the stage.

Ichihara met him halfway. He was holding another type of samurai sword called a *katana.*

Bond wondered if the stage props would be sharpened. Even if they weren't, the tips could certainly pierce a body.

Ichihara swung the sword in a long arc, slicing the air in front of Bond. Bond dodged, drew his own sword and dropped the sheath. The two men engaged in quiet, but deadly, combat while the Kabuki play continued, the performers oblivious to what was happening behind the scenery.

The *bosozoku* adopted a traditional and common *Chudan no kamae* stance, holding the sword at middle height, pointed forward, while all Bond cared about was simply defending himself. The weapons clashed, this time making some noise. The sound of scraping metal carried through the house, but neither the audience nor the actors knew what it was. The two men continued to spar and parry, inching their way back through a large opening that led to the scene shop. Carpenters and painters stopped what they were doing and stared in disbelief.

The fight continued, now noisier than before. Ichihara shouted a *kiai* when he struck at Bond, a tactic used to frighten opponents and focus energy. The metal clanged. Several of the spectators implored them to stop. One said that he was calling the police.

Bond went on the offensive, moved forward and swung his sword back and forth. The blade was heavier than it looked, and Bond was merely adequate at the skill. He had taken two kendo classes and one basic training session in *kenjutsu,* but lacked the years of practise of a professional.

Luckily, Ichihara was not much better. He too was an amateur who knew only a few moves. He was reckless and didn't have the discipline or stamina to be effective. Instead, he swung the sword with abandon, hitting whatever objects were in his way.

Bond backed him to a staircase that descended to the basement level. Ichihara lost his balance and fell, rolling down the steps as he went. Bond followed him down, but Ichihara got up and ran beneath the stage. Before Bond could stop him, the killer had jumped onto the *seri,* a platform that could be raised and lowered from below the stage to make actors appear and disappear. Ichihara flipped the switch and the platform began to rise. A trap door on the stage floor opened as the killer rose up into the unfolding drama on display in front of the audience.

People gasped and shouted at Ichihara. The actors froze, not sure what they should do. Stagehands immediately ran out onto the stage to apprehend the intruder, but Ichihara jumped away and ran down the *hanamichi,* the ramp extending through the audience along the aisle from the stage to the rear of the theatre. Actors often used this area of the stage for intimate rapport with the spectators. Several women screamed as the killer hurried to the back of the house and theatre staff pursued him. Ichihara turned and swung the sword, holding them at bay. Then he burst through the auditorium doors and into the lobby.

Police sirens were wailing in the distance. Bond was about to run to the stage as well, but several stagehands blocked his way. They were understandably angry and were shouting at him to drop the sword. He realised that there was no eloquent way out of this one, so he dropped the sword and tried to explain that he was a law enforcement officer.

Ichihara, on the other hand, escaped out of the front doors of the theatre and disappeared into the throng of pedestrians.

Reiko had alerted Tanaka when Bond left her. Tanaka had traced Bond to the theatre with the homing device in Bond's mobile and was able to get through to the police and issue instructions before Bond was put through the humiliation of a ride to the police station. A police sergeant found Bond's Walther PPK amidst the spilled costumes in one of the hallways, grilled him for three hours in the theatre administrative offices and finally released him as the sun was on its way down.

Bond used his phone after he got to the street.

Tiger's voice came through loud and clear. "Bondo-san? Are you all right?"

"Fine, but it's been a bloody wasteful day," Bond said. "How's Reiko-san?"

"She will be all right," Tiger replied. "She had to have a few stitches. She has been released and ordered to rest for a day or two. She will be back on the job in no time."

"Well, that's good to hear. What's the score with Noburo Ichihara?"

"We are looking for him. We have tried all of his usual haunts, but he seems to have disappeared. It's not surprising. I suggest you go back to your hotel and call it a night. There is one other bit of news. The CureLab board of directors was in an emergency meeting all day today. Many of them left at the end of the day in disgust. I predict that some kind of announcement about the company will appear in the papers very soon."

"Have you tried calling Shinji Fujimoto and asking him what went on?"

"Yes, but there was no answer."

"Then I will sign off, grab a bite to eat and go back to the Imperial. Good night, Tiger."

"Good night, Bondo-san. I will contact you first thing in the morning."

Bond rang off and started walking through the Ginza towards the Imperial. The neon had already fired up, and the area was a gridlock of traffic and pedestrians. Not surprising, since this was one of the more fashionable and expensive areas of the city. There were couples dressed up for the evening, walking quickly to make their dinner appointments; salarymen and office ladies on their way home or to the local bar; and at least a handful of ad hoc product giveaway booths set up where pretty young girls dressed in short skirts handed out samples of the latest perfume, soap or deodorant. These were always accompanied by banners or placards displaying the company's logo and mascot, which was almost invariably a much-too-cute cartoon animal with large eyes.

Bond stopped at a noodle shop and had a quick bowl of *udon*, then continued walking to the hotel.

"Mr. Bond?" a voice said in English.

Speak of the devil . . . ! Bond turned to see Shinji Fujimoto sitting in the passenger side of a Toyota Celsior that had pulled over to the curb. A young man was in the driver's seat.

"Konban wa," Bond said, bowing slightly.

"Good evening to you too. I thought I recognised you walking down the street. May I offer you a lift?"

Bond's internal radar flashed a warning. "Thank you, but it's not much farther. I prefer to walk."

"Actually, I'm glad I saw you. I have something I would like you to see. It concerns my great niece, Mayumi."

Bond was wary, but he decided to hear what the man had to say.

"What is it?"

"It is at my office. It's not far. Won't you get in? You haven't seen the CureLab headquarters yet, have you?"

Why not? Bond thought. Now was as good a time as any. He opened the door to the backseat and got in.

"I am hoping you can interpret the message I received. It is from Mayumi, but I am not sure I understand what she says," Fujimoto said.

"Why would I?" Bond asked.

"It's written in English!"

The car drove a few blocks into the Ginza as Fujimoto spoke rapidly into his mobile phone, then the driver stopped in front of a twenty-four-storey building. Fujimoto got out and issued some instructions to the driver.

"This is it, Mr. Bond," Fujimoto said, opening the back door. Bond got out and stood on the pavement with him.

"Our offices are on floors eighteen and nineteen. Come with me. I imagine the building is fairly quiet this time of night."

Bond followed him through the front door and into a lobby where a security guard acknowledged Fujimoto and greeted him.

"He's with me," Fujimoto said, indicating Bond. The guard bowed.

They got into a lift and Fujimoto pressed the button for floor nineteen.

"I might as well see Peter McMahon's office while I'm here," Bond suggested.

"Good idea," Fujimoto replied.

The lift arrived and Fujimoto gestured for Bond to exit. "Please, after you."

It was an ultramodern building, very high-tech and designed in a pseudo-futuristic decor that seemed to be popular with sophisticated Japanese corporations. The walls lining the corridor were a shiny stainless steel and the carpet was plush. There was an antiseptic quality to the place that reminded Bond of the infirmary at MI6.

Closed steel double doors stood at the end of the hallway. An engraved sign read "CureLab Inc." in both English and *katakana*. Fujimoto took a key card out of his pocket and swiped it through the slot in the wall. The doors slid open with a soft hum. They stepped into a thoroughly modern reception area with a space-age design scheme. Fujimoto swiped his card again, and another set of doors slid open.

"This way," he said.

Bond followed him past several offices and a conference room and finally to a closed door marked with Fujimoto's name and title. The card was swiped once more, and the door opened. Fujimoto stepped aside and again gestured for Bond to enter first. Bond stepped through the door, and a heavy object came crashing down on his head.

A slap in the face roused him.

His head was pounding and his eyes were blurry, but eventually he focused on Fujimoto's face.

Another slap.

"I think he's awake now," Fujimoto said to someone else.

Bond took in his surroundings. He was in Fujimoto's spacious office, complete with a stylish glass-top desk, computer, filing cabinets and bookshelves. There was a portable fan standing next to the desk. A large picture window looked out onto the bright lights of Ginza. There were three other men in the room, all teenagers or very young adults, dressed like yakuza. One of them was Noburo Ichihara.

"Close the curtains," Fujimoto ordered, and one of them pulled the cord that shut the drapes.

Bond saw his Walther lying on the desk, along with the Palm Pilot and DoCoMo phone, but they had left the antacid blister pack and the cigar holder in his jacket pocket. They had placed a plastic painting sheet on the carpet underneath Bond's chair.

"Hold him," Fujimoto commanded. One of the gang went behind Bond, bent down and grabbed their captive's forearms. He pulled them back tightly and held them in a vice-like grip. Fujimoto nodded at Ichihara.

The killer slowly slipped on black leather gloves as he grinned, revealing a large gold tooth. Then he stepped in front of Bond and punched him hard in the face. Bond felt a shockwave from his jaw to the top of his skull. His mouth began to bleed.

"Again," Fujimoto ordered.

The angry fist smashed into Bond's lips a second time.

"Again."

This went on repeatedly for several minutes. When Fujimoto decided that his captive had had enough, Bond's face was a bloody mess.

"What do you want, Mr. Bond? Why are you in Japan?" Fujimoto asked.

Bond groaned, barely able to keep his head up. "You . . . know . . . why . . ."

"Well, officially you are here to investigate the deaths of Peter McMahon, my niece and their daughters. You are to try to find the wayward girl, Mayumi. We know all that. But what else are you after? Talk, Mr. Bond, or this will become very unpleasant."

"I don't know what the hell you're talking about, Fujimoto," Bond said, his words slurring. He had difficulty enunciating.

"You are in Japan for another reason, Mr. Bond. What is it?"

Bond had to think. The summit conference? Was that what the bastard was on about?

Wait . . . ! How classified was that information? It was a secret *G8 meeting, wasn't it?*

"Nothing," Bond said. "I just want to find your great niece and get the hell out of this country."

"My great niece's whereabouts is none of your business, and it is none of your country's business. Her father may have been a British citizen, but she is not. This is family business, and I shall take care of it myself."

"You have taken care of it, haven't you?" Bond whispered.

"What did you say, Mr. Bond?"

"You killed them. You were responsible for their deaths. You murdered your own niece and her family."

"And why would I do that?"

"So you could control the company. You were always jealous of your older brother's success and resented him for not leaving CureLab to you. I would bet that you're going to sell out completely. You're going to sell your shares of the stock to Yonai Enterprises. Aren't you?"

"You are in no position to ask questions, Mr. Bond," Fujimoto said. "Peter McMahon outlived his usefulness. He was just a barbarian foreigner who had seduced the daughter of the company's chairman. He took over a Japanese company—what should have been *my* company— and he finally met his karmic destiny."

"So you admit killing them?"

"I admit nothing. Tomorrow is a new day, Mr. Bond. Things will be different. Tomorrow, under the eyes of the *Daibutsu*, CureLab Incorporated will rise to a new level of existence and be entirely controlled by Japanese. CureLab will be under new management. And you, Mr. Bond, will be dead."

"What is the yakuza paying you, Fujimoto?" Bond spat. "What kind of deal did you make with them?" Fujimoto shook his head and started to walk out of the room. He stood beside a rather large rubbish bin that janitors used to wheel around the building when they cleaned offices.

"Ichihara, you know what to do. Try not to make a mess of my office. Put the body in here when you're done, and you can wheel it to the van. Take him somewhere where he won't be found."

"Hai!" Ichihara barked, and then he turned to Bond and smiled. The gold tooth sparkled in his mouth.

11

Smoke Screens

Bond was alone with the three hoods. Blood covered his face and clothes, and he was dazed from the beating, but he knew that he had to snap out of it and defend himself. Bond willed himself to concentrate, commanding his senses to be alert. Timing would be everything, and if he couldn't use the element of surprise then all could be lost.

Ichihara moved toward him, fists ready. Bond clumsily attempted to leap out of the chair and attack the thug, but Ichihara easily punched him hard in the face. Bond fell on top of the plastic sheet and lay still.

"What did you do?" one of the others asked.

"He's out," the other one ventured.

Ichihara laughed. "Some tough guy. Come on, let's pick him up and get him out of here."

"Shouldn't we kill him first?"

"We can have more fun doing that where we're going."

Bond's body was limp. The three men hoisted him off the floor and carried him to the rubbish bin. One man managed to open the lid and then they dumped Bond inside. He crumpled like a rag doll. They shut the lid and began to wheel their cargo out of the office.

Inside the container, Bond reached into his pocket and

grabbed the antacid blister pack that Major Boothroyd had given him. He extracted two pink tablets and then knocked on the lid.

"He's awake," one man said. "Let's take him out and kill him!"

"I told you we should have done that in the first place," the third man said.

"All right," Ichihara replied.

They closed the office door again and moved the bin back to the middle of the room. Ichihara stood away and reached to open it, just in case the *gaijin* tried something funny.

As soon he saw the fluorescent strip lights on the office ceiling above him, Bond shut his eyes and threw one of the tablets as hard as he could. It struck the ceiling and burst, and a dark cloud of smoke quickly enveloped the area. Water immediately shot out of sprinklers built into the ceiling.

The three men shouted in surprise and moved back, temporarily blinded by the flash. Under the cover of the smoke, Bond climbed out of the bin. He couldn't see through the smoke, but at least he could discern shapes. One of the thugs was three feet away from him, waving at the smoke in an attempt to clear it. Bond slugged him hard in the stomach. The man went "Ooompf!" and doubled over. Bond clasped his hands together and brought them down hard on the back of the man's neck. He heard the bones crack.

One down, two to go.

"What was that?" Ichihara shouted.

"He's escaped!"

"Get him!"

Bond moved quickly to the desk and picked up the Walther and his other items. Then he moved around the room in a circle, carefully avoiding the two men.

The building's fire alarms went off. Bond knew that they would have company very soon.

Ichihara, still unable to see, drew a Browning 9mm and pointed it into the smoke. He fired twice, aiming nowhere near Bond.

"Are you crazy?" the other man shouted. "What are you doing?"

Ichihara didn't listen. He started turning around, firing a bullet every couple of feet. Bond moved to the portable fan that was beside the desk, pointed it towards the centre of the room and flicked it on. The blades began to whirr, blowing the smoke away.

The black billows immediately dissipated, leaving the two men standing and rubbing their eyes. Ichihara was pointing his gun in the opposite direction from where Bond was now.

"I'm over here," Bond said. It was one of those rare moments when he received utter and complete satisfaction.

Ichihara turned, and the Walther recoiled. Bond performed what was known as a Mozambique shot: "Three shots—two to the chest and one to the head, knocks him down and makes him dead." Ichihara slammed backwards into a filing cabinet and slid to the floor.

The other man saw what had happened. His eyes wide with fright, he thrust up his hands. "Don't shoot!" he cried.

Bond levelled the pistol at him. "Get inside," he said, gesturing to the rubbish bin. The man didn't have to be asked twice. He quickly climbed over the side and got in. Bond put the lid on and snapped it shut. He then pulled the plastic sheet out from underneath the chair and wrapped it around the bin so that the man would be unable to open it from the inside.

Now he was ready. Bond listened at the door; satisfied that no one was nearby, he opened it. Two security guards appeared at the other end of the hallway, running towards him. Bond counted to four, then stepped outside the office.

He threw another pink antacid tablet into the hallway, where it struck the metal wall hard and exploded. Another cloud of black smoke filled the corridor, blocking the security guards' vision. Bond then inched along the wall as the two men blindly walked right past him.

As he approached the main reception area, he heard the lift bell chime and the doors open. There were several voices.

Bond ducked into a conference room and shut the door. He heard the rushing footsteps down the hallway, started to open the door but stopped when he saw what was in the room.

Large anatomical colour illustrations of mosquitoes had been posted on three walls of the room. It was also furnished with a round conference table and chairs, a podium and a computer. The monitor was on and there appeared to be some kind of PowerPoint slide presentation in progress. Someone had been in the room working on something and had left very recently. A pad of paper and a pen, a mug of coffee and an ashtray full of cigarette ends were next to the computer, and a sports jacket was draped around a chair.

Bond decided to risk taking a look. First he examined the posters. All of the text was written in *kanji* except for the words "Hokkaido Mosquito and Vector Control Centre" in the bottom corner of each illustration. The posters had been stamped with an address in a town called Noboribetsu. The mosquitoes were of different species, slightly different in shape and colouring. Bond turned his attention to the computer. A Palm Pilot was sitting in a cradle that was hooked up to the CPU; it was downloading the files. The slide show in operation also featured mosquitoes. There were shots of a female mosquito laying eggs, shots of eggs hatching into larvae, the larvae shedding skins to become pupae and then finally adult mosquitoes emerging from the pupal skins. Some *kanji* text appeared on the screens, then more pictures of mosquitoes—biting a human arm, mating and alighting on water.

Finally a slide appeared that featured a miniature bonsai waterfall like the one he had seen at the McMahon home. Bond knew that he had found something important.

Bond removed the Palm Pilot on the table and replaced it with his own. He quickly pressed some buttons and began to download the entire slide show onto his device. While he waited, he took the sports jacket that was hung over the chair and used it to wipe off blood from his face, hands and clothes.

He heard shouts and more people running through the hallway.

Hurry up! he silently commanded the device. He dropped the now-bloody jacket onto the chair, then took his DoCoMo phone out of his pocket. He punched the speed dial button for Tiger, who answered it after one ring.

"Bondo-san?"

"Tiger, I've made a slight detour."

"Where are you?"

"CureLab office in Ginza."

"Ah, yes, I see the indicator on the map. Your homing device is still working. Do you need help?"

"Affirmative. I need an escape route quickly."

"Can you make it to the front of the building?"

"I can try."

"Give me ten minutes."

There was a voice directly outside the conference room door. Bond shut off the phone, quickly moved to the wall beside the door and drew the Walther. He levelled it so that whoever came in would get a face full of lead.

The door opened and a man started to walk in, but

someone called him from down the hall. Bond only got a glimpse of him. He was a Japanese man of about thirty, slight of build, with glasses and a crew cut. Whatever he was, Bond knew that he was no killer: a scientist, perhaps, or a doctor. He looked very familiar.

"What?" the man shouted back.

The voice called him again.

"Hmpf," the man said, then closed the door without coming in.

Of course! It was Fujio Aida, the missing molecular biologist! What the hell was he doing at the CureLab office? Hadn't he been fired for being a spy and traitor? What was the big mystery with him being "missing"? Here he was, alive and well, and apparently working on a project involving mosquitoes.

How long before he'd be back? Bond wondered. He ran back to the computer and saw that the download was eighty per cent done. Bond glanced at the pad of paper on the table but couldn't understand a word of what was written on it. He tore the page off, folded it and put it in his pocket.

Finally the download ended. Bond retrieved his Palm Pilot and then moved back to the door. He listened but wasn't able to discern how many men were in the hallway. There was no way that he was going to be able to walk out of the room without being seen.

Time for another antacid.

Bond palmed a pink tablet in his left hand and kept the pistol in his right. He pushed the button and the door slid open. He looked out and saw several men at the end of the hall near Fujimoto's office. The other way, in the direction of the lifts, was clear. Bond stepped out and walked swiftly toward reception but someone saw him and shouted.

"You! Stop!"

Bond turned and threw the tablet, bursting it against

the wall. The dark smoke filled the corridor once again, and Bond ran for it. He reached the lift as bullets flew in his direction. He punched the button and pounded on the door. There were shouts in the hallway as the sound of running boots grew louder.

"Come on, damn you!" Bond said aloud.

The lift chimed and the doors split open just as the men began to swarm through the smoke. Bond jumped inside, turned and fired the Walther once at a guard who had made it to the lift. The guard jerked back, dropped his weapon and fell back into the arms of another man. The doors closed and Bond was on his way down.

When he got to the ground floor, he was surprised to see that no one was there. The security guard who had let him and Fujimoto into the building was not at his post. *Probably upstairs on the nineteenth floor,* Bond thought.

Bond casually went through the front doors and out to the street. A fire engine was already there, and he could hear more sirens approaching.

"Bondo-san!"

Tiger was in the Majesta, which was parked by the curb nearby. Bond ran and got into the back, then the driver sped away just as another fire engine and police cars swerved around the block and pulled up to the building.

"Do you need to go to hospital?" Tiger asked, his brow wrinkled with concern.

"I'm all right," Bond said as he held a cloth filled with ice to his face. "I'll probably just look like Frankenstein's monster for a few days. Nothing's broken. I can still talk."

"At least you didn't let him live to tell the tale." Tiger handed him a glass of whisky from the mini-bar in the back of the Majesta. Bond took a long, burning drink and gasped with pleasure. "God, that felt good," he said. *"Arigato."*

Tiger laughed. "Bondo-san, you have the highest tolerance for pain of anyone I know."

"I'll take that as a compliment."

"Bondo-san, you must realise that all of these murders involving Abo and Umeki could have absolutely nothing to do with the McMahons. It could very well be yakuza and *bosozoku* business."

Bond pulled out the Palm Pilot and gave it to Tiger. "We have to take a look at what's on here. CureLab has something going on with mosquitoes, that's for certain." He related everything that he had seen in the conference room, including his identification of Fujio Aida.

"So what is Aida doing back at CureLab?" Tanaka asked.

"Obviously working on mosquitoes. Tiger, that bonsai contraption was just like the one we found at the McMahons'."

"I believe you. I will ask our lab to rush the analysis of it." Tiger took the Palm Pilot and flipped a switch on the armrest. The back of the driver's seat pulled down to reveal a laptop computer. Tiger booted it up and placed the Palm Pilot in the cradle.

"This should only take a few moments."

"I also got this," Bond said, pulling out the piece of paper from the notepad. Tiger took it and gave it a cursory look.

"It says, 'Life cycle from eggs hatching to adult mosquito has been reduced to one week. Still need to work on transovarial transmission.' What does that mean, Bondo-san?"

"I'm not sure. Something to do with the female's eggs. Did Reiko-san tell you what Abo told us?"

"About Yoshida?"

"Yes."

Tiger nodded. "Very worrisome. My superiors are beginning to take all of this a bit more seriously."

The car pulled up in front of the Imperial Hotel and parked. They waited until the computer had finished uploading the files from the Palm Pilot. Tiger typed on the keyboard and the slide show began. It was just as Bond had seen in the office: photos of mosquitoes going through their natural life cycles accompanied by *kanji*.

"This is all about mosquito biology," Tiger said. "Cure-Lab does work with disease-carrying insects."

"But Fujimoto told us that they didn't work with mosquitoes, remember?"

"Ah, you are right, Bondo-san. We will turn this material over to someone who understands it and obtain a proper evaluation."

"I'm convinced that bastard was in on the McMahons' deaths. He practically admitted it." Bond told Tiger what Fujimoto had said about Peter McMahon. "And he said that 'tomorrow, under the eyes of the *Daibutsu,* CureLab will rise to a new level of existence and be entirely controlled by Japanese.' "

"The *Daibutsu*? That's in Kamakura."

"What's a *Daibutsu*?" Bond asked.

"The Great Buddha. It's the largest bronze Buddha in the world. He's been sitting in Kamakura for over seven centuries."

"How far away is that?"

"Not far. About an hour's train ride."

"Why Kamakura?"

"Because Fujimoto has a home there, as I understand it. He keeps a flat in Tokyo but goes to Kamakura on the weekends. I've always wanted to see the *Daibutsu* again. It has been a long time. Get some rest, Bondo-san. Put some antiseptic on those cuts, and we will pick you up in the morning at seven o'clock."

Bond left his friend and walked into the Imperial lobby. Ignoring the stares from the concierge and other staff, he went straight to the lift and took it to his floor in the tower.

Once he got into his room, Bond finally looked at himself in the mirror. The damage looked worse than it was, but it was bad enough. He cleaned and doctored his face, took a scalding hot shower, crawled into bed and was asleep in less than a minute.

12

The Distant Pain of Death

Yasutake Tsukamoto awoke abruptly to the sound of his private phone ringing. He glanced at the digital clock beside his bed and was horrified to see that it read four-fifteen. His wife stirred and grumbled sleepily.

"Moshi moshi," Tsukamoto said into the phone, not too pleasantly.

"Tsukamoto."

He shuddered. It was the *Yami Shogun.*

"Hai!"

"Did I wake you?" Goro Yoshida asked.

"It is all right. Please, let me change phones." He pushed the Hold button and hung up.

"Who is it?" his wife asked.

"Business problem. Go back to sleep."

Tsukamoto got out of bed, went out of the room and walked into his study. While most of the house was traditional Japanese, this room looked like it would be more at home in a British law firm's office. Besides a traditional desk and filing cabinets made from Hakone polished wood, the walls were covered with books. Over half of them were law books. Tsukamoto had long ago decided that he should know a thing or two about the law.

His home in Sapporo was a large one, very luxurious and very well guarded. His men kept vigil around the compound twenty-four hours a day, for being the *kaicho* of the Ryujin-kai not only afforded him great opulence but also brought danger. There were plenty of other yakuza who hated him.

He sat at the desk, picked up the phone and pushed the button to get back on the line.

"I am here," he said.

"Good. Is everything ready for the transfer of Cure-Lab?" Yoshida asked.

"Yes. Kano is going to Kamakura today to meet with Fujimoto."

"What's this I hear about some trouble at the CureLab office in Tokyo?"

Tsukamoto drew in a breath and said, "*Saaaa* . . . Fujimoto took matters into his own hands. Very bad situation. There is an Englishman in Japan. He is here to investigate the deaths of the McMahon family. Fujimoto tried to have him killed last night."

"And the Englishman got away?"

"Yes."

"What does he know?"

"We are not sure. He may have seen things. We have no way of knowing."

There was silence at the other end. Finally, Yoshida said, "We can't afford to have undue attention on CureLab at the moment. Fujimoto has outlived his usefulness."

"I agree. Shinji Fujimoto is a bumbling fool."

"Then see to it that he experiences great pleasure today," Yoshida said. "He will go to Kamakura and make the deal he has been preparing for all these many months, and for a short while he will be a very wealthy man. But as my mentor, Mishima-san, once wrote: 'The distant pain of death refines the awareness of pleasure.' We must ensure that Fujimoto knows both of these sensations."

"It has already been arranged," Tsukamoto said.

"Good. Now what about the Englishman?"

"I will take care of it. Do not worry."

"I won't. Tell me, how did yesterday's tests go?"

"Splendidly. We cut the incubation time down to exactly six days. The life span of the insects is still very short, but it's long enough for them to do the damage we seek. The best news is that with the latest delivery from CureLab, we have been able to further mutate the virus so that the onset of symptoms is much faster. Laboratory animals became sick within an hour."

"That is good news. Keep the engineers working on it. After this phase is completed, we must be ready to unleash a new and improved version of our product."

"Yes, I understand."

"What about the McMahon girl? Has she been eliminated?"

"Not yet."

"Why not?"

"With all due respect, I have been asked by the *sohonbucho*, Kubo, that I speak to you about this. The girl is a big earner. She is one of the most popular girls in the establishment. And he wanted to have her around for the send-off of the carriers. You yourself instructed us to give the carriers a night on the town that they wouldn't forget."

"I did indeed, but that was two days ago. You can find other girls. There are always other girls. Get rid of her. She is dangerous to have alive."

"Very well. She will not live to see the weekend."

After a short pause, Yoshida said, "Good night, Tsukamoto."

"Good night, Yoshida."

Tsukamoto hung up the phone and contemplated the original painting by Ogata Korin that hung on the wall between sets of bookshelves. He knew now that he would not be able to get back to sleep. He lit a cigarette and rang the servant whose duty was to stay up all night in case the master of the house needed anything. Tsukamoto ordered some coffee and yoghurt, then settled back in his chair to meditate.

It was going to be an interesting week.

Bond and Tiger arrived in Kamakura around nine the next morning. One of Tiger's men had been posted at the *Daibutsu* since the grounds opened at seven, but he reported by mobile phone that he had not yet seen Shinji Fujimoto. Tiger instructed the driver to take them directly to the Great Buddha and to park the car somewhere. Tiger and Bond got out in front of the main gates.

Bond was stiff and sore from the beating he had taken the night before and his face was a mess. There were contusions around his mouth, an abrasion on his left cheek and swelling around the left side of his jaw. He had noticed the hotel staff grimacing at him behind his back when he had strolled through the Imperial lobby to meet the Toyota out in front before the hour-long drive.

"Have you been to Kamakura before, Bondo-san?" Tiger asked.

"If I have, I don't remember it."

"It's a beautiful place. It was an early capital of Japan and there is an abundance of Buddhist temples and some shrines here. The *Daibutsu* has been here since 1252. It used to be housed in a huge hall, but the building was washed away by a tsunami in the late 1400s."

They walked up the path to the entrance, which was guarded by two statues on either side that portrayed the Buddha at two different stages—at the beginning of life and at the end.

Tiger stopped at the pavilion to purify his hands and mouth. Bond did the same; the cold water felt good on his wounds as he swished it around in his mouth and spat it out. They continued into the courtyard where the impressive bronze Buddha sat, all knowing and all seeing. The metal was discoloured but the statue was in remarkably good shape considering its age. The figure towered a little over eleven metres tall.

"Look at the curly hair, Bondo-san," Tiger pointed out. "There are 656 curls altogether and it has a white hair curl on the forehead. This symbolises wisdom."

Abbreviated tea ceremonies were performed at regular intervals on one side of the courtyard. A group of tourists had already begun to gather there and some were looking at the souvenir kiosks on the opposite side.

"Do you see our man?" Bond asked.

"No. We should sit down over there and wait. And we should keep you out of sight." He pointed to some benches at the back of the courtyard.

"I look that bad, do I?"

Tiger laughed. "I meant in case our friend shows up soon. We don't want him to see either of us. Don't worry, Bondo-san, you will be a handsome man again. Those cuts and bruises will heal in no time."

They sat under the shade of a large cherry tree. Bond inhaled deeply, enjoying the fresh air. The weather was pleasant and not too hot. The tranquillity of the place was infectious.

"Quite a peaceful place for a business deal," Bond said.

"Yes, I'm not surprised by the choice. So many people come here, and since Fujimoto lives in town, no one would think twice about him coming to pay his respects to the Buddha. The question is, where is the actual meeting going to take place?"

"I think we'll know in a few minutes," Bond said, gesturing with his head. "There he is now." They held open newspapers to cover their faces.

Shinji Fujimoto entered the courtyard alone. He looked around nervously, then continued walking toward the Buddha. He pretended to show great interest in the statue, then walked over to the tea ceremony area and sat down. Obviously his contact was not there yet. Bond and Tiger watched from across the courtyard as Fujimoto was served green tea by the women wearing kimonos.

"He appears ill at ease," Bond noted.

It wasn't long before two men entered the courtyard and Tiger perked up. "Here we go," he said. "That's Masuzo Kano, the president of Yonai Enterprises." He was referring to a tall grey-haired man who walked as if he owned the world. With him was what appeared to be a dwarf. The small man was the strangest looking human being Bond had ever seen. From this distance, Bond thought that the dwarf's head must be deformed, for it was oddly shaped. The top of his head was bald except for a few long strands of hair that had been greased and combed over the scalp. His skull had an unusual bowl-like depression in the top. They were too far away to study his facial features but it wasn't difficult to see that he had the face of a monster.

"Who's the other fellow?" Bond asked.

"I don't know. He looks like a frog."

The dwarf was carrying a large metal briefcase. Like Kano he was dressed in a suit, which made him seem all the more out of place. The man reminded Bond of something. He was short, frog-like . . . *of course!* The kappa. Takuya Abo had mentioned a kappa, something out of Japanese supernatural fairy tales.

"Tiger, do you know what a kappa is?" Bond asked.

"Of course I do, Bondo-san." Tiger paused a moment as he considered what Bond was getting at. "You are right, Bondo-san! That man does look like a kappa! I will have to call in his description and see if the police have anything on him. I have a feeling that one should not be deceived by his size. That little fellow is probably quite formidable or else he would not be accompanying Kano."

They watched as the two men approached the souvenir

stand and made a show of looking at the trinkets, which included charms like the ones sold at the Meiji shrine in Tokyo, miniature replicas of the Buddha, postcards and other items. Fujimoto finished his tea and bowed to the women, left the tented area and walked to the Buddha. Without acknowledging the other men, he paid the admission fee to go inside the statue, then went around the back of the monument to the entrance.

The dwarf bought something from the kiosk, then he and Masuzo Kano nonchalantly walked to the Buddha, paid the fee and disappeared behind the statue.

Tiger punched a number and put his mobile to his ear. "My man posted on the other side of courtyard," he explained. He spoke quietly into the phone, listened, then rang off. "He says that they are inside the Buddha. Now we wait until they come out."

Ten minutes later, Masuzo Kano came out alone. He purposefully strode away from the Buddha and out of the courtyard. A few minutes later, Shinji Fujimoto emerged, carrying the metal briefcase. He, too, walked toward the exit but took his time in doing so. He stopped at a souvenir kiosk and pretended to study the trinkets, then finally left the grounds.

"What happened to the kappa?" Bond asked.

"He must still be inside the Buddha," Tiger replied. Bond got up and walked around the courtyard, then paid the twenty yen required to go inside the statue. He ducked his head in the short doorway, then stood in the centre of the metal figure. The interior looked nothing like the Buddha. It was just discoloured bronze. The idol's head was but a cavity in the metal. There was scaffolding set up inside where some repair work was in progress, but no workmen were there, and there was no sign of the kappa.

Bond emerged and met Tiger at the front gate. "I don't know what the hell happened to the little fellow," Bond said. "No one was in there."

Tiger asked his colleague on the phone about it. The man replied that he never saw the dwarf leave the statue.

"Come on, let's follow Fujimoto," Tiger said.

They left the *Daibutsu* grounds and saw Fujimoto walking up the hill towards Hase-dera, one of Kamakura's more popular Buddhist temples. Bond and Tanaka followed him from a distance.

"I suspect there is money in the briefcase. What is he going to do, make a donation to the temple?" Tiger asked sarcastically.

They entered the temple grounds, which contain several buildings that date from the 1300s, a beautiful garden and a fascinating collection of statues of Jizo, who, as Tiger quietly explained, is the guardian of the souls of departed children. The two men made their way around the garden over a wooden bridge and then shadowed Fujimoto to the front of Kannon Hall, where the image of Kannon, the Bodhisattva of the goddess of mercy, is represented by a statue with eleven faces.

Fujimoto appeared to be praying. He rang a bell and placed several wads of bills in the collection box.

"That man has a guilty conscience," Bond remarked.

Fujimoto turned suddenly and almost saw them. Bond and Tiger ducked behind a post and waited until the man moved away. They started to follow him over the bridge and into the garden when they saw the dwarf again. The kappa had appeared from nowhere and was trailing behind Fujimoto by a few metres.

"Where did he come from?" Bond asked.

"I don't know!"

Fujimoto went around a group of cherry trees and was soon out of sight. The dwarf walked in the same direction.

"Let's go," Tiger said. They continued their surveillance, moving over the bridge and stopping behind the trees. They saw Fujimoto, but the dwarf was gone.

"He's disappeared again!" Tiger exclaimed. "That thing really *is* a kappa!"

"Don't be ridiculous, Tiger," Bond said. "He's obviously skilled in stealth."

"I have a very bad feeling about this, Bondo-san."

Fujimoto left the temple and walked down the hill toward the street. Bond and Tiger carefully scanned the area but saw no sign of the dwarf. They got down to the street and surveyed the line of cars parked along the curb. Fujimoto was on his way toward the main thoroughfare, where several side streets intersected. He turned a corner and was gone.

"Come on," Tiger urged.

They moved swiftly toward the first cross street and there it was—Fujimoto's Toyota Celsior. Other than that, the street was deserted.

Bond and Tiger stepped up to the car and looked inside. The driver was slumped forward over the wheel. Fujimoto was in the backseat, lying at an awkward angle. Tiger opened the door and they saw that the vice president of CureLab had been stabbed numerous times. Blood covered the seat and dripped onto the floor. The driver's throat had been cut.

"We're too late," Tiger said. He got out his mobile and immediately called for the police and an ambulance.

Bond examined the car as best as he could. "That briefcase is gone," he said. "And look here."

He pointed to Fujimoto's hand. All of the fingers had been sliced off. Next to it was a miniature replica of the Great Buddha—the trinket that the kappa-man had bought from the souvenir stand.

13

Loose Ends

They were in a satellite Koan-Chosa-Cho office located in the elaborate Takanawa Prince Hotel complex in the Shinagawa district of the city. The room was on the top floor of one of the newer hotels, Sakura Tower. Bond could look out of the window and gaze at the famous city landmark, Tokyo Tower, Japan's larger equivalent of the Eiffel Tower. The service owned the small private workspace, and Tiger liked to use it since his pseudo-retirement. There was a complete linkup to the main headquarters so Tiger didn't have to deal with any bureaucracy when he wanted to access electronic files. He also had full use of the hotel's room service, which wasn't a bad deal.

Tiger and Bond had spent the remainder of the previous day in Kamakura, working with the local police investigating the murder of Shinji Fujimoto. Frustrating as it was, they both remained on the scene as the police worked and later gave statements at the police station. The police were unsuccessful in unearthing anything useful. Other than the miniature Buddha, no other clue was found at the crime scene that might indicate who the perpetrator was.

But Bond and Tanaka had a pretty good idea.

Now they sat in the small office that overlooked the busy commercial district and worked on tying up loose ends. Tiger typed on a PC in an effort to identify the strange dwarf they had seen, and Bond watched the news on television, waiting for the expected story on CureLab.

"My agents have confirmed what I suspected all along," Tiger said, punching up a report on his computer. "The so-called private individuals who own the twenty per cent of CureLab stock are all on the board of directors of Yonai Enterprises."

"What a surprise," Bond said. "That fits with the news we got last night. Shinji Fujimoto sold his shares the day before he was killed. That makes Yonai a significant shareholder of CureLab. Pieces of the jigsaw are falling into place. I wonder if our little killer in Kamakura is one of the shareholders."

"I'm telling you, he was a kappa," Tiger said facetiously, hoping to get a rise out of Bond.

"Would you shut up with that kappa nonsense? Look, I think it's coming on."

The first thing that appeared on the screen was the logo and name, "Yonai Enterprises." The reporter said, "Big news in the business sector today. Yonai Enterprises, a Sapporo-based conglomerate, has announced a merger with CureLab Inc., a Tokyo-based corporation. The move was not a surprise to analysts, as Yonai had made several public bids for acquisition of the company that had been run in recent years by Englishman Peter McMahon. Peter McMahon and his family died of an unknown illness eight days ago."

Peter McMahon's portrait flashed on the television.

"The deal was further complicated by the murder of CureLab vice president and acting chairman Fujimoto Shinji yesterday in Kamakura. He had stunned his board of directors the day before at an emergency meeting by announcing that he had sold his own twenty per cent of CureLab stock to Yonai Enterprises."

They watched as a familiar scene appeared. It was Shinji Fujimoto's Toyota Celsior, parked on that side street in Kamakura. Police tape was stretched around it and several uniformed men could be seen hovering around.

The programme cut to a clip of Yonai's president, Masuzo Kano, speaking into a microphone and saying that together the staff of Yonai Enterprises and CureLab would work to reach even greater heights than either of their two companies had done thus far.

The reporter continued, "Police are not saying if Fujimoto's murder is related to organised crime. Yonai Enterprises has long had to fight the accusations by some that it is allegedly involved in yakuza business."

A new clip: Yasutake Tsukamoto, walking with bodyguards in front of his office in Sapporo. Several reporters hounded him. Bond recognised him from the file that Tanaka had given him.

"No comment. Go away," Tsukamoto said into the camera.

The *kaicho* got into a Mercedes as the picture cut back to the reporter. "CureLab Inc. is known for its work in pharmaceuticals and cures for diseases. Kano-san says that the company will fit in nicely within the chemical engineering areas of Yonai Enterprises. Now on to sports . . ."

"There you have the motive," Bond said. "Fujimoto was killed once he'd sold his shares and agreed to the merger with Yonai. The yakuza is behind it all. They orchestrated the McMahons' deaths all right."

"I agree with you, but all we have to go on is speculation," Tiger replied. "No proof. Ah, wait, here we may have it." He punched up a new e-mail. "The report on the bonsai waterfall came in. You were right, Bondo-san, there were traces of mosquito eggs and shed pupa skins in the reservoir where the water sits. Mosquitoes need water to hatch, right? Since the motor had malfunctioned, the water had been still for a week. That was enough time to hatch those eggs, apparently. The question is, did someone put those eggs inside it? And did Fujimoto know about it?"

"Tiger, it has to be the answer. It was part of his grand plan to sell his stock to the yakuza. I wonder what they promised him besides a great deal of money."

"He did not even receive that in the end," Tiger observed. He read some more of the report. "The egg remains and other organic material have been sent to toxicology to see if they can determine if the virus came from there."

"I think we have to go on the assumption that it did. Someone has invented a deadly biological weapon with an ingenious delivery system—those mosquitoes. It takes a molecular biologist to do something like that, doesn't it? Someone like Fujio Aida? With everything I saw at Cure-Lab about mosquitoes, can you have any doubts?"

"Aida's probably capable of creating the virus. It took the merging of Yonai and CureLab—their separate technologies—to make this weapon."

"But there had to have been insiders at CureLab for some time. The McMahons were killed last week, so if Yonai or the yakuza were responsible for this, they would have had to possess the virus technology before yesterday."

"I think we know who the insiders were, Bondo-san," Tiger said, his eyebrows raised.

Bond nodded and said, "Shinji Fujimoto and Fujio Aida. Tiger, this weapon—we have to stop whatever these people might want to do with it next and destroy it. You don't want another incident like the sarin gas subway attacks a few years ago. I suggest that you set up a meeting with a mosquito expert as soon as possible. We need a crash course in insect biology."

"I agree. I must consult with my colleagues at headquarters and inform them of our hypothesis. If this is true, then the yakuza has become even more dangerous than ever."

He picked up his mobile and made a call.

Headquarters was located in Kasumigaseki, the district adjacent to Nagata-cho, where the Japanese Diet Building sits. It was an unusually nondescript government building on the exterior; however the interior possessed an energy that Bond thought was reminiscent of the Tsukiji Fish Market. The only difference was that the personnel wore business attire. The level of beehive-like activity was just as chaotic at the Koan-Chosa-Cho as it had been at the market, but once again, when Bond looked closer he could see the order and mechanical efficiency of the Japanese people at work.

Reiko Tamura had quickly arranged to bring in an entomologist to give them an overview of mosquitoes. She had been discharged from the hospital when Bond was in Kamakura and had reported for duty, even though she had been given a few days' leave.

"This is Dr. Okumura," Reiko said, introducing an unusually tall, slender woman in her thirties. Tiger and Bond bowed to her and exchanged business cards, then the four of them went into a conference room.

"I have been studying the samples that Tamura-san provided to me," the doctor began, "and I have come to the conclusion that the mosquitoes involved here are *Aedes aegypti*. This is a species that lays eggs above water and can breed in small containers. The eggs can remain dry and survive for a considerable amount of time, and they hatch when they come into contact with water."

"Instant mosquitoes, just add water," Bond said.

"Something like that," she said. She showed them pictures of mosquito eggs. They resembled black caraway seeds. "It normally takes a week to ten days for them to go through the cycle from eggs to adult mosquitoes; some species take longer. Eggs hatch into larvae that live in water for several days. Stagnant, standing water is the best environment for these things."

"So it was fairly easy for mosquitoes to breed inside that bonsai waterfall contraption," Bond said.

"Yes, as long as they had food. Larvae eat just about anything with protein, usually microscopic organisms that live in the water. The larvae eventually become pupae and then after a few days, the adult mosquitoes emerge. The females are the only ones that bite. They immediately need to find a blood host, which gives them the protein needed to lay eggs. The male mosquitoes feed off things that provide sugar and are basically harmless to humans. The males and females can mate at any time after they emerge from the pupal state. Females live longer than the males, so some entomologists call them 'red widows.' "

"I've known a couple of those in my time," Bond muttered.

"How long do the adult mosquitoes live?" Tiger asked.

"Males live less than a week. Females can live longer if they're not killed by the elements, slapped by a human hand or eaten by other creatures, which is what usually happens. Very rarely do we see mosquitoes live to be a ripe old age, which conceivably could be three or four weeks."

Bond asked, "If someone were to have the ability to change the genetic structure of a mosquito, what advantages could be gained?"

Dr. Okumura shrugged. "I understand that many companies in the pesticide business are working on that type of technology. If you could genetically engineer a mosquito not to bite, I suppose that would be good, yes?"

Bond frowned. "But if that is possible, then is it also possible to genetically engineer a mosquito's behaviour in other ways? Say, to bite even more zealously?"

"Yes, that is possible."

Bond and Tiger shared a look.

"Is this *Aedes aegypti* able to transmit diseases?" Bond asked.

"Oh, yes," the doctor said. "They are one of the main species that is a vector, or carrier, for yellow fever, encephalitis and West Nile disease. There are others, but this one is known for that."

"How does that work?" Reiko asked.

"The female mosquito bites an infected host, becomes infected herself, then goes and bites a human. Simply a transference of blood."

"Wait a second," Bond said. "So the mosquito isn't born with the disease? It has to pick it up somewhere else?"

"That's right."

"Is it possible for mosquitoes to pass the disease onto their young, via the eggs?"

The doctor made a face and said, "Some species can do that, but not this one. Thank goodness."

"Then is it possible for them to be genetically engineered to do so?"

"Perhaps. Although I don't know why anyone would want to do that," the doctor replied.

"Is there a name for that?" Reiko asked.

"Yes, it's called 'transovarial transmission.' "

Again, Bond and Tiger shared a look. This time Reiko joined them.

The meeting with the entomologist went on for a few more minutes; Dr. Okumura left after offering her help for any other inquiries they might have. Bond had a look at some of the literature she had given them, found a picture of the *Aedes aegypti,* and studied it.

"From the notes you found at CureLab the other night, Bondo-san, it seems that they are working on producing a strain of mosquitoes that can transfer the disease to their eggs," Tanaka suggested.

"Red widows," Bond added.

"We've had a look at that slide show that James-san brought from CureLab," Reiko said. "There's nothing suspicious in it. It's basically a crash course on the biology of a mosquito. Toward the end, it talks about how the company should genetically engineer the mosquitoes for the good of mankind. Knock out their reproductive instincts or make them so they don't bite. That kind of thing."

Tiger's mobile rang. He answered it and listened, then he rang off and said, "We have found our kappa. I'll be right back." He got up and left the room.

"Poor James-san," Reiko said. "You must be in terrible pain. Those are nasty cuts on your face."

"It only hurts when I kiss someone," Bond said. It was true that he still looked battered.

"I would still kiss you, James-san, but I am afraid that you would find it painful," she said.

"Perhaps we should experiment?" Bond asked. "How's the wound?"

"Much better. Still hurts a little."

"Reiko?"

"Yes, James-san?"

"How about when I'm finished with this assignment, we go somewhere on a holiday, just the two of us?"

Reiko's eyes widened. "Oh my, James-san. I don't know what to say. Where do you suggest we go?"

"Is there somewhere you've always wanted to see?"

She thought a moment. "I have always dreamed of going to the Hawaiian Islands."

"What a coincidence. I have too. Hawaii it is. Will you think about it?"

She nodded quietly and looked down as Tiger came back into the room.

"Look what I have," Tiger said as he went to the computer and inserted a floppy disk into the drive. He used the mouse and brought up an image of the kappa killer. "This is him."

"It certainly is," Bond said.

"His name is Junji Kon. Nickname: 'Kappa'! He has a police record, all right. Kon was an orphan; his parents probably got rid of him because of his deformities. Historically in Japan children who were born deformed were either killed or left to die somewhere. It was a sad fact of life. Junji Kon managed to survive, working in a circus until he was in his teens. That's when the arrests began. Shoplifting, burglary, assault and a number of more serious charges. He was arrested once for murder but was released for lack of evidence. He was known to be a *shatei,* or younger brother, of the yakuza by the time he was twenty. Sometimes the yakuza will accept misfits from society because they're the only family that will have them. It makes sense."

"Indeed."

"It says here that Kappa is very good with a knife and always carries a balisong, what we call a 'butterfly knife.' "

"I'm familiar with it," Bond said. It was a nasty weapon used by many gangs in the Far East. It consisted of two hinged handles that fitted around the blade, which could be exposed by spinning one handle around in an arc with a flick of the wrist. Bond had seen men who could manipulate the balisong with blinding-fast manoeuvres.

Tiger continued, "Because of his size, he is adept at stealth skills. In the circus he performed as a freak in a sideshow but also as a magician's assistant."

"That explains why he seemed to appear and disappear

at will in Kamakura," Bond said. "He walked out of that Buddha under our noses, and we didn't notice."

"It also says that Kappa is suspected of being a hit man for the Ryujin-kai. Very interesting. I will file a report stating that we suspect him of being Shinji Fujimoto's killer. He will be wanted for questioning."

"If anyone can find him," Reiko said. "Where does he live?"

"It does not say. He is known to be in Tokyo but has been seen in Sapporo as well."

Tiger's phone rang again. He rolled his eyes and answered it. He listened and said, *"Hai!"* He hung up and said, "There is news about the summit conference. They've finally picked a site."

"It's about time," Reiko said. "It's only six days away."

"It is to take place where I suggested. It is a remote location in the Inland Sea, on Naoshima Island. It is just off the shore south of Okayama, just east of the Seto-Ohashi Bridge. It is perfect for a G8 meeting. Benesse Corporation bought a portion of the island and turned it into 'Benesse Island,' and they built a beautiful art museum and hotel there called Benesse House. It is one of Japan's little treasures that not too many people know about. The conference will be held at the art museum and the guests will stay in the lodgings there."

"When do we have to be there?" Bond asked.

"The day before. My people will already be on the island days earlier, of course, to make sure that security is well placed. This location is top secret, so I cannot imagine that the threats we have received can be credible. Still, one cannot be too careful. I have been put in charge of the security. And as this is an international gathering, I have made you my second in command, Bondo-san."

"Thanks, Tiger. I'm honoured," Bond said dryly.

"You are welcome!" Tiger said, enjoying the moment.

Bond looked back at the mosquito documents that were on the table. "You have people in Sapporo, don't you?"

"Of course. I have a very good man in Sapporo. He's Ainu, a very interesting fellow."

Tiger was referring to the race of people who are believed to be the original inhabitants of Japan. The Ainu live mostly in the northern parts of the country and in the Kuril Islands.

"I think it's time for me to go north and try to find Mayumi McMahon," Bond said. "Put a word in to your man that I'm looking for her and see what he can dig up. I'd also like to put in a visit to this Hokkaido Mosquito and Vector Control Centre. Those posters I saw at the CureLab office came from there. Where is Noboribetsu, exactly?"

"That's a resort town south of Sapporo with a lot of hot springs and spas," Reiko replied. "Hotels. Tourists. The Hokkaido Mosquito and Vector Control Centre is a public health facility located just outside the town."

Tiger said, "Very well. We shall send you to Hokkaido, Bondo-san. I think you should have Miss Tamura accompany you, what do you think?"

"I'd be delighted," Bond said. "It helps to have a native speaker along for the ride."

Reiko blushed again and looked away. "I will have my assistant check on flights," she said as she fiddled with her Palm Pilot. "When do you want to leave?"

"Today if possible," Bond said. "But no flights. I have a feeling that our friends in the Ryujin-kai might be watching the airports. Let's take a train. We can do that, can't we?"

Reiko shrugged. "Sure. There's an overnight train from Ueno Station. We could have sleeper compartments. It's not as fast but it gets us there."

"I adore train travel," Bond said. "Book two sleepers. For tonight."

14
Night Train

Reiko was successful in securing two sleeper suites on the two-storey *Cassiopeia,* touted as Japan's most luxurious train. It travelled between Tokyo's Ueno Station and Sapporo three times a week on a journey lasting seventeen hours. All carriages were first-class sleeper cars. The train also offered shower rooms, an observation lounge and an excellent restaurant car that provided French or Japanese dinners.

Bond checked out of the Imperial, had a quick dinner with Tiger, then met Reiko at the station half an hour before departure time. Bond had the "Cassiopeia Suite," the only one of its type on the train. It was located at the very front of the lower floor and had all the amenities of a hotel room: two double beds, a private bathroom and a small sitting area by the front windows that could be used for work or dining. The suite took up the entire width of the train. Reiko got the slightly less luxurious "Deluxe Suite" just down the corridor from Bond. It contained two single beds, a private bathroom and fold-up tables. The beds could be turned into day seats, and the room was on one side of the train.

"Why did you get me the most expensive compartment on the train?" Bond asked her.

"Because you are our special guest in Japan," she said. "You said that you adored trains, so I provided you with the best."

"You know, we could have shared one room and saved the Koan-Chosa-Cho some money."

She wagged her finger and gave him one of those looks that suggested that he was a naughty boy. "James-san, you know that if we did that, the people who process our expense reports would spread rumours about us!"

Bond shrugged and smiled.

The train departed precisely on time, something that Japan Rail advertised proudly. Bond had to admit that the country's rail service was indeed the best in the world.

Bond spent a half hour in his suite enjoying the view of the landscape rushing at him. It was after dark, so there wasn't much to see in terms of scenery but there was something hypnotic and soothing about watching the parallel lines of train tracks, illuminated by the engine's headlamps, whipping towards him. The train was steadily shooting towards its destination, northward to the upper tip of Honshu, where it would go through the Seikan Tunnel to the island of Hokkaido. *The tunnel would be interesting,* Bond thought. It was the longest rail tunnel in the world at more than fifty kilometres between the two ends and had taken twenty-four years to build. Bond had always been interested in architecture and structural engineering, but more from a practical point of view than an artistic one. He appreciated the thought that went into the way buildings, bridges and tunnels were designed and constructed and admired the men who could do it.

He opened one of the small bottles of sake that Tiger had given to him as a parting gift and poured a glass. He thought that perhaps he should ask Reiko to join him, but at this point he wasn't sure how she really felt about him.

It was true that she had allowed him to kiss her, but it was sometimes difficult to discern whether a Japanese girl was serious in her flirting or not. Reiko was a professional, and she would probably behave like one until the assignment was over. But they were all alone on an overnight train! How much more romantic could life get? Bond wondered if she might be willing to entertain such notions. Should he get up, go and rap on her door?

A knock at his compartment answered his query.

Reiko stood in the corridor, having changed into a *yukata.* She too held a bottle of sake.

"I thought you might be lonely," she said. "I know I was."

"Come in!"

She went past him into the suite, walked straight to the sitting area and placed the bottle next to Bond's.

"I see you started without me," she said. "I have some catching up to do. *Sugoi,* what a view!"

"Isn't it?"

"I have an idea. How about we order room service and stay here?" She swallowed and batted her eyelashes at him. He could see that she was a little nervous. He walked to her and stroked her smooth black hair.

"I think that's a lovely idea," he whispered. He leaned in to kiss her and she hungrily embraced him.

It was nearly midnight.

Reiko's skin felt warm and smooth as she wrapped a slender leg around him and snuggled into his chest. She playfully rubbed at the hair there.

"I like this stuff," she said, almost giggling. "We Japanese women don't see that very often."

"Are we so different from Japanese men?"

"Yes and no. I mean, you have hair in places that Japanese men don't, and you obviously look different. You're very tall, so you're a bit of a giant compared to most Japanese men. What about us?"

"You mean Japanese women? Possibly the most beautiful in the world."

She hit him lightly on the shoulder. "You know how to flatter. Will we really go to Hawaii?"

"If you'd like."

"We could lie on the beach all day and make love all night."

"We could pick a different beach each day."

Reiko laughed. She was ready for him. The gentle rocking of the train added to their pleasure. Reiko wrapped her legs around his waist and locked him against her, allowing the motion of the train to do all the work.

Bond was sleeping soundly when Reiko awoke a couple of hours later. The wound on her side hurt; she must have rubbed it accidentally during the lovemaking, which at one point had become rather turbulent.

Damn, she thought. The painkillers were in her suite. She didn't really want to have to get dressed and leave, but she was afraid that she would be unable to go back to sleep if she didn't. She quietly got out of the bed, put on her *yukata* and slippers and tread softly towards the door.

"Reiko?" Bond mumbled as he stirred.

"It's all right," she whispered. "I'm going back to my room for a minute. I'll be back."

"Take my key," he said. "There on the counter."

She found it, blew him a kiss and went out of the room.

The train corridor was quiet and dark. As it was probably two o'clock in the morning, everyone with any sense was asleep. She walked down to her room, unlocked the door and went inside. Once there, she found her pills and looked for something to take them with.

Oh no, she thought. Nothing to drink. The restaurant car was closed at this hour, but the lounge had a vending machine. Come to think of it, there were snacks in the machines there too. She was a little hungry. The room-service box dinner had been tasty but not very filling. Bond had complained that he had still felt hungry after they had eaten too. Reiko decided that she'd make a quick trip to the lounge and bring back some sweets and drinks to share with him, and then perhaps they would be ener-gised for another round of passion.

She put on a pair of blue jeans and a T-shirt and went back into the corridor. The lounge car was on the top floor of the train, all the way at the back. She made her way out of their car and into the second one, then up the steps to the next level. A conductor was walking her way and greeted her. She asked him if there was any food left in the vending machines, and he replied that there was. Reiko thanked him and went on.

She went through several cars, past the many regular twin suites that filled the train, until she came to car eleven. She was about to open the sliding metal door to car twelve, the lounge car, when she saw something that sent a chill up her spine.

Through the window, she could see a small man in the lounge car putting money into a vending machine. He was a dwarf with a bald, misshapen head.

It was Kappa.

What was he doing on the train? Did he know they were on it? She had to go and inform James immediately!

But wait, she thought, perhaps she should find out what sleeper he was in.

Kappa retrieved a can of juice from the machine and began to walk towards her. Reiko ducked and squeezed herself into a cranny that held a pay telephone. Thinking quickly, she turned her back to the corridor, picked up the receiver, and began to talk to a nonexistent party. The door opened behind her, and she heard the man leave the lounge car and walk past her. Reiko waited a few seconds, then hung up the phone. She peered into the corridor and saw Kappa opening the opposite door and going into the next car.

She ran to follow him, waited a moment and then opened the door. She went into the car and watched him unlock one of the compartments and step inside. Once she was certain that he had closed and locked the door, she crept down to see what number it was. Car ten, compartment twenty-two.

All thoughts of hunger had vanished and her heart was pounding with excitement. Without returning to the lounge car, Reiko went back to Bond's suite and let herself in with his key. He was still in bed, breathing deeply. She took some of the unfinished sake and swallowed her pill, then sat on the bed beside him. She ran her fingers through his hair until he stirred.

"Hey wake up, mister," she said.

"Hey." He turned and smiled at her. "You're dressed."

"I have some news. Guess who is aboard the train."

"The Emperor."

"No. Kappa. Junji Kon himself."

Bond sat up. "Are you sure? How do you know?"

"I just saw him. And . . . I know what compartment he is in."

"Good girl." Bond thought a moment and said, "So, is he on this train because we're on it, or is he simply travelling to Sapporo with no idea that we're here? Did he see you?"

"I don't think so."

"I would love to get into his compartment and take a look around. What time is it?"

"I don't know. It's the middle of the night."

"He'll have to come out in the morning. Do you think he'll go to the restaurant car for breakfast?"

"Hard to say," she said. "Since he looks the way he

does, he may try to avoid people. He might order room service, like we did last night."

"We have to think of something."

"Let's go talk to the conductor. I saw him walking through the train earlier."

Bond quickly put on some clothes and the two of them went out into the corridor. They made their way through the car to the stairwell, then up to the second floor. They caught up with the conductor in car seven.

Reiko showed him her identification card. "Excuse me, we are with the Public Security Investigation Agency. We have learned that there is a dangerous criminal aboard the train."

The conductor looked alarmed.

"Don't be frightened. We could use your help. He's a dwarf and he's in compartment twenty-two, car ten. Have you seen him?"

"Yes," the conductor said. "Strange fellow. Gives me the creeps."

"Will you be up the rest of the night?" she asked.

"Yes, I'm on night duty until we reach Hokkaido."

"Could you possibly keep an eye on his compartment? We would like to have a look around his room should he happen to leave. Would you do that for us?"

"That's not exactly legal, madam."

"Please? It might mean the safety of your passengers." She batted her eyelashes at him and gently placed a hand on his upper arm.

The conductor blushed and bowed. "Yes. I will try."

She gave him hers and Bond's compartment numbers, bowed and left with Bond to go back to his suite.

The conductor smiled as he walked through the train to his own compartment, which happened to be in the same car that contained Bond and Reiko's suites. *What a pretty girl!* he thought. Sometimes it really paid to work for Japan Rail.

He unlocked the door to his little room. Inside there was a place to sit down and not much more. An emergency pull cord was located in every conductor's compartment, and this could be used to stop the train if he had to do it. There were also communication phones to the other posts on the train and to the engineer and control panels for the lights and doors. The conductor opened a cabinet and pulled out his carry-on bag. He dug inside for the sandwich his wife had packed for him.

There was a knock on the door.

He put down the bag and opened the door. At first he didn't see anyone. It was only when he looked down that he gasped.

The butterfly knife in Kappa's hand whipped viciously back and forth without making a sound.

15

The Desire for Death

It had happened again.

Goro Yoshida awoke in his bunker and had to shake off the remnants of another nightmare. It was a recurring one, something that normally wouldn't have disturbed him if it hadn't been for Yukio Mishima's role in it.

In the dream, Yoshida was kneeling on the floor, naked to the waist, and was prepared to commit ritual *seppuku*. Mishima, his mentor, stood over him with a sword, ready to cut off Yoshida's head. The problem was that when Yoshida attempted to plunge the dagger into his belly, the skin wouldn't budge. The blade just wouldn't penetrate. Mishima would get angry and yell that Yoshida was a coward. And just as Mishima raised the sword to lop off Yoshida's head, Goro would wake up.

There was no morning sun in the bunker. That had been the most difficult thing about going into exile and having to live underground. Yoshida used to enjoy rising with the sun. It was said that dawn was the ideal time to commit *seppuku*. At the end of one of Yoshida's favourite books by Mishima, the hero gallantly commits ritual *seppuku* on a mountaintop, plunging the dagger into his belly just as the "bright disk of the sun soared up and exploded behind his eyelids."

The digital clock indicated that it was indeed morning. It was time to get up. There was much work to be done, but instead Yoshida lay there wallowing in memories of the man he admired so much.

Yoshida had been a part of Mishima's Shield Society, the private army that the poet and novelist had formed in the late 1960s as a token of his dedication to the emperor and to the traditional values of Japan. Yoshida had looked up to Mishima-san and revered the *sensei's* every word. He volunteered to be a cadet in the Shield Society and trained along with Mishima and the rest of the students. He worked to improve his body and mind with kendo and other martial arts. He read the doctrines prescribed by his mentor. He was prepared to follow Mishima in whatever the *sensei* chose to do.

Then Mishima learned that Yoshida was involved with the yakuza. Even though he was an intelligent and free-thinking individual, Mishima did not approve. It was true that Mishima had right-wing tendencies and believed in many of the same principles as the yakuza did, such as the purification of Japan, but he drew the line at organised crime. Mishima told Yoshida that he must leave the Shield Society.

Yoshida had never felt so disgraced in his life. The man he looked up to had dismissed him. Yoshida had wanted to commit *seppuku* then and there, but his friends in the yakuza convinced him not to. He was persuaded to use his knowledge and skills for the good of the Ryujin-kai, where he could someday become a *kaicho*.

And so Yoshida turned his back on the Shield Society and tried to forget about Yukio Mishima until that fateful day in November of 1970, when Mishima and his four most trusted cadets boldly walked into the army's command headquarters and held General Kanetoshi Mashita hostage. Then, as twelve hundred soldiers gathered on the parade ground, Mishima stepped onto the balcony and delivered a rousing, impassioned speech that most of the men heckled. He questioned the troops' motivation for guarding the constitution that, he claimed, denied them the true essence of what was once Imperial Japan. He pleaded with the men to "stand up and fight" or "die together" for the sake of nationalism.

But his words fell on cynical ears. Finally giving up the cause, Mishima shouted, *"Tenno Heika Banzai!"*—"Long live the Emperor!" He stepped back from the balcony and proceeded to perform in precise detail the traditional *seppuku* ceremony. He went into the office where the general was being held, stripped to the waist and knelt on the floor. He probed the left side of his abdomen and put the ceremonial dagger in place. Then he thrust it deep into his flesh. Standing behind him, Morita, his most trusted cadet, raised his sword to cut off Mishima's head. He missed the first time, gravely wounding Mishima. It took two more tries and the help of another cadet before Mishima's head rolled onto the floor. To complete the ceremony, Morita plunged a dagger into his own stomach and yet another cadet lopped off Morita's head. Shedding tears, the three surviving cadets saluted the two dead men and surrendered to the general's aides. It was reported later that Mishima's seventeen-centimetre incision displayed a "degree of mastery over physical reflex, and over pain itself, unparalleled in modern records of this ritual."

Goro Yoshida's admiration of Mishima increased tenfold after the incident. What a brave and noble thing to do! Mishima had been serious about his convictions all along. He had made the ritual act of *seppuku* a part of his art. While many critics might have thought that what Mishima did was insane, Yoshida felt that he was a man who never forgot his wartime catechism: the doctrine of Japan as a ritually ordered state, the samurai way of life characterised by manly courage and feminine grace and the vision of imminent death as the catalyst of life.

Yoshida finally got up off of the futon and walked away, leaving his woman sleeping. Naked, he walked across the *tatami* and took the ceremonial dagger from a drawer in his desk. He knelt on the floor in the correct position and placed the point of the dagger against his skin, touching the bright red tail of a tattooed dragon that wrapped around his waist. He pressed the blade, ever so slightly, feeling the sharp tip's desire to penetrate his body and wondered if his blood would be distinguishable from the crimson artwork adorning his belly.

When the time came, would *he* be able to do what Mishima had done? If everything that he and his followers had worked for ended up failing completely, then he would have no other choice.

"What are you doing?"

The woman had awoken and looked at him in horror.

Yoshida answered, "Nothing. Go back to sleep."

She frowned but after a moment finally turned over and put her head down.

Yoshida could see her bare shoulders and back. For many men, such beauty would be enough, but he was reminded of Mishima's words: "A man's determination to become a beautiful person is very different from the same desire in a woman; in a man it is always the desire for death."

How true, Yoshida thought. How true.

Bond finished the *natto* Reiko had insisted on his trying. The bloody stuff was awful. This putrid concoction created from fermented soybeans nearly made him gag. It had an atrocious nutty flavour, a disturbing aroma and stickiness, all held together like a spider web by gooey strands.

"I can see you enjoyed that!" Reiko said brightly. "I told you it was good."

"Mmm," Bond said with a smile.

She finished the last bit of her own bowl of *natto* and looked past Bond, across the dining car toward the entrance. Her eyes gave her away.

"James-san, another guest for breakfast," she whispered.

Bond knew whom she meant without looking.

The dwarf known as Kappa waddled into the dining car, was greeted by the hostess and then shown to an empty table for two. He was dressed in a suit and tie, as if he were ready for a day at the bank. He wore no hat, so his glistening misshapen head was in full view. Virtually everyone in the dining car was staring at him, for he was an extraordinarily bizarre sight. Behind Kappa's back, the hostess gave a wide-eyed look to the waiter, who bowed to the dwarf before taking his order. After the waiter walked away, Kappa unfolded a newspaper and began to read.

"Does he know we're here?" Bond asked.

"He hasn't looked at us," she said. "He hasn't looked at anyone but people are sure looking at *him*."

"He's ordering breakfast?"

"That's what it looks like."

"You have your mobile with you?"

"Of course."

She patted the pocket of her business suit. They were both dressed a bit more formally since they would be arriving in Sapporo later in the morning.

"You stay here. Have some coffee or something. Watch him and if he gets up to leave, call me."

"You're going to his room now?"

"Hush."

Bond got up from the table, turned, and casually walked across the compartment. He passed the dwarf and bowed slightly to the hostess. Kappa did not look up from his newspaper.

Bond went into the corridor of the next car and continued through the train until he came to car ten. He found compartment twenty-two, looked both ways to make sure the hallway was clear, then lifted his left foot so that he could access the heel of his shoe. He used his index finger to find the slight impression next to a seam and press it. A thin metal wire released itself into his hand.

Bond gently inserted the lock pick into the keyhole. He twisted the wire carefully until he heard a snap. The door opened. He stepped inside, closed the door and replaced the lock pick in his shoe.

The room was a standard twin with two bunks at a ninety-degree angle to each other. On one of the fold-down trays sat a bottle of orange juice, an empty paper cup and a plate with three slices of cucumber.

Bond went straight for the luggage and began to rummage through it. He found mostly clothes, personal effects, nothing of interest.

Under one of the bunks was a square box. It was like a hatbox, but much smaller. Bond pulled it out and lifted the lid. Inside was a glass jar with a strange seal on the top. There appeared to be a hinge attached to the rim of the seal, and the top surface contained several mesh-covered holes. The seal couldn't be unscrewed or popped open. Bond looked for a keyhole that might release the hinged top but didn't see one. He held the jar up to the light and peered into it.

It contained live mosquitoes and an inch of water. The insects were crawling on the inside of the jar and lid, perpetually trying to find a way out. Bond counted ten.

His mobile rang, startling him. He pulled it out of his jacket pocket and answered the call.

"James-san, he's getting ready to leave," Reiko said.

"Thanks." Bond rang off and put the mobile back in the

pocket, then replaced the square box under the bunk. The glass jar he stuck in his other pocket.

Bond took a quick look around the room to make sure that nothing appeared out of place, then he quickly opened the door and scanned the hallway. All clear. He stepped out, closed the door and made sure that it was locked. Then he began to walk back to the dining car.

As he went through one set of doors between cars, Bond saw Kappa coming from the opposite end towards him. They would pass each other in the centre of the car.

Since it was too late to turn back, Bond kept going. He expected to make eye contact, but Kappa never looked at him. Bond had to stop and allow the little man to squeeze past him. Bond said, *"Sumimasen,"* but Kappa didn't acknowledge him. The dwarf kept walking and was soon going through the automatic door at the end of the car. Only after he had cleared the door did Kappa look back and grin to himself, but Bond didn't see this. He had gone on to the dining car and found Reiko still at the table.

"Did you see him?" she asked.

"Uh-huh, and he ignored me," Bond said. "I have a funny feeling about it. It's like he's making a show out of not noticing us."

"Did you find anything?"

"Yes, but I had better let you see it back in the suite. Let's go."

She held the jar close to her face as she examined the movements of one mosquito crawling up the side of the jar.

"So those holes are in the top so they can breathe?" Reiko asked.

"That's right."

"I bet that one's pregnant," Reiko said. "She's dragging a big belly."

The insects were a dull red colour but otherwise were

not unusually large or out of the ordinary in appearance. Reiko pondered the significance of a small cube with a tiny tube extending from it that was attached to the side of the glass.

"You know what?" she said. "I think that little thing on the side had food in it for the larvae. This is a mosquito incubator, James-san! There were eggs in here, then they hatched into larvae, grew into pupae and became mosquitoes. I'm not sure how it opens."

"It has some kind of locking mechanism. See the hinge? The top flips up but I can't determine how it's done. Not that I'd want to. I think we're just fine with those things safely trapped in the jar."

"I agree with you. What do we do now?"

"I guess we wait and see," Bond said. "Either he'll discover it's missing and do something about it or he'll get off the train in Sapporo and we'll follow him."

She continued to peer at the insects. "Do you think these bugs might have the virus?"

"What do *you* think?"

"We'd better hide it."

"Give it to me," Bond said. He took the jar and squatted beside the bed. He reached under the frame and balanced the container on top of a metal support that was a part of the structure.

"That will do for now. I suggest we remain in the room until we reach Sapporo."

Reiko smiled. "Sounds good to *me*."

Junji Kon smiled to himself. Perfect timing. The mosquitoes had shed their pupal skins thirty hours ago. The insects' shells would be hard now and they could fly. The fool had taken the container back to his compartment. The mission would be a success. Everything was going as planned. He would bring great honour to his name. The world would look at him with respect, something he had never experienced except from other members of the yakuza. Junji Kon was no longer an outcast. He had integrated into a new society and found acceptance. He made good money, and he enjoyed what he did.

Kappa looked at his wristwatch just as the train entered the long Seikan Tunnel. All light from the outside was extinguished as the locomotive sped under the sea on its way to Hokkaido. It was time to act.

He put on his jacket, took his luggage and walked through the door. He made his way to the lower floor and walked to the first car. He listened at the conductor's compartment. It appeared that no one had discovered his handiwork yet.

Then he stood outside Bond's suite. First making sure that no one was looking, Kappa removed a small radio transmitter from his pocket. He pulled out the two-inch antenna and turned on the power. There was only one other button, and Kappa pushed it to transmit a signal.

He could see it happening in his mind's eye. Inside the suite, where the *gaijin* lay with the secret service woman, the signal was received by the ingenious device housed in the top of the jar of mosquitoes. The hinged lid silently opened. The mosquitoes, suddenly discovering that they were free, crawled out of the jar and began to fly around the room. All females, especially hungry for a blood host.

The next thing Kappa did was move to Bond's door and insert one of the keys on the ring he had taken from the conductor. It went into the lock easily. Kappa turned it once, then clasped both hands and slammed them down on it as hard as he could. The key broke in the lock.

Kappa went back to the conductor's compartment, unlocked it and stepped inside. It was difficult avoiding the mess of the bloody, crumpled conductor's body, folded into a corner of the cubicle like origami.

The dwarf examined the control panel on the wall and

found the switch to turn off the lights in the car. Nearby was the mechanism that opened the outside car doors.

He looked at his watch and reached for the emergency brake cord that hung in a little recess on the wall. He grasped the handle and waited.

A few more seconds, he thought, as he looked at his watch.

This was going to be *fun.*

Reiko snuggled against Bond's neck as they relaxed into the gentle rumbling motion of the train. They were enjoying the last few solitary moments on the train in each other's arms, their clothing discarded about the room.

"I hear that Maui is the best island," she said as she tightened the hold around his chest.

"Well, the big one, Hawaii, and Oahu are supposed to be charming."

"We'll have to hit them all. Go to a luau or two."

"There are other people at luaus. Don't you want to be alone together?"

"At least ninety-five per cent of the time. We could go there and, hey—!" She interrupted herself with a slap on her arm. She lifted her palm and revealed a smashed mosquito.

"James-san!"

Bond leaped out of bed and looked under the bed.

"The damned thing is open!" he said in horror. He pulled out the jar. The hinged top was indeed at a right angle to the container. Bond went to the door and tried to open it. He struggled with it and said, "We're locked in."

"Oh, God, look, I see another one!" she cried, pointing at the air. Bond attempted to see where she was pointing but the light and movement of the train inhibited his ability to spot the wretched insects. Then he saw one and batted at it.

"Get dressed—cover your arms!" Bond shouted.

They both leaped around the room grabbing their respective articles of clothing and raced to put them on. Reiko then picked up one of the train brochures to use as a weapon.

"There's one!" she said, swatting the insect on the mirror. It left a wet, stringy smudge.

Suddenly, the train lurched violently, screeching with a horrible noise. Bond and Reiko were tossed forward. Reiko slammed into the table and cried out as Bond fell on the floor. The train quickly lost its forward momentum, audibly kicking and screaming as it went. Finally, it slowed to a crawl and eventually stopped. The exhaling sound of compressed air that followed was loud and jarring.

"Are you all right?" Bond asked, standing and helping her up.

"I think so. Oww, I hurt my side again," she said. "What just happened?"

Before he could answer, the lights in the compartment went out and they were plunged into darkness.

16

In the Tunnel

To stop unexpectedly inside the Seikan Tunnel was cause for alarm for the passengers who were aware of what it might mean. Trains didn't just stop in a tunnel two hundred metres underground, especially when the tunnel was beneath the tons of water in Tsugaru Straits. Japan Rail staff immediately attempted to determine who stopped the train and why. Many passengers came out into the corridor to inquire what was going on, and the staff did their best to keep things calm. As the scene was reasonably chaotic, none of the employees noticed that they were missing a conductor.

Inside the dark suite, Bond and Reiko attempted to keep their cool but knew that they were in a predicament. They had no idea where the mosquitoes were but as a precaution they both continuously rubbed their arms and necks—any patch of bare skin that was exposed to the air. Bond had tried banging on the door to no avail. Even the phone was dead.

"Reiko, where are you?" Bond asked.

"Over here, by the bed," she said in the blackness.

"Okay, stay there and sit down. I'm going to try something."

Bond reached into his pocket and found the cigar holder that Major Boothroyd had given him, then he felt his way to the door. Using his sense of touch, Bond popped the lid off the container, removed the cigar and squeezed out a small amount of the toothpaste-like explosive and lined the lock with it. Satisfied that he hadn't applied too much, Bond dropped what was left of the cigar and set the timer. He thrust the canister into the paste and moved back to where Reiko was sitting.

"You might want to hold your ears," Bond whispered as he mentally counted backwards from ten and pulled Reiko to the floor.

The entire door blew off in a loud, trembling blast that rocked the train. Pieces of wood and plaster flew about the room and a thick cloud of smoke obliterated any sight line to the corridor.

"Sugoi," Reiko said after it had settled.

"Okay, so I used a little too much," Bond said. He pulled her up and they waved the smoke away. They could see the corridor now and were surprised to find it just as dark as the room.

"So much for containing the mosquitoes. If they survived that blast, they're in the rest of the train now," Bond said.

"Let's go find out what has happened," Reiko said.

They came out into the corridor and felt their way along the wall to the exit alcove. The doors were wide open. At least the tunnel lights were on so they could see something at last.

"I'll bet he got off the train," Bond said. "I should go after him."

"All right. I will stay and look for the mosquitoes, James-san," Reiko said. "I will crush them when I see them."

"At this point they could be anywhere. Are you sure?"

"Yes! Go!"

Bond looked into the tunnel. "They could have flown out. Let's just hope they die soon." He turned to her and said, "If we get separated, you know the rendezvous location."

She nodded.

Bond kissed her on the cheek and then bolted out to the narrow platform. Unsure which way to go, he looked back and forth, finally gambling on what appeared to be the closest of the passages that ran at right angles to the main rail tunnel, and went that way.

Two conductors carrying torches burst into the car. They were extremely agitated and began to shout at Reiko, demanding to know what had been going on. Reiko flashed her official identification and did her best to explain that they had been locked in the suite by whoever it was that stopped the train. One of the men banged on the door to the conductor's compartment. When there was no answer, he unlocked it with his own key and opened it. He cried out in alarm.

The torches illuminated the little room so that everyone could see the horrid display of butchery.

"Who did this terrible thing?" one man whispered.

Reiko replied, "A very bad man."

The torch revealed the damaged panel that controlled the lights in the car.

"Call the police," a conductor told another man. "And apprise Control Centre of the situation."

Reiko inched away from the men who were now preoccupied with the scene in car one. She turned and went through the doors into the next car, which was, thankfully, well lit. Passengers were standing in the corridor; some of them asked what was happening.

Reiko played dumb and said that she didn't know. One man wanted to go past her into the first car, but Reiko stopped him. "I don't think that is a good idea," she told him. "The rail people are in there trying to figure out what happened. They said not to bother them and that they would make an announcement in a moment."

"I want to find out what's going on!" the belligerent man shouted.

Reiko's eyes went wide. A mosquito was flying lightly near the man's face. Reiko watched it intently as the man babbled about how Japan Rail trains never break down and this was the first time it had happened to him. The insect circled the man's head, as if trying to find a good landing site. The man continued to rant as the mosquito finally lit on his neck. Reiko lifted the train brochure that she still had in her hand and slapped the man, squashing the insect. The man shut up and looked at Reiko in horror.

"Hush up and calm down," she said. "They are doing the best they can!" Then she pushed past him and continued down the corridor, leaving the man dumbstruck.

The Seikan Tunnel is actually made up of a grid-like series of interconnecting tunnels. Besides the main tunnel, which is wide enough for two sets of train tracks and a track for maintenance vehicles in the middle, there is also a service tunnel running parallel and attached to it by "connecting galleries"—short tunnels spaced at intervals along the main passage. Shafts run from the surface on Honshu and Hokkaido to the tunnel—vertical ones for hauling machinery and materials in lifts and inclined ones for cable cars and for walking. In case of emergency, passengers can be evacuated out of the main tunnel, through the nearest connecting gallery and into the service tunnel. From there they can walk to the closest end and then go up the inclined shaft by foot or cable car to the outside world. There are two undersea train stations on either side of the strait as well in case trains need to stop in the tunnel. At the moment, the *Cassiopeia* was stopped a mile past the Tappi undersea station on the Honshu side.

Bond hurried through a connecting gallery and found

himself in the service tunnel. There was enough illumination from the work lights to allow him to get a good look around. The tunnel stretched as far as he could see. Bond noted the many connecting galleries that lined the way and also the cameras that appeared to be set every forty metres. No doubt the Japan Rail people in the Control Centre could switch on any of the cameras to see what was going on in the tunnels.

Bond ran down to the next connecting gallery, then shot through it, across to the main tunnel once again.

It was a world of concrete, steel and plaster. Service pipes and cables were neatly painted and attached to the sides of the tunnels, giving the appearance of one solid surface. There was a musty smell to the place, but the air was cool. Bond knew that care had been taken to ensure that the tunnel had adequate ventilation as well as an efficient drainage system to pump out water in case any leaked in. The tunnels were remarkably clean, if a bit damp, cold and lifeless.

He ran towards the Tappi station, hoping that he could catch up with the dwarf. After witnessing Kappa's tricks in Kamakura, Bond wondered if pursuing the killer might have been folly on his part. The runt could hide anywhere and eventually make his way out of the tunnel unseen, even under the gaze of the cameras. Perhaps he should go back to the train and get on it before it left.

The attack startled Bond, who normally took great pride in his ability to avoid being surprised. Junji Kon dropped onto Bond's head like a sandbag. He had been hanging on to one of the large pipes that ran along the tunnel ceiling several feet overhead. The two men fell to the pavement and rolled. Before Bond could react, Kappa had bounced to his feet and twisted like a top until he had positioned himself to deliver what was a stunning aerial kick at Bond's face. The dwarf then dropped to the ground and used his arm to springboard back into the air to kick with the other leg, this time into Bond's chest, which was being propelled backwards from the force of the first kick. Bond fell, the pain searing through his sternum. It had been a strong blow but not one meant to kill. Bond knew that if this man had wanted to, he could have shattered his breastbone.

The dwarf known as Kappa stood casually on the pavement like a pixie, watching to see what his victim would do next. Bond turned and got to his hands and knees, which was always a bad position to be in, but he had no choice. Before he could get up, he saw the glint of steel in Kappa's right hand.

The Balisong came swishing at him with the speed of a snake. Luckily, Bond had recovered just enough to summon his lifesaving skills of self-defence. He too had trained many years to be lightning fast. When an opponent attacked with a knife, you had to be.

Bond's left hand, the one that Kappa hadn't expected Bond to use, shot out and grabbed Kappa's wrist like a lizard's tongue catches a fly. The impact of his palm on Kappa's arm sent the Balisong flying across the pavement and onto the tracks.

The dwarf didn't let that subdue him. He jumped, allowing Bond's grasp to hold him in the air. Then he swung out and kicked Bond again in the face. Bond reflexively let go of Kappa's wrist and fell back. Bond rolled on the pavement, shook his head and looked up.

Kappa was gone.

The staff in the Hakodate Control Centre were monitoring the situation in the tunnel very closely. Their job was to get the train moving again as quickly as possible after determining that there was no danger to passengers. They had visual links to all of the cameras in the tunnel, but they could turn on only selected cameras at a time. Communications equipment was still working properly, and they had established a dialogue with the train staff.

Hiroki Yamanote, the operations manager on duty that morning, considered what had been reported. A passenger had stopped the train and jumped off after first murdering a conductor and locking another passenger in his suite. The second passenger was a government law enforcement agent and had taken off on foot through the tunnel in search of the killer.

Fine, he thought. As long as the rest of the passengers were safe, what did he care if killers butchered each other? He got on the phone to the train's engineer.

"Close the doors and leave," he ordered. "We have already delayed some trains behind you."

The engineer on the *Cassiopeia* announced to the staff that they were going on, and an announcement was made over the train's intercom. Passengers were told that the staff were sorry for the interruption of service and that they would try to make up for lost time on their way to Sapporo.

In the meantime, Yamanote arranged for the train to be met by police at Hakodate, where it would make a short stop before continuing its journey.

One of the technicians alerted Yamanote that he had a visual on one of the camera view screens. The operations manager stepped behind the display and saw the figure of James Bond walking through the tunnel. The *gaijin* looked dishevelled and appeared confused. He had a pistol in his hand and was obviously searching for someone.

"Better send police down the shaft," he told an assistant.

Meanwhile, on the train, Reiko was continuing her reconnaissance mission through the cars looking for near-invisible flying insects. As the announcement that the train was leaving came on the intercom, Reiko muttered a

Western swear word under her breath. She wished that she had talked James-san out of chasing that killer.

A mosquito! She saw it out of the corner of her eye, flying alone near one of the windows. The train's engines fired up and the locomotive began to move as Reiko followed the insect down the corridor. Wait, she lost it! Where did it go? Reiko looked around frantically. It was like searching for a speck in the sand.

A passenger came out of a room and looked at her. "Are we finally leaving?" he asked.

"Yes!" Reiko snapped. She continued creeping along the wall, not caring how she might have looked to the passenger. The man gave her a funny stare and went back into this room.

There it was! The little thing was gliding along the perimeter of a window, instinctively looking for a way out. Reiko raised the train brochure and swatted the window. She removed the brochure and saw that she had squashed the insect.

Oh no, she thought. The smear on the window and brochure was red with blood—human blood.

Bond rubbed his chest with one hand as he moved silently along the tunnel wall. The Walther was in his other hand, safety off, ready to shoot the first thing that moved. The little attacker had enraged him. It was one thing to be beaten by an opponent; it was another thing to be beaten by someone so small. Bond wanted to pick the runt up by the neck and shake him, then give him a taste of his own medicine. The killer probably got away with a lot as it was likely his opponents held back their punches.

But that wasn't going to stop Bond at this point. He was ready to wring the bastard's little neck.

He heard a rumble and the blast of a train's horn. The *Cassiopeia* was leaving. Bond stood on the platform and watched it pass by. He waited there for a minute, watching its red taillights disappear into the endless tunnel.

Then he was alone with the silence. He moved on, looking for any telltale clue that Kappa might have left behind. But he knew that was probably futile; Junji Kon was a master of stealth. He could hide in any nook or cranny, and his speed was freakish. He could be in any of the dozens of interconnecting tunnels. Perhaps Tiger had been right—the man *was* a supernatural being!

There was a sound in the distance that resembled a can being kicked. It was difficult to discern where it had come from. Bond peered down a connecting gallery to the service tunnel. Yes, it definitely had come from there. He turned and moved in that direction, his gun steady. He inched to the edge of the wall and looked around. Nothing there. He rounded the corner and continued on, his ears attuned to the slightest sounds. All that he heard were occasional drips and the faint blowing of air, what they called "tunnel effect."

There! Something moved! Bond fired the Walther and it reverberated in the tunnel, the shot repeating itself down the length of the shaft until it faded away.

Bond moved carefully to the next connecting gallery, searching intently for his prey.

In the Control Centre, Operations Manager Yamanote could see Bond's back on the view screen as he moved away from the camera that was pointed at him. Then he saw the second figure creeping up behind Bond. At first he thought it was a child until he saw the way the man was moving. It was a little person, or a dwarf, some kind of strange person. Was he the criminal who had killed the conductor on the *Cassiopeia?*

The little man was nearly upon the *gaijin.* Yamanote had to warn Bond somehow. He reached over the shoulder of the technician and flipped a switch.

Suddenly, the tunnel's sprinkler system shot on above

Bond and Kappa's heads. The water surprised them both, and they reacted by jumping back. Bond saw Kappa just as the little man leaped at him. Bond fired but missed as the dwarf slammed into him. Bond dropped the PPK but managed to take hold of the dwarf's shoulders and, using the killer's own momentum, hurled Kappa over his head and into the wall. The plaster crumbled slightly as the small but solid body struck it. Bond let him fall to the pavement as he scrambled to retrieve the Walther. But Kappa bounced off the concrete and sprung at Bond, fists clenched. The two bodies collided and fell to the cement. They rolled twice, the little man punching Bond hard wherever he could land a blow. Bond did his best to push Kappa away and connect a punch too, but the dwarf was just too fast. He moved like a whirling dervish and was impossible to pin down.

The men separated and got to their feet. The evil pixie stood facing Bond with hatred in his eyes. The image was surreal: water filled the depression in the dwarf's head as if it were a bowl. Then, before Bond could plan a strategy, Kappa leaped into the air like something from the nether-world. His right foot connected with his opponent's jaw with such force that Bond went reeling backwards. Bond stepped into a puddle of water and slipped. Kappa landed but kept up the offensive, kicking and punching until Bond was on the ground. Bond tried to grab the killer's foot, but this time it didn't work. Bond was too stunned to react with the speed that was required.

Kappa delivered two, three, four hard kicks to the head. Bond attempted to raise himself to ward off another blow, but the fifth kick sent him into the black hole of un-consciousness.

17
Old Ghosts

Reiko reached the last car on the lower level of the train. Other than the two she had already killed, she hadn't seen any more mosquitoes.

Looking for the things was worse than threading a needle, she thought as she stopped for a moment, removed her glasses and rubbed her eyes. She had a splitting headache that had come on suddenly a few minutes ago.

How long had it been since the train left? Five minutes? Ten? And what about James-san? Was he all right? She wondered if Tanaka-san had been contacted and—

Oh no! she thought to herself. *She* should be calling Tanaka-san! What was wrong with her? Why hadn't she done that immediately! Her head was so cloudy it was difficult to think. She *had* been a bit preoccupied. That was it. She chalked it up to the urgency of finding the deadly mosquitoes. If they *were* deadly.

Reiko leaned against the wall and looked at the stairwell in front of her. Could there be mosquitoes on the top floor? Reiko didn't want to think about it. At the moment she had no energy and felt drained. Why was she so disoriented? She should get going, climb the stairs, look for invisible insects and talk to Tanaka-san on her mobile as she searched.

The effort that was required to take that first step up surprised her, but she took a deep breath and willed herself to go on. It felt as if each step took a lifetime.

As she climbed, she reached around behind her neck without thinking and scratched an itch.

At first Bond thought it was thunder.

The roar of a train reverberated in his ears. He opened his eyes and saw a blur. There were some pinpoints of light in an otherwise dark mass of nothing. But the noise was growing louder.

What the hell? Bond thought. *What happened?*

Then he remembered. He was fighting with Kappa and must have been knocked unconscious. He was still in the Seikan Tunnel.

Bond instinctively attempted to reach up and rub his face but found that his wrists were bound in front of him. He could move his arms up and down freely; it was just that they were tied together.

The volume of the approaching storm intensified. He tried to move his body and discovered that he was secured to something.

Wait a minute . . . ! Bond couldn't feel the floor. There was a strong tugging sensation on his upper torso.

My God! he thought. He was suspended from the tunnel's ceiling! A rope had been harnessed around his chest under his arms and then looped up and around a pipe running along the top of the tunnel. He was dangling four or five feet above the tracks.

That's when the adrenaline kicked in. Bond's senses became fully alert as he forcibly cleared the haze. He pushed the pain in his head away and focused sharply on his surroundings.

The sound that was growing louder and louder had to

be a train headed his way. In fact, those pinpoints of light were its headlamps. How far away was it?

Think! If there was a time that he had to move fast, it was now.

Bond momentarily flashed on the absurd notion that the service had never trained the Double-Os what to do in case they were tied up over a bloody railway track and a bloody train was coming.

But they had trained him to use the tools at his disposal. Painfully, Bond raised his bound wrists to his shirt collar. He felt underneath for the slit and pulled out the special collar stay that Q Branch made available to field agents. He removed the thin plastic sheath that covered it, and then made sure that the sharpened edge was facing the right way. Bond then held the thin blade down to the rope that was around his chest. He began to saw, pressing the knife into the rope with his thumbs.

The train's headlamps were getting bigger. The entire tunnel was shaking with a deafening roar.

Cut through, damn you! he willed. He moved the blade back and forth, pushing it into the hemp as hard as he could. It was awkward and uncomfortable and the muscles in his hand began to hurt.

One strand split! He was halfway through!

Bond immediately moved the blade to another loop in the rope, one that, if cut, would assure his freedom. He began to saw again when the collar stiffener slipped out of his hand and fell to the tracks below.

No!

Bond reached up to his neck and pulled out the other collar stay. If he dropped this one, he was done for.

Now he could see the outline of the train. It was no longer merely two dots of light.

He sawed while pushing with his thumbs and fighting the cramp that inched up his thumbs and into his wrists. Every second counted now. The locomotive's fierce bullet-shaped nose was growing larger and larger. There was the blast of a horn. Could they see him? It was doubtful. The light was too dim in the tunnel. Only when it was too late would the engineer be able to see that something was hanging in the middle of the tunnel. It would not register that what he saw was a man. It would be the last thing the engineer would think of.

The blade was almost through. Just a little harder . . .

The tunnel vibrated with intensity. The train was now clearly visible. Bond could see that it was red. He figured that if he could tell what colour it was, then it was too damned close.

Finally, the blade was through! The bindings loosened around his chest. Before he dropped, Bond grabbed the strands and began to swing on the rope. The clamour of the approaching hulk of power drowned out all other thoughts. One more arc and he would have enough momentum to swing over to the edge.

Now! Bond let go of the rope, landed and rolled to the side of the tunnel just as the train roared past him.

He lay there a moment and caught his breath. His heart was pounding. His head hurt like hell. Ever since Bond had received a particularly bad head injury during an assignment a few years ago, he had been more susceptible to the effects of blows to the skull.

Time to get up.

Bond sat on the pavement. He took stock of the damage and found that aside from the minor cuts that had reopened on his face, the lump on his head was the only thing that needed immediate attention.

He stood and began to walk toward the Tappi station. Five minutes later, he heard voices. The police and rail authorities had finally arrived.

The *shatei-gashira* watched as one of the men from the north fed bills into the pachinko machine. Many of them had played nonstop since they got to Tokyo the night before. It was as if they suspected that they would never be able to play pachinko again.

"Phone call, boss," his right-hand man called from the other side of the parlour. It was a busy morning. The kids were out of school and had filled the place, so it was difficult to hear what his man was saying. His colleague raised a mobile phone and pointed to it.

The *shatei* walked across the busy arcade and took the mobile. "I'll take it in the back," he said as he went behind the door marked "Private" and into a small office.

It was Yasutake Tsukamoto, calling from Sapporo. The *shatei* had been expecting him.

"Hai!" he answered.

"Is everything satisfactory?" Tsukamoto asked.

"Yes, *kaicho*," the man said. "The twenty men arrived last night. The equipment just arrived this morning. Everything is in order."

"That's very good, the *Yami Shogun* will be pleased."

The *shatei* said good-bye to his *kaicho* and hung up. He walked through another door in the office and into a large storeroom and lounge area. Some of the "carriers" were relaxing there; three of them asleep on cots. The two trunks marked "CureLab Inc." sat on the floor unopened. That event wouldn't occur until this afternoon, at CureLab headquarters.

One of the men approached him and asked when lunch would be served.

"Very soon, my friend. How did you sleep last night?" the *shatei* asked.

"Good. I was very tired. We have been on the go for several days."

"I hear you had a nice night out on the town in Sapporo?"

"Oh, yes! Tsukamoto-san was our host. We had a wonderful expensive dinner and then spent several hours at a soaplands! It was the best I have ever had!"

"I envy you!" The *shatei* gestured to the cases. "So what's in those things?"

The man shook his head. "I am sorry, but I cannot reveal that. It's part of our mission."

The *shatei* bowed. "Forgive me. I understand." He looked at his watch. "Another hour before lunch, and then this afternoon the cars will come to pick you up and take you all to CureLab for your meeting."

The man laughed. "More meetings. I wish we'd just get on with it. We are all well trained, and we know what to do. I don't see why we have to wait five days."

"It's because the materials are not quite ready," another carrier said. He was the leader, a man named Ukita. "And stop talking about our mission."

The other carrier bowed rapidly, "I apologise, *sempai*." He walked away quickly. Ukita looked at the *shatei* and said, "I am sorry. We are under orders not to talk about it."

"I understand," the *shatei* said. When Ukita walked away, the *shatei* shrugged, left the lounge and strode back through the building to the public pachinko parlour.

Yasutake Tsukamoto picked up the phone in his Sapporo office and dialled the number that only three people in the world knew. The other two were the *Yami Shogun* himself, and the Ryujin-kai's *wakagashira,* or number-two man.

Goro Yoshida answered.

"Ohayo gozaimasu," Tsukamoto said.

"Ohayo to you too, Tsukamoto," Yoshida said.

"I am calling to report that everything is in order. The carriers arrived at the distribution centre in Tokyo on schedule and the equipment was delivered this morning. It will go to CureLab this afternoon."

"That's good news. I trust that the new version will be completed within five days?"

"If it needs to be completed in five days, then it will be completed in five days."

"Ah, but will it work? What do you think, Tsukamoto?"

"You have always known my feelings about this project, Yoshida. Our chief engineer tells me that it will work, but I am not a man of science."

"Tsukamoto, you surprise me. You still have doubts about our motives, don't you?"

If they had been with each other in person, Tsukamoto would have bowed to his master. The *Yami Shogun* was displeased.

"Forgive me, Yoshida. I have complete faith in you and in the project. I never meant to question it."

"Very well. And what of our British friend who has been sticking his nose into our business?"

"Kappa arrived this morning, master. According to him, our British friend is now the front ornament on the *shinkansen*."

Tsukamoto heard Yoshida chuckle, and he wished that he could see it. Goro Yoshida rarely laughed. He hardly ever smiled, for that matter.

"And the McMahon girl?" Yoshida asked. Tsukamoto had been anticipating the question.

"Kubo at the soaplands tells me that she has been eliminated."

"Good. We couldn't afford to have her around."

"Yes, you are right, as always."

After they rang off, Tsukamoto sat back in his leather swivel chair. He looked out the window at a patch of azalea in the park across the street. The lavender colour was a staple of Hokkaido. In the country, especially, it spread over the landscape like spilled paint.

Why did he feel so wretched? Tsukamoto wondered. Why didn't he feel comfortable with the project? Because it was wrong? Because he *knew* it was wrong? That was ridiculous. He had done many things that were wrong. He had killed men. He had stolen money. He had committed crimes that could put him away for life, but the wall of the yakuza organisation protected him from that fate. He was untouchable.

So why did this particular project disturb him? Was it because it involved a deadly biological weapon? Was it because they would be delivering a strike against several countries, including Japan herself? Why should he feel bad about that? After all, it was the established Japanese government that still catered to the West. The project was meant to be a blow to the enemies of traditional Japan, and that included those within the boundaries of the country itself.

Tsukamoto stood and walked to the window. He stared into the park, fourteen storeys below, and watched a pair of birds fly over the purple blot of azalea. A mother was wheeling her baby in a stroller. It was a beautiful day.

It was no use pretending that he didn't know. What bothered him about the project was the fact that it was completely mad. It was a symbolic strike, to be sure, but one that could possibly bring the wrath of foreign nations and the Japanese government down upon their heads. It had no further purpose but to make a statement. There was no profit to be made from it, it was extremely dangerous and the yakuza had no business waging a war of terrorism on the rest of the world. It was total, utter madness.

But it's what the man with the red tattoo wanted and that was what he was going to get.

Bond had been picked up by the authorities and put onto the next train at Tappi station. He disembarked at Goryokaku station in Hokkaido and made phone contact with Tanaka, who had helped clear his activities with the police. Unfortunately, Tanaka had not heard from Reiko. The

Cassiopeia had stopped at Goryo-kaku as well because "some passengers were ill." That was all that he knew.

Now that the train had arrived, perhaps he could find out something. Two officials who introduced themselves as Eto and Akira met him on the platform. Eto explained that they worked for the Public Security Investigation Agency, and that they needed to debrief him.

"What about agent Tamura?" Bond asked. "Has anyone heard from her?"

The two men exchanged glances. Eto inhaled through his teeth and frowned.

Bad news.

"Tamura-san was one of the ill passengers," Eto said. "She was taken to the hospital."

"Take me there now," Bond commanded. "We can talk in the car."

They walked through the small station and got into a Suzuki Wagon-R. As they drove the short distance to the medical centre, Eto revealed more.

"Three passengers and Tamura-san came down with a serious illness on the train," he said.

"What were the symptoms?"

"High fever, bad headaches and finally, loss of consciousness. We will find out more when we talk to the doctors."

It took them only a few minutes to get to the busy Hakodate Municipal Hospital, which was located very close to the rail station. It was a large, six-storey building that was the principal medical facility in southern Hokkaido.

Eto and Akira led Bond inside the brown and grey structure and took the lift to the fifth floor, where they found the doctor in charge of the passengers who had been brought in. He was a man in his thirties who appeared to be overworked and under a great deal of stress. When Eto asked about Reiko, the doctor looked grave.

"Come with me," he said. He led them into a small office and shut the door. "We are trying to figure out what happened to these people. One man has died, just minutes ago. He had a temperature of a hundred and six. He was in his seventies, so it's not surprising that he didn't survive. The other passengers are younger and healthier, so it is difficult to say whether or not they will pull through. From the small amount of information we have, it appears that these people were stricken with some powerful virus, an encephalitis of some sort."

"West Nile disease?" Bond asked.

"Very similar," the doctor said, nodding. "Only much stronger. I understand it came upon them suddenly and reached a peak very quickly."

"Do you happen to know if any of them have mosquito bites?"

The doctor squinted at Bond. "Do you know more about this? What is it that you are not telling me?"

"Doctor, I don't know a lot, but I believe that there were some genetically engineered mosquitoes aboard that train. They escaped and might have bitten these people. I can't tell you what that virus is, but it's probably manmade."

"Then we will examine the patients and see what we can find. Why don't you gentlemen wait here, and I'll be back in a few moments after I give instructions to the nurses. They are afraid of touching the patients for fear of catching whatever it is."

"So far we have no reason to believe that the disease is contagious," Bond said. "But I suppose you can't be too careful."

"We don't touch them without wearing gloves and masks. Pardon me."

He left the room and Bond got back on the phone to Tanaka. Tiger listened as Bond explained the situation and then said, "She is strong, Bondo-san. If anyone can pull through this, Miss Tamura can. Try not to worry."

"I'm going to stay here until we know for certain."

"Thank you, Bondo-san. I am sure Miss Tamura will appreciate that. Now, have you had your head looked at?"

"Not yet."

"Do it. I don't want you walking around with a concussion."

"What about Sapporo?" Bond asked, changing the subject. "Is my contact expecting me?"

"Yes. His name is Ikuo Yamamaru. He's the Ainu gentleman I told you about. Very good man. He will meet you at the Sapporo Beer Garden tomorrow for lunch."

"How will I know him?"

"He will know you. Now go and have a doctor take a look at you. Since you are working under my authority I can say 'that's an order,' Bondo-san. But it's also for your own good."

"All right, Tiger."

When the doctor came back, he said, "You were right. Tamura-san has a mosquito bite on the back of her neck. The elderly gentleman who died has two bites on his arm. The other two patients both have bites on their arms as well. They look like fresh mosquito bites."

"So what do we do now?"

The doctor shrugged. "I have done all I can for now. We have to pray and wait." He looked at his clipboard and noted something. "It says here that you received a head injury, Mr. Bond."

Bond nodded reluctantly. "Really, I'm fine."

"Let's go in an examination room and let me take a look."

The doctor performed the necessary tests to make sure that there was nothing seriously wrong with Bond. There was indeed a small lump above his right temple where the dwarf's shoe tip had struck. The doctor gave him some painkillers and said in English, "You have very hard head. You lucky man."

"May I see Tamura-san now?" Bond asked.

"I suppose it would not hurt." He led Bond into the critical ward and to a bed where Reiko lay. An IV was in her arm and she was wearing an oxygen mask. Her skin was pale, but she was breathing slowly and deeply. She looked so helpless and fragile that Bond wanted to take her into his arms, hold her close and protect her from whatever was in store for her.

He placed his palm on her forehead. The skin was hot but dry. She was burning up. Bond leaned over and kissed her above her eyebrows. He whispered in her ear, "I'm here, Reiko-san. I will wait for you. Be strong. You have to pull through, you know. We have that date in Maui."

Reiko remained still and quiet. Could she hear him? Bond didn't know.

Then the doctor asked him to wait in the lounge.

Bond spent the next half hour talking to Eto and Akira about the dwarf and the incidents on the train. They took copious notes, Bond signed a statement and then the two men left him alone.

The day turned into night as Bond sat in the lobby staring out of the window first at the matchbox-like cars on the streets, then at the lights in the various buildings that could be seen from the hospital. He was dead tired.

So this was the score, he thought. The ghosts had struck again. Just when he began to invest a little of himself in someone, something happened to wreck it. Was he forever going to be bad luck to anyone he came close to? All the women whom he had loved had come to a bad end. Vesper, Tracy, Kissy . . . Was this the price he had to pay for the lives he had taken throughout his career? Was this his fate, to be forever alone because whatever he touched turned to dust?

Stop it, he commanded himself. *Don't be morose. Reiko will pull through. As Tiger said, she was strong.*

As he looked at his reflection in the window, Bond remembered the doubts and fears he had experienced before coming to Japan. Those old ghosts that he didn't want to see were certainly nearby.

"It is not your fault, Taro-san," Kissy said. She sat next to him, gazing out the window, dressed in the *yukata* she had always worn before bedtime.

"Yes it is," Bond replied. "I bring death wherever I go. It's a curse."

"No, Taro-san," she said, softly. "It is merely the hand of fate. You travel in a dark and dangerous world, but you do so because it is your destiny. You could not exist in any other world, Taro-san."

"I should never have left you," Bond said. "Life was simpler on that island."

"It may have been, but you must not feel bad," she said. "You would not be complete if you had changed your path. Trust me, Taro-san."

In that illogical way that things happened in a dreamworld, Kissy became Reiko. Bond could feel her gazing at him longingly. Then, she slowly smiled and put on her glasses. He thought that she whispered *"Arigato,"* but he wasn't sure.

Bond felt his heart being squeezed. He turned to look at the person beside him but there was no one there.

The doctor woke him just after midnight. Bond had fallen asleep in the lobby in front of the large window.

"I have bad news," the doctor said.

Bond sat up and prepared himself for what he knew was coming.

"Tamura-san died ten minutes ago. I am sorry."

18
The Search for Mayumi

"Did everything go well regarding the girl?" Tsukamoto asked Kubo, the *shatei* who ran the Casanova Club, the most exclusive and expensive soaplands in Sapporo. He was calling from his office, having put off the inevitable for long enough.

"Yes, *kaicho*," Kubo said. "Everything has been taken care of."

"Good. I assume that any traces of her existence have been destroyed?"

"Yes."

"Do I need to send some men there tonight to have a look around?"

Kubo was quiet for a brief moment and then said, "That is not necessary, *kaicho*. I will personally see to it that there is no evidence."

"Very well."

Tsukamoto hung up and drummed his fingers on his desk. Should he trust Kubo to do a proper job? Perhaps he should go ahead and send some men anyway. If it were known that the McMahon girl had been at the soaplands, there could be a lot of trouble that even the Ryujin-kai might not be able to clear away.

He picked up the phone again and made the call.

• • •

James Bond was subdued when he arrived at the Sapporo Beer Garden and Museum grounds, which were located in the northeastern corner of Sapporo, Hokkaido's largest city. He still felt punished by the previous night's events. He had been unable to sleep in the brief time available to him. The sun had risen when he left for the train station, and he had only managed to nod off for a short time on the morning express train to the city.

Now, having arrived in Sapporo, he fully understood how hard Reiko's death had hit him. He had gone to Japan with the misplaced notion that the assignment would be a holiday. Instead, they had made it personal and Bond was grimly determined to avenge Reiko's death. She had been an ally, a professional colleague; they had shared wounds and danger and briefly something more. He vowed not to leave the country that had brought him so much personal pain without smashing Yoshida's plans and—if possible—liquidating the evil man himself.

It was time to leave the pain behind and move on.

Bond got out of the car in front of the beer garden entrance and surveyed the area. There were several red brick buildings that made up the museum, the complex of restaurants and the breweries. Bond was well aware of Sapporo Beer and preferred it when he did drink beer in Japan. He therefore recognised the company's emblem, a red star, painted on a tall brick smokestack that rose above everything else. The Beer Garden was a popular tourist haunt that had been around for a hundred years; visitors could tour the breweries, taste beer, learn about the beverage's history in the museum and have their choice of a few kinds of Japanese barbecue for lunch.

Bond walked into the information centre and gift shop, where one could purchase various souvenirs and tickets for the museum and make reservations for lunch. He was greeted with an enthusiastic *"Irrashaimase!"* from every employee in the place, a greeting spoken in businesses throughout Japan, welcoming the customer.

Bond smiled and bowed slightly, then approached the reservations desk. He confirmed that there was a table for two under the name "Yamamaru," and was led to a table in the Classic Hall on the ground floor.

It was done up like a German beer garden and, in fact, the words *"Sapporo Bier Garten"* were painted above the bar. An elaborately painted wooden street organ was prominently displayed on the floor of the restaurant, and wooden tables and benches surrounded it. The kitchen's smoky grills were visible on one side of the room, staffed by a number of chefs dressed in white.

He was led to a table near the organ where a man was sitting. He rose when he saw Bond and said, *"Hajime mashite,* I am Ikuo Yamamaru. Welcome to Sapporo." He offered his business card and bowed.

Bond repeated the ritual, and then they shook hands and sat down.

He was immediately taken with Yamamaru. Bond usually had good instincts about people, and he knew that this man was made of the same stuff as he.

The Ainu are believed to be indigenous to Japan but very little of the original lineage remains. They are often compared to the Native American Indians and possess some striking cultural similarities.

Yamamaru had bushy eyebrows over large blue eyes, and his round full cheeks gave his face a lot of character. His long hair, tied into a ponytail, was black and streaked with grey. Bond guessed him to be about fifty years old. Yamamaru wore a *ruunpe,* a traditional garment elaborately embroidered with delicate appliqué in Ainu patterns, which were similar in style to those of Native Americans.

"I understand you lost your partner from Tokyo," he said in English. "I am very sorry."

"I am too."

The waitress came with a tray of drinks.

"I took the liberty of ordering beer for us," Yamamaru said. "I hope you don't mind."

"No, not at all."

They were each served a three-beer sampler consisting of large glasses of types of Sapporo beer, displayed in a lazy-Susan carrier that neatly held all three glasses. The Classic Draft Hokkaido Limited and Yebisu Draft were light beers; Bond particularly liked the third, Black Draft, a dark beer that had a strong caramel taste.

Yamamaru insisted on ordering for them and asked for the grilled platter for two.

After the waitress left, he pushed a package across the table to Bond. "From Tanaka-san," he said. "It is a replacement firearm. A Walther PPK, correct?"

"Yes, thank you," Bond said as he took the parcel and put it in his pocket.

"Now, Bond-san, how can I help you?"

"I need to find Mayumi McMahon. She is supposed to be in Sapporo, probably the girlfriend of a high-ranking yakuza. One source suggested that she might be working for the yakuza in the water trade."

Yamamaru nodded. "I have a contact in the yakuza. When Tanaka-san first asked me to try and find this girl, I contacted this man. He is usually able to find out some things and will talk for a price. We've worked together before. I imagine that the yakuza would keep her whereabouts a secret these days."

"If she's still alive," Bond said.

"Yes. At any rate you are just in time. I have a meeting with my contact this afternoon. He has already indicated that he has some news for me. I would ask you to accompany me, but I am afraid that he would feel more comfortable seeing me alone."

"I understand."

The food came and was served on a flat heated grill that was placed on the table. The food was fresh off the kitchen's barbecue grill and consisted of beef, lamb, shrimp, king crab, scallops and sausage, all complemented with sauerkraut and German style potatoes. Once it was in front of him, Bond realised how ravenous he was. He began to eat with fervour.

"Have you been to Sapporo before, Bond-san?"

"No. I'm not familiar with Hokkaido at all."

"You must try to visit our Ainu village while you are here. Have dinner, stay the night. We'll let you feed the bears."

Tiger had told Bond that the Ainu were animists, that is, they deified certain animals, especially bears. Most Ainu villages had at least one bear kept in captivity to serve as their god, mascot and sightseeing attraction for tourists. Some villages had several.

"Where is your village?"

"South. Noboribetsu. Very near Bear Park, which my people operate. I'm originally from Shiraoi. I have an apartment here in Sapporo, but my family is in Noboribetsu."

"Do you know where the Hokkaido Mosquito and Vector Control Centre is in Noboribetsu?"

"Sure. It is outside of town. Tucked away in the woods, out of sight. It is interesting that you mention it. In the past several months, unusual things have been going on there."

"What do you mean?"

Yamamaru shifted his eyes around to make certain that no one was near enough to hear him. "It is a public health facility, isn't it? It used to be that anyone could go there and walk in. Now they have a high fence around it. Locked gate. Employees need a key card to get inside. Very strange."

"Can you get me in?"

"Very difficult. Security is very tight there. It is almost

as if it is run by a completely different organisation." Then the Ainu grinned broadly. "But I enjoy a challenge! I will see what I can do."

Bond was silent for a moment as he relished the taste of a king crab leg on his palate, then said, "Just tell me how to get there and I'll worry about getting inside."

"I'll draw you a map."

The food was delicious and the beer took the edge off Bond's emotional fatigue.

"How did you get involved with the Koan-Chosa-Cho?" he asked the Ainu.

"When I did my military service back in the dark ages, when I was a young man, I was posted in an intelligence unit. I met Tanaka-san there, and we became friends. He invited me to join later. The fact that I am Ainu is actually very good cover. There are not many Ainu who work in the Japanese government. Most of us operate replicas of traditional Ainu villages for tourists. We are a race that is slowly dying out, or rather, we are integrating more and more into modern society and are losing the Ainu ways."

"Is there much intelligence work for you to do up here?"

"Oh yes," Yamamaru said. "Mostly watching the Russians. They are always smuggling stuff in or out. We keep track of what their mafia is doing. There are some Korean criminal elements operating in Hokkaido. We keep an eye on them too."

"What about Goro Yoshida? Any idea where he is?"

"Hiding somewhere in the Northern Territories. He's another one who has been causing some trouble. Reportedly he has a small private army with him, and yet our intelligence forces have still been unable to exactly locate him. The Russians don't make it any easier for us. They don't like it when we do reconnaissance flights over the islands. Perhaps that's why I enjoy them! Some of my colleagues tell me that I am reckless. Anyway, I have my suspicions about where he is, mainly from what I hear through the Ainu grapevine. I believe he is holed up on the island of Etorofu. It's large enough and it's covered with natural camouflage. Lots of forest. Many Ainu live there."

After the meal, they left the restaurant, strolled through the Beer Garden grounds and had a smoke. Yamamaru offered Bond one of his cigarettes, made from tobacco grown by the Ainu. Bond found the taste pleasant but not strong enough.

"What dealings have you had with the Ryujin-kai?" Bond asked.

"Not much. I know Yasutake Tsukamoto. Well, a little. We met at a trade show for chemical engineering suppliers."

"What do you think of him?"

The Ainu shrugged. "He is a very powerful *oyabun*. Very rich. Getting old. When we met, he barely looked at me. I have heard from many sources that he can be a very honourable man. For a criminal."

Yamamaru eventually looked at his watch and said that he had to leave for his appointment. They agreed to meet that night at Bond's hotel. If all went well with his contact that afternoon, the Ainu would have some information for him.

Bond's next target was the Yonai Enterprises office in Sapporo. It was located in the city centre in an office building not far from Odori Park, the dividing line between the north and south sides of the city. Unlike other Japanese cities, Sapporo was conveniently divided into a grid, named and numbered according to the points of the compass. The street names reflected how many blocks and the direction they lay from the city's centre. Yonai Enterprises was on South 1.

It was a shiny twenty-four-storey building that took up half a block. To Bond it looked like any other ordinary office building in Japan: there was no indication that the occupants might be in bed with organised crime. He circled the block and made his way to a loading dock area behind the building. There he found men loading boxes and crates into a lorry.

Two security guards eyed him suspiciously as he approached. Bond smiled at them, but they remained expressionless. He came closer to the lorry and stopped to make a show of lighting a cigarette. As he did so, he studied the address labels on the boxes and crates and saw that along with the Japanese characters a legend in English read: "Hokkaido Mosquito and Vector Control Centre."

That explained why the public health facility had recently added a fence and tight security. This confirmed his suspicions that it was now being run by Yonai Enterprises.

"May I help you, sir?"

It was a woman with a clipboard, standing on the loading dock. She had spoken in English.

"Oh, hello," Bond said, assuming the role of the stupid *gaijin*. He introduced himself as a tourist from Britain who was lost.

"Please go around the building that way," the woman said. "There is a tourist information office one block to the west."

"Right, I'll do that. Pardon me, I didn't mean to intrude."

"That's all right."

Bond caught a cab that took him straight to the Sapporo Prince Hotel, where Tanaka had arranged for him to stay.

After he had left the loading dock area, the woman with the clipboard made a phone call to her superior. As she had been instructed, the woman reported that a *gaijin* had been seen snooping around. Her boss thanked her for her diligence and hung up. This message was then passed

on to his boss, who, in turn, passed it on to Yasutake
Tsukamoto.

Kubo was extremely nervous. He had disobeyed a direct
order from the *kaicho*. He had deceived the yakuza. He
would surely lose a finger or two. Maybe even his life.

As he sat in the small office of the Casanova Club and
nursed a flask of Japanese whisky, he went over the various options he had available to him. Unfortunately, there
weren't many.

Why had he fallen for the girl? She was no different
from any other soaplands girl in the business. *Well, that
wasn't entirely true,* he thought. In fact, it wasn't true at
all. Mayumi McMahon was *very* different. She was an
angel, a goddess sent from heaven! Kubo had never mixed
business with pleasure before she had arrived at the soaplands, but he had been completely bewitched by Mayumi.
Perhaps it was her independent streak that had attracted
him, something that was uncommon among most soaplands girls. She had come to the Casanova Club declaring
with a determined swagger that she was going to be the
best soaplands girl in the business. Too bad it hadn't
worked out that way for her. Now the yakuza wouldn't let
her leave. Kubo knew that she was unhappy and was des-
perate to break away, even though she was making lots of
money for the club.

Why did they want to kill her? It was unfathomable!
Such an exotic creature and such a good earner too! When
Kubo received the order to have her done away with, he
couldn't bring himself to follow it. One day he would pay
for his disobedience.

Now he had to hide her somewhere else. She could no
longer stay in the upstairs room he had provided for her.
She had believed him when he had told her that it wasn't
safe for her to go home to her apartment, but now she was

restless. She had been complaining about having to stay there.

Kubo had a lead on another apartment outside of Sapporo. He had just enough time to go out and talk to the landlord and arrange it. Then, later that night after the guards were asleep and the soaplands was closed, he would move Mayumi out.

Her freedom, as well as his peace of mind, was worth a finger or two.

Tanaka had put Bond in the corner suite on the top floor of the Sapporo Prince Hotel Annex, which was newer than the main building across the road and its rooms were the hotel's best. As Bond waited for his appointment with Yamamaru, he sat and looked out of the window, watching the sunset and the Sapporo lights as they began to dominate the skyline. Mayumi McMahon was somewhere out there.

The phone rang. Bond answered it, acknowledged Yamamaru, and told him to come up.

"*Konban wa,* Yamamaru-san," Bond said.

"Please," he said. "You may call me Ikuo. I like dispensing with formalities every now and then."

Bond offered him some of the sake that was in the refrigerator, compliments of Tiger, and then they sat around the low glass table and clinked glasses.

"I have some good news," Yamamaru said. "I found Mayumi McMahon."

"I was hoping that you would say that. Go on."

"She is a soaplands girl. In one of the biggest and most expensive establishments in Sapporo run by the Ryujinkai. Apparently, Ms. McMahon came to Sapporo and changed her name to Tomoko. She was put up in a very nice apartment. She can come and go as she pleases."

"Then how come she hasn't been found up until now?"

"Because even though she has freedom of movement,

she is guarded. And she has a new identity. The yakuza have men watch her. It took my friend several days to locate her. There is another problem. The girl has not been seen for several days."

"Does that mean . . . ?"

Yamamaru put up a hand. "No, Bond-san. She is alive. My friend put me in touch with another girl who works there. She goes by the name of 'Norika.' I was able to speak to her today before she went to work. Norika says that Mayumi is being kept in a room on one of the upper floors and has not been allowed to work for a few days. For ten thousand yen, Norika said she would try to arrange for you to meet Mayumi."

"Then I had better go to the soaplands to see her."

"I suspected you would say that. Usually this place does not let *gaijin* in except for VIPs. Take this card."

He handed Bond a business card with *kanji* on it.

"This will get you in. Show that to the man at the front. You have to pay twenty thousand yen to get in."

"What does the card say?"

"It says that you are an important *gaijin* doing business with Yasutake Tsukamoto. Ask for Norika. Do you know Susukino? It's easy to navigate. It's the entertainment district." He pulled out a map and pointed to the location. Bond could walk there easily. "What do you plan to do with Ms. McMahon once you have found her?"

"If I can get her out, I'm taking her back to Tokyo," Bond said.

Yamamaru looked skeptical. "She may not want to go. Have you thought of that?"

"Yes, but she may not know that her parents have been killed."

Yamamaru was silent for a moment, as if considering how much of an impossible task it might be.

"Good luck, Bond-san," was all that he said.

• • •

Susukino was Sapporo's equivalent of Tokyo's Kabuki-cho. At night it was yet another spectacular display of neon and noise, and Bond felt that it was a little more "wild west" than Tokyo's red-light district. Here, things seemed looser, more in the open. Billboards and sidewalk placards on major streets prominently advertised the variety of sexual entertainment one could sample, from soaplands to strip clubs to hostess bars. The area was also full of restaurants, bars and pachinko parlours, exhibiting the same level of energy and decadence that Bond had found in Tokyo. Touts were just as aggressive, perhaps more so because Susukino catered to foreigners, especially Russians. A *gaijin* would probably have an easier time gaining access to some of the establishments here than in Tokyo.

Bond found the soaplands in question, the "Casanova Club," and approached the doorman, a bulky strong-arm with a punch perm. Before Bond could utter a complete sentence, the man held up his hand and said, "No *gaijin*." Bond showed him the card that Yamamaru had given him. The bouncer studied it, rubbed his chin, and said, "Just a minute." He went inside and left Bond standing on the pavement. A pretty girl walked by and tried to hand him a flyer. He smiled and refused, but she insisted. When the bouncer returned, she quickly walked away.

"All right, come in," the doorman said. "You are welcome."

Bond climbed a set of stairs to the first floor, where he was met by a couple of sleazy-looking yakuza who were all smiles. By now, Bond had learned to recognise the trademark punch perms, the gaudy suits and the swaggering manner. Neither of them spoke English. Bond told them that he had heard about a girl named Norika who worked there.

One of them said, "There is a house charge of twenty thousand yen."

Bond paid it and was led to a lounge area with a velvet-lined sofa, a coffee table with some skin magazines and an ashtray on it and a couple of comfortable chairs. They asked Bond what he wanted to drink. He asked for vodka on the rocks and then lit a cigarette.

"Would you like to see the selection of girls available?" one of the punch perms asked.

"No," Bond said. "Just Norika, please."

The man shrugged, handed Bond his drink, and left the room. Five minutes later, a young woman walked in and sat down in front of him. The punch perm was right behind her.

"This is 'Norika,' " the man said.

She was attractive and dressed in the type of outfit that might be worn by a bareback rider in a circus — the top-coat and tails of a tuxedo, very tight shorts, fishnet stockings and high heels.

Bond realised that he was supposed to indicate that she was indeed his choice.

"She'll do," he said to the man.

The punch perm nodded to the girl, who rose and gestured for Bond to follow her. She led him to a small room that contained a number of items: a double bed, a Japanese shower area on a tile floor, a bathtub, a vinyl inflatable mat, a cabinet and a locker.

Norika closed the door and looked at him expectantly.

"I'm here to see Tomoko," Bond said. He reached into his jacket pocket and pulled out ten thousand yen. "I believe that was the arrangement?"

Norika nodded, counted the money quickly, stuffed it into her shorts and left the room after taking a look out into the hallway.

Bond sat on the bed and waited. A few minutes later the door opened and a young woman he recognised as Mayumi McMahon came in.

She was stunningly beautiful. Her photo did not do her

justice. Bond had seen many lovely women in Japan, but none possessed a face as elegant as Mayumi McMahon's. The blend of Japanese and European features created an exotic portrait; she certainly looked more Asian than not, but Bond could see hints of Western influence in her genes. For one thing, her almond-shaped eyes were blue, not brown. She had a wide, sensual mouth and a complexion that was as pure and creamy as buttermilk. Her long black hair was shiny and silky and full of body.

She was short, probably about five feet, two inches, with a compact, hourglass figure. She wore a *yukata* over loose silk pants and was barefoot.

"Norika says you want to see me," she said. "Who are you? What's this about?"

"I just want to talk," Bond replied.

She grimaced and nodded. "Oh, you're one of those. Listen, I'm not working now. The boss — he hasn't let me work for the past few days. I don't know why." There was very little Asian accent to her speech. She could have passed for someone raised in Britain.

"I just need a few minutes of your time. I'll pay you."

She considered this a moment, looked back into the hallway, then shut the door. "What's your name?" she asked.

Bond didn't mind telling her the truth. "James."

She sat beside him and crossed her legs. Bond could see why a girl like her could make a fortune. She was practically perfect in every way.

"So what do you want to talk about, James?"

19
Secrets

"Listen to me, Mayumi," Bond said. "I have something to tell you."

The girl's eyes widened. "Who are you? How did you know my name?"

"My name is Bond. James Bond. I work for the British government. I've come to take you home."

At first she almost burst out laughing. "Are you crazy?" she asked. Then her demeanour changed and her eyes flashed with anger. "Did my father send you?" she spat. She stood and put her hands on her hips.

"In a way," Bond replied. "Calm down and listen to me."

"No. Who the hell do you think you are? You think you can just waltz in here and take me home? Do you know who runs this place? Do you have any idea what they would do to you if they knew you were talking to me like this?"

"Please, Mayumi, just listen to me for a minute."

She looked appraisingly at him for a moment, and said, "All right. I'm listening. I'll give you a minute but talk fast. You should know that all I have to do is push the button on the intercom over there if you cause any trouble."

"Can they hear us?" Bond asked.

"No."

"You had better sit down."

"I'm fine right here."

"Very well, then I shall tell you straight out. Your parents are dead."

Mayumi looked as if she had been slapped. "What?"

"Your parents and both of your sisters are dead. I'm sorry. I was hoping I would be able to break the news to you gently, but you didn't give me much choice."

She moved to the bed and sat beside him.

"How did it happen?" she whispered, obviously shocked.

"We're pretty sure that the Ryujin-kai killed them."

She looked at him with disbelief in her eyes.

"Yes, the people who run this place, the men who employ you. They did it. The yakuza you work for. They wanted to take over your father's company. Your great uncle was a part of it. He's dead now too."

Mayumi trembled a little. She swallowed and asked, "When . . . when did all this happen?"

"A little over a week ago."

"A *week ago?*" She stood again and began to pace around the room. "Why didn't anyone tell me? How come I didn't know?"

"Mayumi, it was in all the papers and on the news."

"I don't look at any of that stuff," she said.

Bond considered whether or not he should risk blasting his way out of there and taking her with him. What were the odds? There were the two men at the front. There could be others. Did he want to cause a disturbance at this point? Was there another way? It would certainly be better to get her out discreetly and quietly.

"Why don't you sit down?" he urged.

"I don't *want* to sit down!"

She was obviously very upset about the news, but was

struggling to master her emotions. The girl obviously had a fiery resolve; she was used to being in control in this room and was fiercely resisting Bond taking it from her.

"Mayumi," he said, "Can we leave and talk somewhere else?"

"No," she said. "They've been keeping me here for the past two days. They won't let me leave the building. I've been staying in a room upstairs. I don't know what's going on."

"Did they give you a reason why you couldn't leave or work?"

"They said my life was in danger. I was told that it was some business-related thing between a jealous client and Kubo, the manager here. Apparently this client threatened to have me killed because I'm the Casanova Club's most valuable asset. Kubo said that I had to stay here for a few days and not go home because my apartment was being watched."

"Mayumi, your life is just as much in danger if you stay here."

Her eyes narrowed as she studied him. He could see the thoughts passing through her head. Could he be trusted? Was he telling the truth? What was this *really* about?

She sat down again on the bed. "Tell me what is going on."

Bond took her hand. "My government sent me to Japan to investigate your parents' deaths. They died of a deadly man-made virus manufactured by Yonai Enterprises. They needed your father's company for its technology— specifically, the virus itself—and they use genetically engineered mosquitoes to transmit it."

"But why . . . why my mother and sisters too?"

"So no one would control the family's stock. The board of directors was free to agree to a merger with Yonai. Your great uncle Fujimoto masterminded the plan—he had a letter from your parents granting him power of attorney in the event of their deaths. I'm guessing he forged it. Then he was killed by the Ryujin-kai, after he had outlived his usefulness."

"This is too incredible . . ." she whispered. His words were beginning to sink in.

"I've been asked to bring you back to Tokyo," he continued. "With you back in the picture, the merger could be made void. To tell you the truth, I find it amazing that you're still alive."

"But I don't want to go back to Tokyo. Especially now. Besides, from what you're telling me, the Ryujin-kai is not going to let me go even if I wanted to."

"Mayumi, don't you see that you're a slave?" Bond said.

Those words seemed to hit a nerve. "I never wanted to look at it that way," she said. "I was brought here by one of the *oyabun* of the Ryujin-kai. For a while I was treated in style as the girlfriend of a powerful yakuza. Then he was killed in a gun battle with a rival gang. I wanted to go back to Tokyo, but they put me to work here. They 'provided' for me, because the man I was with was well respected. At first I thought I couldn't work here, but to tell you the truth, I became determined to become the best soaplands girl in the business. And I am. Then . . . I don't know . . . things changed."

Bond waited a moment for her to continue.

She shrugged, unwilling to admit the truth. "Let's just say that it's not as glamorous as I thought it would be."

Bond sensed that there was pain behind her pride. He elected not to press her on it. "What can you tell me about the Ryujin-kai? Have you heard anything about something they might be planning?"

"Listen, Mr. Bond, is it? This is crazy. Why would the yakuza suddenly turn against me? I have remained loyal to them."

Bond felt exasperated by her delusion. He said, rather

brutally, "Mayumi, many people will die if you don't talk to me about it. This has become bigger than you or your family."

Suddenly she put her hand to her mouth and clenched her face, fighting the urge to cry. She clearly didn't want to do so in front of Bond. He waited patiently, giving her a few moments.

Finally, she took a deep breath, composed herself and said, "A lot of high-ranking men come here. A few nights ago there were men from the Northern Territories here and I had to help entertain them. Kubo made a big deal out of that. Yasutake Tsukamoto, the *oyabun,* was here with them. He was giving them a send-off. They were on their way to Tokyo on some kind of secret mission for the Ryujin-kai."

"This is very important," Bond said. "What else do you remember?"

But Mayumi couldn't concentrate. She rose once again and walked over to the sink. She gazed at her reflection in the mirror and said, "I hated my parents for so long. But now that they're gone, I . . . I just don't know how I feel . . ."

"I understand."

"And my sisters. I didn't get to say good-bye." Her voice cracked but she still refused to cry. Bond could see that this girl had an iron will. She was tough, unpredictable and very attractive. She was also very young, vulnerable and in terrible danger.

She took a tissue and wiped her nose. "About a month ago, they took me to some place outside of Noboribetsu," she said.

"Go on."

"It was a place that had a lot of tanks full of insects. A laboratory of some kind. I had a peek into a big room where I probably wasn't supposed to be. Anyway, there was some kind of high-level meeting there with Ryujin-kai top-ranking officials. I was hired, along with four other girls, to service them there. I heard a bit of their conversation, but I didn't think anything of it then."

"What did they say?"

"They were talking about infectious diseases. In a very general way. But I remember Tsukamoto asking someone about *their* disease. I distinctly recall being struck by his choice of words, like it was something they were in possession of. The other man replied that it was 'ready.' "

Mayumi came back to the bed and sat down beside him.

"Don't you feel used, Mayumi?" he asked gently. "You can't want to stay here. It's not the life for you."

"How do you know that?" she asked him casually, with no anger. "You are not in London anymore. You do not understand Japan. The conditions are not as bad as one might think. Some of my clients are celebrities. All of them are rich. I already have a reputation for being the best girl in the place. My apartment is very nice; I can come and go as I please. Some people might say that I'm a bad girl, but I like to think of myself as a party girl, Mr. Bond. I prefer it that way. My family never understood that. I didn't want their lifestyle. I have everything I want here."

Bond allowed his eyes to travel around the characterless yet faintly sordid room. She saw this and her face tightened. "I'm paid very well."As she spoke, Mayumi's eyes betrayed her. She didn't believe what she was saying. These words were meant to convince her as well as him.

"You know that's a delusion," Bond said gently. "You don't have your freedom. Mayumi, they're going to kill you."

There was a moment's pause, and she whispered "Then what should I do?"

"Is there any way that you can get out of here?"

She thought a minute and shrugged. "There's a fire

escape in the room upstairs. The window is locked, but I can always break it." She got up again. "What am I talking about? I *can't* leave! I have nowhere to go."

"I'll see that you get back to Tokyo safely."

"I don't want to go to Tokyo! Anywhere but there. Look, I can't believe they're going to kill me. James? That's your name?"

"Yes."

"I'm too valuable a commodity. I look Japanese but I speak English. I have blue eyes. I'm exotic. I have a lot of important clients. From Russia, from Korea, from America. From *Britain*."

"You're mistaken, Mayumi," Bond said. "You are a trophy. You are the daughter of a rival, and your presence here makes them feel superior. You are the spoils of war and a prisoner."

She was quiet after that.

"I'm not leaving until you tell me that you're going to come back with me to Tokyo," he said.

She sighed and said, "I need to think about all of this. I can't promise anything. If I try to leave, I had better do it very early tomorrow morning. Where shall I meet you?"

"I'll come back here and wait for you."

"No," she said. "I want to get away from here. Let's meet somewhere in the city centre."

"All right. Let's meet at the Tokei-dai clock tower," Bond said.

"You've been reading too many guide books. All right. *If* I decide to believe your story and *if* I make it out of here, I'll be there at four o'clock. Now go away. Maybe I'll see you later."

He nodded. "Trust me. If you can get that far, I'll get us out of Sapporo safely."

They stood and went to the door. Bond reached for his wallet but she put a hand on his arm. "No," she said. "You have to pay Norika."

Norika met them outside the door. Mayumi went past her and up the stairs, not looking back. Norika then quietly said, "Thirty thousand yen, please."

Bond didn't flinch. He pulled the bills out of his wallet and gave them to her. She took the money and put it in a small purse. Then she led Bond back to the reception area, where, in front of the men, she kissed him demurely on the cheek. She said good-bye and for him to "come back again soon." The two punch perms glared at Bond as he bowed to them and left the premises.

Mayumi went up to her room, shut the door and considered everything that she had just been told. Was she really in danger? Did the Ryujin-kai really kill her family?

Her family . . . mum . . . dad . . . her sisters . . . Oh God, what had she done . . . ?

She finally broke down and cried.

20

Escape from Sapporo

At three o'clock in the morning, Mayumi McMahon, dressed in jeans and a T-shirt, opened the door to her room on the top floor of the Casanova Club and peered into the hallway. Everything was quiet and still. Kubo had been gone since the afternoon, leaving only the two men downstairs to watch over the place . . . and her. They had been there every night since she was told that she couldn't go home.

She crept down the stairs and inched around the corner to take a look. Both men were asleep in their chairs, mouths open, snoring away.

Some guards, she thought.

Mayumi went back upstairs to her room and shut the door. For the fifth time, she examined the locked window that gave access to the fire escape.

What did they think would happen if there really was a fire? she wondered.

The last few hours had been tough. The full impact of what the Englishman had revealed to her had not hit her until a few hours later. Then she stayed in her room and cried herself to sleep. She woke up disoriented.

She felt shell-shocked and numb. It was very confusing.

Mayumi had spent the last five or six years absolutely hating her parents. Her teenage years had been miserable and she blamed them. They had been so controlling and strict, much more so with her than they had been with her older sisters. Of course, Kyoko and Shizuka were model daughters. They never complained, were always dutiful and well behaved.

As an adolescent, Mayumi had done as she pleased. Although her IQ was high, she was a poor student in school because she simply didn't care. She often skipped classes. More often than not, she was hanging out with other young troublemakers in pachinko parlours. When she was fifteen, she posed nude for a photographer who specialised in pornography. She got in with a rough crowd.

Things really started happening when she met Kenji Umeki through her association with the photographer. Umeki was part of a *bosozoku*, and Mayumi had found that exciting. He worked as a bouncer at a soaplands in Kabuki-cho, and she got to know how those places operated.

By the time she was sixteen, she was enjoying the lifestyle of a gangster's girlfriend. She got into all the best clubs, dabbled with drugs and had a great time living on the dark side of life.

Mayumi McMahon had thought that she had it all under control until that one night. The night that opened her eyes to the truth about her father.

But now that he was dead, Mayumi wasn't sure how she felt about him. She grieved for her mother and sisters, as they weren't so bad. But her father? After the years of his being "disappointed" with her and the hundreds of times he had shouted at her that she was "no damned good"?

God, how she hated him. What a hypocrite.

Still undecided about what to do, Mayumi paced the

floor. She still couldn't believe that the gang would want to kill her. Kubo liked her. He wouldn't let any harm come to her. Kubo wouldn't—

There was a knock at the door.

"Who is it?" she asked.

"Kubo."

Wary, Mayumi unlocked and opened the door a crack. He was standing alone in the corridor.

"What do you want?"

"Get your things," Kubo said. "I'm moving you out. We have to be quiet. The guards are asleep."

"What are you talking about?"

"I was gone most of the day trying to find you a new place to live."

"But I like my apartment. Why can't I go back there?"

"It's too dangerous!" he hissed. "Hurry! Get your things, now!"

She was confused, but she also picked up on Kubo's nervousness. Something was wrong.

"All right. Wait a second." She shut the door and quickly piled some clothes into a small bag that she had brought from her apartment a few days before.

Then she heard a door slam downstairs, followed by shouting. Mayumi recognised Kubo's voice and then heard some scuffling. She set down her bag and opened the door. As she lightly stepped down the stairs, she could hear Kubo talking to other men. When she got near enough to hear what they were saying, Mayumi stopped on the stairs, unseen by the men.

"No, you can't go upstairs!" Kubo was saying.

"Get out of our way, Kubo-san. The *kaicho* gave us orders."

"But she is already dead, I tell you! I killed her myself!"

"Then why won't you let us go upstairs?"

"You can't! She—"

Then there was the sound of a struggle that went on for several seconds until a gunshot made Mayumi jump out of her skin. She heard Kubo groan. Another shot silenced the fighting.

Now trembling with fear, Mayumi strained to listen to the newcomers downstairs. They were talking with the two guards. When she heard a guard say, "She's upstairs," she quickly backed up the stairs and ran to the sanctuary of her room, prison cell that it was. She locked the door and turned her attention to the fire escape window. It was her only hope.

Mayumi picked up a wooden chair and threw it at the window. The glass shattered, leaving shards within the frame.

It had made much more noise than she had thought was possible. They must have heard it.

As she climbed through the window she cut her calf and cried out. She fell onto the fire escape platform, clutching her leg. It was dark but she could see that her jeans were torn and that she had a pretty bad cut. It was bleeding profusely.

She swore softly and got up. She limped down the stairs—one floor, two floors—and then she heard voices at the broken window above her.

The men were shouting for her to come back up.

Mayumi practically fell down the final flight of stairs, but she made it to the ground and took off, only to slam right into one of the thugs who was waiting for her. He tried to grab her, but she instinctively jumped and delivered an expert *ushiro-geri* back kick into the man's jaw. He fell backwards, dropping something. He hit his head hard on the pavement and stopped moving. Mayumi paused to check if he was still alive but couldn't tell.

Then she saw what he had dropped. It was a pistol, a semiautomatic. Kenji had once shown her how to fire a gun, and he had also taught her a few karate moves such as the one she had just delivered. Mayumi picked up the gun and ran, leaving a trail of blood spots behind her.

Bond arrived at the Tokei-dai clock tower at three forty-five. He stood across the street in front of the tourist information office and watched for Mayumi. Sapporo was asleep. An occasional car appeared on the street, but otherwise the city was quiet and dark.

The clock tower was quite an anomaly. Built in the style of a New England colonial hall, the structure was now a museum and library. It looked very strange set against the rest of Sapporo's more modern and quintessentially Japanese architecture. Stranger still was the fact that it was the meeting place for a British secret agent and a soaplands girl on the run at four in the morning.

At five minutes to four, Bond saw Mayumi come around the corner and walk towards the clock tower. She was limping! He could see blood seeping from a rag wrapped around her right leg.

Bond ran across the street to meet her. "Mayumi!"

She was panting and looked scared. "I cut myself on the window when I climbed out of there. You were right, James-san, they were going to kill me. I overheard them talking about it. They're not far behind."

Whatever else, the girl had pluck. Bond had to admit that she intrigued him.

"I hope you have a way out of here and fast," she said.

Bond looked at his Rolex. Another thirty seconds.

"Here, lean against me." She did and he felt a lump concealed in the waist of her jeans. "What the hell is that?"

"Oh, I took it from one of the guards. Don't worry, I know how to use it. Listen, I'm about to start running again if you don't get us out of here."

Bond looked at his Rolex again. *Where* was *he?*

Suddenly, a Honda Today, to Bond's eyes a ridiculously small commuter car, screamed around the corner and pulled up in front of the clock tower. Ikuo Yamamaru was at the wheel. He threw open the door.

"Get in!" he called.

A black Mercedes swerved around the corner. Bond could see that the man in the passenger seat had a punch perm.

"How are all three of us supposed to fit in there?" Mayumi asked.

"Move, Mayumi! Quick!" Bond shouted.

Bond shoved her into the backseat and he jumped into the front. A gunshot echoed through the street, and they heard the bullet ricochet off the road. Ikuo accelerated and the little car's wheels shrieked. The Mercedes skidded noisily as it torpedoed past the clock tower in pursuit.

Ikuo jumped a red light, almost hitting a lone city bus on its way to begin its early morning route. He slammed on the brakes and turned the wheel sharply. Mayumi screamed and covered her eyes as the car screeched, narrowly avoiding a broadside with the vehicle.

"Sorry!" he said. He turned the wheel violently and floored the accelerator. The car bolted out of the intersection and onto a north-south street containing light traffic. Luckily, the Honda was so small that it could easily run up onto the pavement, which was precisely what Ikuo did.

"Try not to kill anyone," Bond said.

"Especially us," Mayumi said. "Who is this guy, anyway?"

"I am Ikuo Yamamaru, *hajime mashite*," the driver said quickly.

"Did you borrow this car from your mother?" Bond asked him.

Ikuo said, "Laugh if you want, Bond-san, but I have outfitted this little car with an engine that makes your English sports cars seem like golf carts."

The Ainu put the car into fourth, and they sped along the street, heading towards the huge NHK television tower that dominated the skyline in the centre of town. It was in the middle of a paved square with a few park benches. Dozens of pigeons had arrived for sunrise and were feasting on crumbs. The little Honda jumped the curb, scattering the birds in a rush of flapping wings.

The Mercedes was not far behind. They had also driven onto the pavement to bypass the traffic, but the car could not match the Honda's souped-up engine. The man in the passenger seat leaned out of the car and fired a pistol, knocking out a brakelight.

"Get down!" Bond shouted to Mayumi. He didn't have to tell her twice. She was very frightened. "Ikuo, get us out of here!"

But more bullets tore into the front and rear tyres. Ikuo lost control of the car as it skidded towards one of the tower's steel legs. Bond saw it coming through the windscreen and shielded his head just as the car crashed into a girder. The impact threw Mayumi into the front seat on top of Bond.

Ikuo had an ugly gash on his forehead. The window on the driver's side was cracked where he had struck it.

The sound of nearby gunfire jolted them out of the temporary haze. Bond drew the Walther and said, "When I say so, jump out of the car and take cover."

He peered through the shattered back windscreen and saw that there were three of them. The yakuza had stopped the Mercedes about thirty feet away and had taken cover behind the vehicle.

"Now!"

Bond jumped first and crouched behind the engine block, followed by Ikuo. Mayumi rolled out of the car and got behind the steel girder that was a part of the tower's leg. Both men fired at the Mercedes as soon as they were in position. Bond knocked out a headlamp, but otherwise their shots were wildly inaccurate because both men had been shaken by the collision. Bond heard a third gun resound, turned, and was surprised to see Mayumi firing her Browning at the yakuza. She managed to blast a hole through the Mercedes' windscreen.

"We're trapped," Ikuo said. "There is no place to run."

He was right. Bond surveyed the square and realised that they were wide open. The only possibility would be to run beneath the tower, but then they would be moving targets without cover. Bond had to find a way to take them out.

Police sirens were growing louder. They would be on the scene any minute. At this point, Bond didn't want them involved. He had to get Mayumi out of Sapporo without interference or delays.

He loaded a new magazine and ducked low, beneath the Honda's chassis. He could just get a bead on the feet of one of the yakuza thugs, which could be seen below the bottom edge of the Mercedes' door. Bond fired the gun laterally, two inches above the level pavement. The bullet shattered the man's ankle. He screamed and fell from behind the cover of the car door. Ikuo got a clear shot and hit him in the chest.

"One down, two to go," Bond said.

Realising that they needed to get out before the police arrived, the remaining yakuza got back into the Mercedes. The driver gunned the engine and drove towards them. The other man leaned out of the passenger window, ready to shoot whomever he could see as the car shot past them.

"Both of you, go for the gunman," Bond commanded. "I'll take the driver."

He positioned himself on one knee and aimed carefully at the shape behind the wheel. Ikuo and Mayumi concentrated their firepower on the passenger, spraying him with a barrage of bullets. Bond squeezed the trigger once. He saw a spider web appear on the windscreen and then the Mercedes suddenly veered to the left. The shooter jerked violently and dropped his weapon as several rounds hit his upper body. The Mercedes kept going until it rammed into one of the tower's opposite legs. The front end was smashed pretty badly.

Keeping his gun trained on the car, Bond got up and ran to it. He opened the passenger door and the gunman fell out onto the pavement. He ran around to the other side and pulled the dead driver out of the car. Ikuo and Mayumi were right behind him.

"Nice of them to let us borrow their car," Bond said, nodding at Ikuo, who immediately got into the driver's seat.

The police sirens were very near, perhaps a block away.

Ikuo threw the car into reverse, backed off of the girder and then drove into the street. He turned the corner and sped away from the scene just as the police cars began to arrive.

Bond looked over and saw that Ikuo had blood all over his shirt.

"Ikuo, you've been hit," he said.

"I know," Yamamaru replied. "I'll be fine."

Bond reached over and felt Ikuo's chest. The wound was on the right, just beneath the collarbone.

"We have to get you to a doctor," he said. He turned back to Mayumi. "How's your leg?"

"What leg?" she asked.

Bond looked pointedly at her blood-soaked jeans.

"I'm all right," she said. "Really. It looks worse than it is."

Ikuo drove like a whirlwind to the southern outskirts of Sapporo and got on the main highway, but after ten minutes Bond insisted that he pull the car over to the side of the road. Ikuo looked quite pale and was sweating freely.

"I'll drive, Ikuo. Change places with me," Bond said.

Once they were buckled in, Bond guided the car back into the traffic flow.

"There is an emergency medical centre just up the road," Ikuo muttered. "I am afraid we had better stop there. You can drop me off and go on."

"I think Miss McMahon needs some attention too, despite her protests," Bond said. "Perhaps they'll give us a bulk discount."

It was a small clinic that was used primarily for road accidents. The staff were accustomed to those, but had never seen a gunshot wound before. Ikuo showed them an official ID so that he wouldn't have to answer questions. The Ainu was placed on a trolley and wheeled into a room marked "Treatment." Bond stayed with Mayumi, who was looked at by a young female doctor.

"This is a bad cut, how did it happen?" she asked, examining Mayumi's leg.

"Broken glass."

The doctor cleaned the wound, put in several stitches, and gave Mayumi a tetanus shot. After a sterile bandage was wrapped around her calf, the doctor said that she could leave.

"Can we see our friend?" Bond asked.

The doctor told him to wait a minute and then disappeared into the treatment room.

She soon returned with a note from Ikuo, which said: "Go to hotel in Noboribetsu. Will contact you tomorrow morning."

Bond turned to Mayumi and said, "Come on, let's go. We can't do any more here."

Ten minutes later they were in the back of a taxi on their way to Noboribetsu.

Mayumi asked, "Won't they be looking for us?"

"Undoubtedly," Bond said. "But let's worry about that if they find us."

The taxi pulled onto the expressway and headed south, leaving Sapporo and the main hub of the Ryujin-kai behind.

21

Demons from Hell

Tsukamoto picked up the phone and knew instantly that the *Yami Shogun* was on the other end. There was something about the sound of the *air* in the earpiece that was distinctive. He rubbed his hand over his stomach and realised that there was indeed a correlation between the sudden attacks of anxiety he had been experiencing over the last few weeks and talking with the *Yami Shogun*.

"Good morning, Tsukamoto," Yoshida said.

Tsukamoto swallowed hard. "Good morning to you too, Yoshida. How are you?"

"Fine. And you?"

"Very well, thank you," Tsukamoto lied. "I shall leave for Noboribetsu in an hour. The results of the tests are encouraging."

"I am happy to hear that. I have thought of an appropriate name for our plan. Red Widow Dawn. In honour of our insect assasins."

"Very good, Yoshida. I shall inspect the product today, and if it meets our criteria, then Red Widow Dawn will commence as planned."

"The product must meet our criteria."

"The product works as it is now. You could go ahead with today's version."

"Our mission requires the best. The more reliable the weapon, the more foolproof the plan. Tsukamoto, I am waiting for your confirmation that *everything* is prepared."

"Yes, I understand. You need not worry."

There was silence at the other end of the line. Tsukamoto felt his stomach churn. What was the master thinking? Did he know about what had happened in Sapporo?

Finally, Yoshida said, "I sense that something is wrong. What is it, Tsukamoto? You are not hiding something from me, are you?"

Tsukamoto shuddered. "We had a problem," he said. "Kubo was a traitor and disobeyed my orders to have the girl killed. He had kept her alive without any of us knowing. She escaped early this morning, killing one of our men. Now she is with that British agent. Kubo has been taken care of. But more of our men were killed in Sapporo."

There was an ominous silence. Tsukamoto broke it, saying, "I will gladly cut off one of my fingers, Yoshida." He hung his head in shame.

"Tsukamoto, I want them killed, and I want it done now. You have failed in a very simple task. Find them and do the job *right*."

The simplicity of this remark sent a chill down Tsukamoto's spine. He found himself talking too much and too quickly in an effort to dispel his fear. "Our best men are on it. We sent the word out to all of the *honbu* around the country. They have received descriptions of both the Englishman and the McMahon girl. There was a third man with them, an Ainu, someone whom we believe is an employee of the Public Security Investigation Agency. We will kill him too. We believe they are probably on their way back to Tokyo so we—"

"Stop babbling, Tsukamoto," Yoshida snapped. "It does not become you. Just . . . find them. We cannot afford interference at this juncture. You know what happens in four days."

"I understand, Yoshida."

Yoshida raised his voice—something he rarely did. "*I do not think you do!* This is our time of glory! The master Mishima-san is watching over us from heaven. He is proud of our intentions to rid Japan of the barbarians who desecrate and pollute our culture and our land. We must not let him down! The only consequence of failure is *death*!"

Tsukamoto clinched his eyes. His boyhood friend was truly mad. Mishima-san would never have approved of what they were about to do. Yukio Mishima was no terrorist. Yoshida had taken his tenets and twisted them. How was this going to end?

"Yes, *sensei*," was all that Tsukamoto could say.

"Call me from Noboribetsu."

"*Hai!*"

Tsukamoto hung up the phone. He had slipped again and called Yoshida *sensei*. This time Yoshida had not reproached him.

He looked at the clock. He dreaded going to Noboribetsu and taking charge of the operation. He had to follow the *Yami Shogun*'s orders and stand behind them. Supporting Goro Yoshida to victory was going to be a very honourable action, but Tsukamoto felt nothing but dread. Something terrible was going to happen, and he was going to be caught in the middle of it.

Yasutake Tsukamoto, the head of one of the most powerful yakuza crime syndicates in the world, was afraid. He was aware that a day of reckoning would come, sooner rather than later. And that was when he would have to answer for his life of crime.

• • •

The taxi ride to Noboribetsu from the medical clinic had taken a little over an hour. Bond and Mayumi were let off in front of the Dai-ichi Takimotokan, the largest and most luxurious hotel and spa in a town famous for its abundant hot springs. It was a complex made up of four buildings, 399 rooms, two restaurants and a souvenir shop. Tanaka had booked them into the hotel with the reasoning that it was an unlikely place for them to be found. Bond had insisted on investigating the Hokkaido Mosquito Vector and Control Centre outside town before heading back to Tokyo, but he and Mayumi both needed a few hours' rest. Mayumi's face was grey with pain, but she was too stubborn to complain.

The area around the town was volcanic and Bond had to admit that the scenery was extraordinary. A patch of land just behind the Dai-ichi, called *Jigokudani*, or "Hell Valley," was a national park full of steaming, sulphurous vents and streams of hot water bubbling out of vividly coloured rocks. This was the source of the hot springs that fed the hotel's thirty different baths.

The predominant mascot of Noboribetsu was an *oni*, a demon known as the King of Hell. He was a fierce-looking, red, horned ogre who carried a club, and he was everywhere. A huge statue of him guarded the town, sculptures adorned hotel lobbies, and miniature figures of the demon could be purchased in the souvenir shops.

When they entered the hotel, they were greeted in the lobby by a line of chambermaids and bellboys who called out in unison, *"Irrashaimase!"* Tanaka had taken care of the reservations; Bond and Mayumi had separate Japanese-style rooms with futons on *tatami* mats.

"The first thing I'm going to do is get into one of those hot sulphur baths," Mayumi said as they walked away from the lobby.

"Not on your life," Bond replied. "We're going to stay in our rooms. We can't afford to be seen. By anyone."

"What? Come on, the baths are what make this place great. And what about food?"

"We'll have room service delivered. Which I will organise. I mean it, Mayumi. We're not out of danger yet."

"You're absolutely no fun at all," she pouted.

They walked past one of the hotel's main attractions — a uniquely Japanese two-storey-tall mechanical clock shaped like the ogre's club. At various times during the day, the clock would "strike," and it did so now. Several doors on it opened and mechanical fairy-tale figures emerged and danced to an elaborately orchestrated soundtrack that resounded throughout the lobby.

This distraction kept Bond from noticing the two men sitting with drinks in the lounge, which was set apart from the lobby but in plain view of it. Both men had crew cuts and were wearing *yukata* and *tanzen* provided by the hotel. They did not need to exchange a glance when Bond and Mayumi walked through. One man took the mobile out of his pocket and made a call.

It was just before sunset when Bond had a brief conversation with Tanaka over the phone.

"Yamamaru-san is all right and was discharged from the clinic," Tanaka said. "He will rendezvous with you later. Get some rest. However, I must warn you that his Ainu contacts in Noboribetsu have reported that there is a lot of yakuza activity there. Keep a low profile. They are looking for you."

They discussed what must be done with Mayumi McMahon and agreed that Bond should get her back to Tokyo as soon as possible. But both men decided that having a look at the mosquito control facility in Noboribetsu was a good idea, provided that Bond could get inside it without causing a major disturbance. Bond didn't particularly want to wait until nightfall, but he resigned himself to sitting out the next few hours with Mayumi. He hated waiting, and he had done a lot of it in his line of work. Normally he couldn't bear to sit in a hotel room or an airport lobby waiting for instructions or a message from superiors. Now even in these luxurious surroundings, he felt restless and anxious for something to happen.

Bond decided to check on Mayumi. He called her room, but the phone rang and rang. Angrily, he hung up, threw on a *yukata* and glanced at his shoulder holster hanging over a chair. Not practical. Instead, Bond took the small plastic dagger from his field-issue shoe heel and hid it inside the *yukata*. He quickly left his room, walked down two doors to Mayumi's and knocked loudly. There was no answer.

Bond swore under his breath. He looked down the corridor and saw a chambermaid about to enter one of the rooms. Bond sprinted to her and asked if she had seen a young girl come out of room 223. The woman replied that yes, she had. The girl had asked her how to get to the baths.

Bond took the lift down to the *onsen* complex in the hotel. While in some Japanese *onsen,* men and women shared one bathhouse, here it was not so. *To hell with it,* he thought. He was going in the women's side.

The sight of two dressed men entering the women's baths ahead of him hardened his resolve. They had crew cuts and looked like bodybuilders. Bond smelled yakuza.

Bond hurried in to the locker room. Several women in states of undress were upset and calling for help. The two men must have gone on through to the baths. Bond heard screams coming from that direction. He kicked off his slippers and ran through the locker room and into the baths complex. The baths occupied more than one level of the hotel, and guests were allowed to wander from floor to floor trying out the hot mineral pools, waterfalls, walking pools, freezing cold pools, steam room and swimming pool.

Bond found himself in a hot and steamy room. Naked and frightened women were huddled together, clutching their towels. Bond ran across the wet tiled floor searching frantically in the various pools—but a scream that sounded like Mayumi directed him towards the outdoor terrace, where guests could sit in a gigantic hot tub under the stars.

More wet, naked women ran shrieking past Bond as he ran through the door to the terrace. The two yakuza had pulled Mayumi out of the water and were struggling with her. One of them had a cord around the girl's neck and was attempting to choke her to death.

The man who was trying to hold Mayumi down saw Bond rushing towards them. He let go of Mayumi so that he could counterattack, but he wasn't fast enough. Bond pulled back his right fist and put his full weight into a power punch to the man's chin. The yakuza's head jerked back with a snap, and he fell to the ground.

The other man was still trying to choke Mayumi but he was having a very difficult time holding her alone. Bond leaped onto him and locked his arm around the man's throat.

"Let her go," Bond said through his teeth.

But the yakuza ignored him. Allowing his anger to get the better of him, Bond grabbed a tight hold of the man's head and then jerked it to the right sharply and forcefully. The sound of the man's neck snapping was extremely satisfying. The cord loosened and Mayumi fell to her knees, coughing and sputtering. Bond let the man's body crumple to the ground and pushed it into the hot tub with his foot.

But before he could see to Mayumi, someone slammed into Bond's back, knocking him into the water. The heat was intense. He immediately broke the surface to gasp for air and caught sight of three men jumping into the tub

after him. Obviously a second team of killers had targeted
Bond and followed him into the baths.

Bond placed his hands behind him on the edge of the
tub so that he could raise himself out of the water, but the
two men on either side of him grabbed his arms. Bond
broke one man's grip, the one on his right, and lashed out
with a forceful blow to the yakuza's nose. The other man,
however, threw himself into Bond and shoved him into
the hot water. The third man moved across the tub to join
the melee. Bond found himself being held below the surface by all three men as they gripped his arms, head and
shoulders. Bond struggled, but it was no use. If he hadn't
been submerged he might have been able to break their
hold, but the weight of the water slowed his defensive manoeuvres. Fighting in the water was difficult. No matter
how hard he pushed, the speed was always the same.
Strength was about the only tool he had, and Bond was
outnumbered three to one.

Although he was able to hold his breath for an extraordinary amount of time, he could not resist the laws of
physics. His lungs burned as they screamed for air. He
tried clawing and pinching, but the men just tightened
their vice-like grips.

Do something! Bond commanded himself. Wait! The
knife! He had felt it come loose from his *yukata* and
watched it float to the bottom of the tub. Bond felt the tub
floor with his bare foot and finally found it. Grasping it
with his toes, he managed to pull it up far enough so that
he could take it with his hands. He pulled out the blade,
held it firmly, and then slashed the man on his right across
the stomach. From underwater, Bond heard the man
scream. He loosened his grip, allowing Bond to wriggle
out from under the other two through water now thick-
ened with blood.

He surfaced and gasped for air. The two remaining
yakuza lunged at him, knocking him back against the side

of the tub. Bond thrust out his arm and couldn't help making a wild, reckless arc with the knife. It connected with something and one of the men yelped, clutching his face.

The uninjured attacker backed off, giving Bond time to scramble out of the tub. Once he was standing, he attacked the man with the stomach wound, kicking him in the face and knocking him into the water. The second injured man was already blinded, shouting for help. Bond ignored him and focused his attention on the one man who was still standing in the water.

"Here, catch!" Bond said.

He flung the knife at the man. It spun in the air and skewered the yakuza's eye. The man's mouth opened wide in horror as he fell back into the water, which was now foaming with blood.

Bond then knelt beside Mayumi. She put her arms around him, still gasping and sobbing. Her neck bore a livid red welt where the cord had burned her skin.

"How—how did they find us?" she stuttered.

"Determination and the Japanese work ethic," Bond said.

He noticed that she was clutching something in her hand.

"What's that?" he asked.

Mayumi coughed again and tried to breathe deeply. She exhaled loudly and said, "One of them had this in his jacket pocket. I was grabbing at anything and everything and happened to pull it out."

It was an employee identification card. Bond took it from her and examined it. The card read "Hokkaido Mosquito and Vector Control Centre" and there was a photo of the man and a magnetic strip on it.

"Mayumi, this is a key card. These men were from that facility I need to see."

"I never knew that the Hokkaido government employed yakuza hit men," she said.

"Employees of Yonai Enterprises, more likely. Or soldiers with the Ryujin-kai who act as security guards at the place."

The doors to the spa burst open and four hotel security guards shouted at them.

Bond stood and held up his hands. The guards were unarmed, as was the policy in Japan—the police never carried firearms either—but the guards exhibited enough malevolence to convince Bond that he shouldn't try to escape. Besides, Tiger would fix everything.

"Come on, Mayumi," Bond said. "I think it's time to check out."

22

Caught!

"I'm coming with you!" Mayumi said, gritting her teeth and folding her arms in front of her. The angry red welt on her neck seemed to intensify when she asserted herself. She had changed into the T-shirt and designer jeans that Bond had bought her along with a hat and sunglasses from the hotel boutique. She looked like a student.

"It's too dangerous," Bond insisted.

The sun had set and the lights of Noboribetsu were bright and flashy, but the small resort town was nothing like the bigger cities. The shops and restaurants on the main street were alive and open for business, but the areas beyond that were dark and foreboding. The mountains in the distance and the woods surrounding them created the illusion that the little town was in the middle of a deep, dark forest, miles away from civilisation.

"I want you to check into another hotel and wait until I come back," Bond said as he unfolded a map that Ikuo had given him. The mosquito control centre was clearly marked, located on a side road not very far from the Dai-ichi Takimotokan.

"No," she said stubbornly. "I'm staying with you. I owe it to my mother and my sisters to see this through."

"Why not your father?" Bond asked.

She grew silent.

"Him too, I guess," she muttered finally.

"Why do you hate him so much?"

"Because he's a liar and a hypocrite."

"How so?"

"Never mind. I don't want to talk about it."

"Mayumi, if you know something that might help us, then—"

"Shut up!" she spat. "I said I don't want to talk about it!"

"Mayumi, it's simply not safe for you to come with me," he said with a sigh.

"Look, if I don't come with you, I'm leaving," she said, digging in her heels. "And you won't be able to stop me."

Bond shook his head and looked at the heavens. She was an impossible girl. It was no wonder that she had been in constant conflict with her parents. She was perhaps the most wilful girl he'd ever known.

Finally, Bond said through clenched teeth, "Well, if you're coming with me, then I insist that you do everything I say. You're to be quiet and follow my orders, do you understand?"

"Yes, master."

Bond scowled at her, but she simply smiled wickedly at him.

"You can be pretty sexy when you're a bully, James-san," she said.

He ignored her and said, "It's close enough to walk there. It will be safer."

They walked up the hill away from the Dai-ichi and towards the Valley of Hell. A narrow two-lane road jutted off into the woods on the other side of the main street. The couple turned and began to walk in that direction, where there were no street lamps or any other lamps. It was almost pitch black.

An animal ran across the road in front of them and Mayumi shrieked.

"Did you see that? A fox!" she whispered.

"Quiet!" Bond silently cursed the girl. Women could not be relied upon to keep their mouths shut.

They continued until, twenty minutes later, they came to a fork. The larger road continued on, curving to the right, while an unpaved road split off to the left. A sign was marked in Japanese and English: "Private Property, Keep Out."

"Do you recall any of this from when you were here?" Bond asked.

"I remember this road. I was pretty stoned that night so I don't remember much else."

They walked quietly down the dirt path and eventually came to a high steel fence. Bond examined the gate and found that there was an electronic lock and numeric keypad attached to it. The key card Mayumi had taken from the thug at the hotel was not compatible with it.

"I don't suppose you know the code," Bond said.

"Afraid not, master."

"I'm not in the mood for your nonsense," he said. Bond reached into his pocket and removed the Palm Pilot. Major Boothroyd had said that the electromagnetic device was weak but that it might disable small electric appliances. Would it work on an electronic keypad?

"What's that?" she asked.

"Shhh."

Bond opened the Palm and held it next to the lock.

"I'm guessing that there is a fail-safe mechanism on the system," he whispered. "In the event that power is knocked out to the compound, say, because of a fire, they wouldn't want everyone locked in, would they?"

"What are you talking about?" she asked.

"Never mind." He pressed the appropriate buttons and held the contraption steady. It hummed softly and slightly vibrated. The illuminated LED on the gate's keypad flickered once, twice, and then went out.

Bond tried the gate and it opened with a click. He had guessed correctly: the mechanism unlocked when the power was interrupted.

"Hey, it worked!" Mayumi said. "That was pretty cool! How did you do that?"

"Magic. Now be quiet."

The dirt road curved through a group of trees some fifty metres ahead until it stopped at a squat one-storey building made of concrete and stone. The design was typically Japanese and very modern, with diagonal lines and a slanting roof; it looked more like an art museum than a scientific laboratory. The windows were frosted, but light shone through them. There were people inside.

"A late night at the office," murmured Bond. "Let's go round the back."

They circled the building and found a gravelled car park containing nine cars. A door marked as an employee entrance opened suddenly. Bond pulled Mayumi against the wall, unwittingly knocking the breath out of her. She gasped and Bond put his hand over her mouth.

Two men came out of the building, laughing about something. They didn't see the couple in the shadows. Instead, they walked past them to a 4x4, got in it and drove away.

Mayumi breathed deeply for a moment. "You could be a bit more gentle," she said.

"You insisted on coming. You play by my rules. Now, wait for me here while I go inside."

"Screw that, I'm coming with you. Lead on."

Bond thought for a moment. She would be more of a liability outside and restless.

Christ! This girl was a millstone around his neck. "Okay," he said. "Follow me. But keep your mouth shut."

Bond took her key card and swiped it through the slot next to the employee entrance. The catch clicked.

Bond carefully opened the door and peered inside. It was a shiny and sterile, steel-lined corridor. The coast was clear.

"Let's go."

They crept through the corridor and heard voices in other parts of the building. When they reached the end of the hallway, the corridor branched in a T. It appeared that offices were to the right. To the left was a set of double steel doors with small, yellow-tinted windows in the centres. Bond looked through them to see one end of a fairly large laboratory. Men were busy at workstations, all wearing full-body protective suits, much like the kind worn against exposure to radiation. The laboratory consisted of a variety of metal tables, computers, machines and what appeared to be glass cubicles built into the walls. The sterility and stainless-steel furnishings reminded Bond of a surgical theatre.

Two workers began to walk towards the doors.

"Against the wall!" Bond hissed. He pushed her behind the door and he took the position on the opposite side. Bond drew the Walther and held it by the barrel. The doors swung open and the two men wearing protective suits came through. As soon as the doors closed, Bond swung out and struck one man on the back of the head with the butt of the gun. Without waiting to see if his blow was successful, he immediately raised his arm to hit the other man but his target turned to ward off the attack. He was fast: he grabbed Bond's wrist in midair and pushed him against the wall. The first man collapsed onto the floor, out cold. Bond attempted to knee the second man in the groin but the protective suit was too bulky for the strike to be effective. Mayumi, who was standing behind

Bond's attacker, drew the Browning from her waist and slammed the butt down on the man's head. He jerked and Bond could see the man's eyes roll up into his head behind the tinted faceplate.

"Good work," Bond said as the man fell to the floor.

"See? Aren't you glad I came along?" she said, winking at him.

"No. But as you're here, take that man. I'll get this one." Bond grabbed the other man by the shoulders and dragged him down the corridor the way they had come. Mayumi copied him. Bond listened at the first door they came to and after satisfying himself that the room was empty, he opened it.

It was a small office. Bond pulled his man inside, and Mayumi followed. They closed the door and began to strip their victims of the protective suits.

One of the men looked familiar to Bond. He was slight, with spectacles and a crew cut. Where had he seen this man before? In Tokyo? Yes, that was it! This was the man from the CureLab office, the one who had been working on the mosquito slideshow presentation. Bond looked at his ID card and verified that his name was Fujio Aida.

Five minutes later, Bond and Mayumi, dressed in the protective suits, walked out of the office and purposefully headed toward the lab as if they knew exactly what they were doing. They opened the doors and walked inside, turned the corner and beheld the full extent of the complex.

It was huge. The size of the building's exterior had been deceptive. The lab was easily the size of two cricket pitches side by side. Machines and computers dominated the room, but of particular interest were the glass chambers along one side of the lab that appeared to contain flying insects. Terraria lined another wall, and some of these were half-filled with water and appeared to be insect breeding incubators. At least ten other men were in the room, busy at the terminals or working with test tubes and beakers.

Bond and Mayumi nonchalantly made their way to the chambers to get a closer look. In fact, the cubicles were man-sized terraria. Water covered the floors of each chamber, supplemented by plant life and rocks to make the habitat seem more natural. One of the rooms contained a live goat, presumably a host for the mosquitoes inside. Another chamber held mice. Some were running around frantically; others were huddled and trembling in the corner. A couple of them looked dead. Each chamber had an air lock.

As he examined the chambers, Bond put together what he was looking at. Each chamber housed mosquitoes that were in different stages of their life cycle. The first one was empty except for the pond. Bond presumed that there were eggs in the water or attached to some of the plants. The second one was also seemingly empty, probably containing larvae in the water. Indeed, there was an enlarged photograph of mosquito larvae posted on the exterior of the chamber. They were long, transparent, tube-like creatures that hung down in the water with their "mouths" attached to the surface to bring in air. The third chamber held pupae, and through a magnifier built in to the glass, Bond could see that some of the pupal skins had already been shed. Young mosquitoes were gliding in the air within the cubicle, looking for a way out. The fourth chamber was full of live mosquitoes. They were crawling on the inside of the glass, covering the surface of the pond, and flying listlessly.

An extensive workspace separated these chambers from another large room that contained several cages holding various live animals—rats, guinea pigs and goats.

A technician looked at Bond and Mayumi and barked

an order at them. Mayumi bowed to the man and gestured for Bond to follow her.

"What did he say?" Bond whispered. "I didn't catch it."

"He wants us to go into the chamber and check on the mice," she said. "What do we do?"

They walked towards the fourth chamber, the one that was full of flying mosquitoes. Inside, some of the mice were still running back and forth but it seemed that a few more had died since they had last looked. A technician punched a button on his computer and the outer doors opened.

"I'm not going in there," Mayumi whispered.

"We're wearing suits, it should be all right," Bond said. He stepped into the air lock and Mayumi reluctantly followed him. The technician closed the outer door and then opened the inner door to the chamber.

Immediately dozens of mosquitoes landed on Bond's facemask. They crawled over the surface, hungrily searching for a way in to the warm flesh. The insects did the same to Mayumi, and she couldn't stifle a scream.

Some of the other technicians heard her and looked up. They weren't used to hearing a woman's voice in the lab.

"Mayumi, we're blown," Bond whispered.

One of the men stepped forward to get a closer look at them through the glass. Bond and Mayumi turned away so that he couldn't see inside the faceplates, but the man shouted at his colleagues. Two men grabbed phones and alerted security, while the others ran to the chamber.

"Let's get out of here before they bring in the heavy artillery," Bond said. He went for the inner door but found that he couldn't open it. The bastards had locked it by remote control. They were caught.

Bond banged on the glass. "Let us out or I'll break the glass and release the mosquitoes."

"I am afraid you cannot break the glass," said a man as

he entered the room through a sliding steel door, followed by two armed guards. "As it is most certainly bullet-proof, I can assure you that it is fist-proof."

Bond recognised him at once. He had white hair, smiling eyes and a commanding presence.

"We have not been properly introduced," the man continued. "I know who you are, Bond-san, but you do not know me. I am Yasutake Tsukamoto."

He bowed, but not very low.

"Pardon me for not presenting you my *meishi*," Bond said, not returning the bow.

Tsukamoto's demeanour changed rapidly. The smiling eyes vanished as he frowned, obviously insulted.

"Get them out of there," Tsukamoto said to one of the technicians. "The *Yami Shogun* wants to see them helpless before him."

23
Bitter Glory

The first thing they did was to make Bond and Mayumi remove the protective suits, revealing their street clothes underneath. Then a guard thoroughly searched the couple, and their guns were taken from them. When he found the Palm Pilot, the guard studied it, attempting to decide whether or not it constituted a weapon. Bond grabbed the device out of his hand, and the two men struggled for possession of it until another guard raised his rifle and butted Bond on the right side of the face. Bond fell and the Palm Pilot was taken from him.

"Put it over there with the rest," Tsukamoto ordered. The guard placed the Palm Pilot on a table, alongside the two guns and Bond's mobile.

Mayumi knelt beside Bond. He was clutching his cheek in agony.

"James-san?" she asked.

Bond clenched his teeth and forced the pain to dissipate, hoping that his cheekbone was merely bruised and not broken. It felt like hell.

"I'm all right," he muttered, then allowed her to help him stand.

Tsukamoto stood and addressed them. The two guards,

Aida and several lab technicians flanked him. Bond considered the odds. Not great, but it appeared that only the two guards were armed. One of them had an Uzi. If he could just get to his weapon in time, or perhaps wrestle the Uzi away . . .

"The Yonai Enterprises office in Sapporo warned us that you might be coming this way," Tsukamoto said. "I am happy that you have decided to pay us a visit. There is someone who would like to speak with you. This is a tele-conference. He can see and hear you just as you can see and hear him. Please focus your attention on the screen beside you."

A technician brought up an image on a large screen built into one of the walls. A Japanese man came into focus. He appeared to be in his fifties and was dressed in full samurai regalia. A long sword, a *tachi,* hung at his side. The upper edges of a bright red tattoo could be seen on his neck. The man was sitting cross-legged on a pillow.

"Good evening, Mr. Bond," he said. "I am Goro Yoshida." And then he bowed.

Yoshida! At last, Bond was able to gaze upon the man he had been studying for more than a year. This was the man who had built an army of terrorists, who had insti-gated the bombing attack in France and countless other in-cidents around the globe. This was the most dangerous man alive, and yet he was not what Bond had expected. Bond thought the man would be wearing army fatigues, but Yoshida was dressed in a medieval costume. It was a ghastly sight; it confirmed that the man was a deluded psychopath.

Bond stood his ground and refused to bow to Yoshida. The terrorist sat straight and said, "If I had known who you were, Mr. Bond, I would have had you killed within the first twenty-four hours of your stepping foot in Japan. You interfered with a business arrangement of mine in France a while ago."

The man's English was surprisingly refined. "I don't know very much about you, Mr. Bond, but I understand that you have a certain . . . *reputation* that precedes you so therefore I will show you respect." He bowed again.

Bond said, "I think you know what you can do with your respect, Yoshida."

Tsukamoto gasped at the insult. "Do not speak to the *Yami Shogun* that way!" he spat. He gestured for the guard to do something to Bond but Yoshida sat upright, waved his hand and said, "Stop." The guard held his stance. "Mr. Bond, you choose to waste your last moments with insults."

"Let the girl go," Bond said. "This has nothing to do with her."

"You are mistaken, Mr. Bond," Yoshida said. "This has *everything* to do with her. Her father's company was instrumental in the construction of our project."

"She is no threat to you. Let her go."

"Mr. Bond, are you forgetting that she *owns* the majority of shares in the company?"

"Where are you planning to unleash the mosquitoes, Yoshida, in the subway system? Is this another mission from God like the sarin gas attacks?"

"I respect your thirst for knowledge, Mr. Bond. You are a soldier, just like me. I will explain. I don't want you to die ignorant of how we have beaten you, *gaijin*."

Tsukamoto and the others present grinned at that.

"Aida and Tsukamoto, perhaps you would like to tell our distinguished uninformed guest about our new technology," Yoshida said.

Fujio Aida, still rubbing his head and glaring at Bond, said, "Certainly, *sensei*." He looked at Tsukamoto for approval. The *kaicho* nodded subtly.

Aida stepped forward and went to a computer workstation. He used the mouse and keyboard, and the screen's image changed. A magnified, red mosquito replaced Yoshida.

"Until a few months ago, I was head of research and development at CureLab Inc. My task there was to work with known viruses in attempts to create cures for them. One particular virus interested me greatly — West Nile. Unfortunately, I was unable to find a cure for it, but I found that I was able to alter it — mutate it — so that it would do what I wanted it to do. In studying the disease, I began to learn more about the biology of mosquitoes, since they are the primary carrier of the disease."

The movies on the screen began to illustrate Aida's words. Images showing the life cycle of the mosquito flashed before them — from egg laying and hatching to clips of adult mosquitoes mating.

"As I worked on the genetic possibilities of altering the mosquito's physiology, I discovered that I could inject their eggs with certain proteins and chemicals that would affect the mosquitoes that hatched out of them and eventually grew into adulthood. But what I needed was better access to mosquitoes and a laboratory where I could work with them."

Tsukamoto took over the narration. "Yonai Enterprises *owns* this facility. The government contracts its use as a public health organisation. Its purpose is to study mosquitoes and transmittable viruses in an effort to control the spread of those diseases. Since Yonai has a special relationship with the Ryujin-kai, it was no great difficulty for us to take over the management and running of the place. When the *Yami Shogun* learned of the disease research, he instructed Aida to create a mutation of West Nile disease, one with far more powerful and faster effects than the original. At the same time, the Ryujin-kai made Aida an offer."

"I defected," Aida said. "I went to Yonai from Cure-Lab. And I took my research with me."

"We made it possible for him to 'disappear,' " Tsukamoto said. "Tell him about our little assassin."

Aida bowed slightly and said, "What we ended up doing was to breed a mosquito with special characteristics. Using genetic splicing and a great deal of experimentation, we eventually took a normal female *Aedes aegypti* mosquito and genetically altered her so that she would bite furiously. Unfortunately, our mosquitoes have an extremely short life span. The adults, after emerging from the pupal state, live only a few hours. We're still working on solving that problem. Nevertheless, we began to refer to these red widows as 'kamikaze' mosquitoes. They are willing to risk their lives just to bite something living. Well, with power like that, we realised that we should find a way to infuse the mutated virus into the genetic formula. So now we have kamikaze mosquitoes that can deliver a deadly disease to any target, providing the target is contained in an enclosed space."

"A flying death squad." Bond said.

"Something like that," Tsukamoto said.

"The trick is to then set a perfectly timed trap," Aida continued. "You want to deliver the mosquito eggs to the target destination at the right moment, cleverly disguised but able to rest in or near standing water so that at the desired time the mosquitoes will emerge from the pupae and attack. The males, of course, do nothing but fly around and look for food from plants, as they normally do, and mate. The females, however, are full of the virus and crave blood for nourishment. Normal female mosquitoes will bite convenient hosts when they are about to mate or are already pregnant, which in our case, occurs rather quickly."

"The bonsai waterfall in the McMahon house," Bond said. "You planted the eggs inside the porous rocks, which were filled with water. The fountain's motor was disabled when we found it. The water was standing still . . ."

Tsukamoto nodded. "You are correct, Mister Bond. The fountain was delivered to their home as a gift, one week before the McMahon family reunion. The motor was fixed to fail so the water became stagnant. As I understand it, Shinji Fujimoto brought the fountain to the house. When the family informed him the next day that it didn't work, he promised his niece that he would collect it in a few days and return it to the store where he had bought it."

Aida continued. "So the device sat there in the house as the mosquito eggs hatched into larvae, which lived in the water inside the fountain. The larvae fed on food that we provided from a timed-release feeder. They formed into pupae and then became adult mosquitoes—all in seven days. It took another twenty-four to forty-eight hours for the adult mosquitoes' shells to harden, and by then they were, of course, very hungry for a blood meal. They flew out of the granite rocks and found their victims—the McMahons." Bond could hear the sound of a sob escape from Mayumi.

"So Shinji Fujimoto was working with you all along," Bond said. "Why did you kill him?"

"Because he was a fool but a briefly useful one. Fujimoto always felt that his brother Hideo short-changed him with regard to the company. When Hideo Fujimoto died and left CureLab to his daughter, Shinji felt betrayed. The Ryujin-kai recognised a potential ally in him, so he was easily bought."

Mayumi spoke up for the first time. "My great uncle was really responsible for killing my family? I don't believe it."

Yoshida's image reappeared on the screen as Tsukamoto explained, "He didn't know that the bonsai waterfall contained the mosquitoes. He was ordered to deliver the device to the family as a gift. It appears that after they had died, Fujimoto realised what he had done to his niece and her family. He attempted to cover his tracks and obliterate evidence, the fool. He only succeeded in throwing more suspicion to our organisation. Shinji Fujimoto was a nuisance. He was eliminated after he sold his CureLab stock to Yonai."

Now it was clear to Bond. He said, "So the yakuza hoodlums in London, the ones who tried to take Kyoko McMahon's body from the mortuary—they were hired by Shinji Fujimoto. And the arsonists in Tokyo were paid to destroy the bodies of Peter McMahon, his wife and eldest daughter."

Tsukamoto said, "That was all Fujimoto's doing and had nothing to do with us. He was an idiot. We only needed him in the short term. There was another person from CureLab who was cooperating with us, someone who was providing us with everything we needed to instigate our plan."

"Then why was the merger necessary?" Bond asked. "It sounds as if you already had the technology you needed."

"The merger simply solidified our possession of the technology. We did not want to rely on the continuing co-operation or trust the discretion of the insider."

"And are you going to tell us who that was?"

"I don't think so." Tsukamoto grinned.

"Why was Kenji Umeki killed?" Bond asked. Mayumi gasped. Another shock.

Tsukamoto answered, "That was entirely unrelated to our business here. Umeki-san was about to reveal the girl's whereabouts to the authorities. He could not be trusted."

"What difference did it make if they knew where I was?" Mayumi asked. "I wasn't going anywhere. You wouldn't let me leave. After all, I was working for you," she said bitterly.

"Once all of this began, we realised that you were a

valuable pawn—and a dangerous one. We couldn't afford to let the authorities find you before the project was finished. You were supposed to have been killed."

"And just what is the project?" Bond asked. "You have your killer mosquitoes. What do you intend to do with them?"

Yoshida was relishing every minute of this game he was playing. He asked, "What is it, Mr. Bond, that is classified about your assignment in Japan? Why are you here?"

"Why don't *you* tell *me*? You seem to know more about my movements than I know myself." But Bond knew what he was going to say.

"Come, come, Mr. Bond. The G8 summit conference. It's in three days. I don't think I'll go into any detail at this juncture, but you can assume that several world leaders are about to issue their last press statements."

"You're mad, Yoshida," Bond said. "You're going to kill your own people! Japan is a G8 country."

"The Japanese who are cooperating with Western countries deserve to die. Japan needs to remain pure. To retain the former glory that she once enjoyed, we must hold our noses and swallow our medicine. As the great poet and novelist Yukio Mishima wrote, 'Glory, as anyone knows, is bitter stuff.' "

"It will accomplish nothing, Yoshida," Bond said.

"On the contrary," Yoshida said. "The G8 conference is only the beginning. My message will be delivered far beyond the boundaries of Japan. And this morning we have had a technological breakthrough. Aida, please tell Mr. Bond what we are now able to do."

Aida smiled smugly and said, "Transovarial transmission. We have successfully engineered the mosquitoes to pass on the virus to their eggs. This version of our kamikaze insects will mate with zeal upon maturing. Before the adults die, the females will lay eggs, out of which will emerge more infected mosquitoes."

"That's crazy!" Bond spat.

Yoshida chuckled. "A little payback for the Great War in the Pacific, wouldn't you say? Tsukamoto!"

"Hai!"

Yoshida's eyes betrayed the madness behind them. His evil stare travelled through the hundreds of miles of the telecommunication system's fibre optics and clutched Bond and Mayumi's souls. They both felt a shiver run down their spines as he said, "Place them in the mosquito tank. Let them experience first hand the fruits of our work."

24

Earth's Heartbeat

When Bond had struggled with the guard for possession of the Palm Pilot, he had deftly managed to activate the timer for the built-in explosive. The problem was that he didn't know exactly how long he had set it for. He had manipulated the device with his fingers, feeling for the correct buttons while at the same time pulling on the Palm to keep it out of the guard's hands.

Tsukamoto walked away from the centre of the room and was standing by the door. He pressed a button and the door slid open. Aida had remained close to the two guards, while the technicians who had elected to remain in the lab to watch the goings-on stayed at their workstations. The teleconference link was maintained so that Yoshida could view the festivities. Both guards pointed their guns at the captives and gestured towards the air lock attached to the chamber full of mosquitoes. Bond eyed the Uzi and calculated the odds of jumping the man but ultimately decided that it wouldn't work. Before Bond could wrestle the Uzi away from the guard, the other man would have shot him and probably Mayumi as well.

"Open the outer door," Aida ordered.

A technician flipped a switch and the door to the air

lock opened with a *swish*. One of the guards jabbed the barrel of his rifle into Bond's back.

"James-san?" Mayumi asked. Her eyes were full of fear.

"It will be all right," he whispered. "We'll go together."

She finally went into the cubicle with Bond right behind her.

"Close the outer door," Aida commanded.

The technician obeyed the order—the door shut and locked. Bond and Mayumi were standing in the no-man's-land of the air lock. For the moment, they were safe.

"I have yet to see how my mosquitoes will feed upon human beings," Aida said. "So far we have used only laboratory animals for testing purposes. This will be a treat." As a smile played upon his lips, Aida commanded, "Open the inner door."

The technician reached for the control but at that moment the Palm Pilot exploded with such force that he was knocked off of his chair. Three other technicians were thrown across the floor and one of the guards was engulfed by the blast. Tsukamoto ducked out of the room and shut the laboratory door.

Bond and Mayumi were unharmed. The reinforced door had protected them from the explosion, but the glass had cracked. In fact, the lock mechanism was disabled. When Bond kicked it, the door opened and he ran to the guard who had dropped the Uzi. He was blinded, screaming in pain. Bond picked up the Uzi and used the butt to put the man out of his misery.

Bond felt a bullet fly past him, frighteningly close to his face. He turned and saw Aida crouching behind a workstation, pointing a handgun at him. Bond directed the Uzi at that end of the room and let loose with a barrage of firepower. The bullets hit the computers, creating bright eruptions of electrical discharges all over the machines. Aida, his body riddled with holes, screamed and fell to the floor. The technicians who were left alive crouched behind what cover they could find and raised their hands in terror. Bond swept the room with the gun and determined that there was no longer a serious threat.

Bond held out his hand for Mayumi. "Come on," he said. Wide-eyed, she stepped out of the chamber and clasped his hand tightly.

They went to the destroyed table that had held their weapons. It was such a mess that Bond couldn't find any trace of their guns.

"Well, that's two Walthers I've lost on this trip," he said.

He did find the smashed DoCoMo phone in the rubble and picked it up. "It's probably useless, but you never know," he said, putting it in his pocket.

The alarms in the building rang out.

"Let's get the hell out of here!"

Bond ran to the door and slapped a button. The door slid open and he stepped into the corridor. Two more guards were rushing at him with handguns drawn. Bond dispatched them with the Uzi and then gestured for Mayumi.

"Coast clear, let's go!"

They ran down the hall towards the offices and the employee entrance at the back of the building. Another guard appeared at the T intersection and Bond blasted him before the man could raise his gun.

They made it to the back door with no further hindrance. Bond punched the button on the wall, and the door unlocked.

"James!"

Bullets exploded around their heads. Bond grabbed Mayumi and pulled her to the floor. Then, on his side, he fired the Uzi at the guards who had just appeared at the opposite end of the hall. They jumped, taking cover around the corner. Bond reached up and opened the door.

"Stay down!" he cried.

They both rolled out of the door. Bond slammed it shut and helped Mayumi stand. "Are you hit?"

"No." She was panting.

"We have to run. Can you make it?"

"Yes."

They ran across the dark car park and onto the dirt road, but more men had come out of the front of the building, circled around to the road and blocked their escape. Bond attempted to fire at them and found that the Uzi was out of ammunition. He tossed it behind him.

"Into the woods!" Bond led her through the trees, off the main path and into the pitch-black forest. They couldn't see a thing. Gunfire erupted around them, but they had the satisfaction of knowing that the guards couldn't see them either.

Then Mayumi tripped over an exposed tree root and cried as she fell hard. Bond stopped to help her up. "Hold my hand. We have to keep going," he said.

"I . . . I can't!" she gasped.

"You have to!"

More gunfire. Bark flew off of the trees around them. Mayumi struggled to her feet and began to run again at Bond's side.

They bolted through the forest, not knowing in what direction they were headed. They cared only about losing their pursuers and, after a while, it seemed that they had done so. Bond stopped and told Mayumi to be quiet so that he could listen to the sounds around them. In the distance, they heard shouts and some gunfire, but the noise seemed so far away that they might actually be safe.

They continued on, now treading carefully and quietly. The shouts of the guards seemed to fade farther in the distance.

"Where are we?" she whispered.

"I have no idea," Bond said. "Let's just keep going.

We'll come out of these woods eventually. We are still in Noboribetsu, or certainly on the outskirts."

He led her through the forest, but they couldn't help getting scraped and cut by branches and bushes that were too dark to notice. Every now and then Mayumi made a sharp exclamation of pain.

"I think there's a clearing ahead," Bond said. There were some lights glinting through the mass of foliage ahead of them. When they emerged, they found themselves on the main road that led back to the Dai-ichi Taki-motokan.

"You are a genius, James-san!" Mayumi said.

"Animal instinct," he said, wryly. "The wounded fox always finds its way home. Come on, let's hope our friends have given up." They started down the road just as the sound of engines could be heard coming towards them. Bond could see headlamps coming from the direction of the laboratory.

"Damn," he muttered. He took her hand and ran towards the hotel, but a Jeep that pulled out of nowhere blocked their way, some fifty metres ahead of them. Three men got out and gestured at them. One of them began shooting at them.

"Run!"

Bond and Mayumi bolted across the road and found themselves at the edge of the *Jigokudani,* the Valley of Hell. A sign made it perfectly clear that it was very dangerous to go farther. Large spotlights illuminated the area, accentuating the multitude of colours in the rocks and soil. Smoke billowed out of holes in the ground and small bubbling pools of sulphurous water dotted the landscape. Bond estimated that the entire valley was almost half a kilometre across.

"We haven't any choice. Come on!" Bond said, then climbed over the wooden fence that kept people out of the property.

"I'm not going in there!" Mayumi cried.

The continuing gunfire convinced her otherwise. She climbed over the fence and took Bond's hand.

"Tread carefully!" he warned. They stepped gingerly onto the ashen rock. A piece of it gave way under Mayumi's foot.

"Oww, that's hot!" she cried.

"Try to stay off the white rocks. They're fragile," Bond said.

As they zigzagged their way across the alien landscape, the stench of the sulphur made breathing ragged and difficult. They could also hear a faint, deep beating coming from the ground, as if someone were hitting a drum. Bond realised after a few minutes that it was the sound of water squirting out of the holes.

"It's the earth's heartbeat," Mayumi said. She had read his mind.

They heard shouts behind them. Two guards had jumped the fence and were now running recklessly in their direction.

"Don't look back, just keep going!" Bond said.

The heat was intense and almost unbearable. Every now and then Bond stepped on a blazing hot rock. He would curse, quickly spring off it and keep going, directing Mayumi away from the worst places. They eventually came to a wooden wishing well. A planked bridge led from it up to the pedestrian walkway that encircled the valley. Unfortunately, the guards had taken that route and were headed their way.

Bond pulled Mayumi down behind the well. The smoke issuing from the rocks around them was fierce, and they found it difficult to breathe. He held his finger to his lips to quiet her and waited until he heard the guard's boots on the walkway near the well.

Wait for it . . . a bit closer . . .

Bond leapt up and grabbed the man. The guard

shouted, but Bond managed to hit him hard, knocking him over the rail and into the well. His body fell into the bubbling, green boiling water. He screamed horribly as Bond grabbed Mayumi's hand and led her farther out into the valley. They were halfway across.

The remaining two guards stumbled along the rocks in pursuit, every now and then firing blindly at the dark figures who were at least fifty metres away. The floodlights illuminated the valley well enough to expose the spectacular colours and geysers, but they weren't sufficient to adequately light their targets. Bond used this to his advantage by moving in diagonal patterns and staying low.

They reached the top of a hill and Mayumi slowed, completely out of breath. "I must rest a second, please."

"We can't stop, Mayumi."

But she turned her ankle on a rock and stumbled, striking her bare forearm on the ground. She cried out in pain and immediately jumped to her feet, holding her arm. Even in the dim light, they could see that her skin was seared.

"Right," she said, "let's keep moving."

They rounded the hill just as they heard a guard scream. Bond turned to see that the man had stepped onto one of the fragile ashen rocks. It had collapsed and he had fallen into a pit of blazing hot stones.

They moved on, finally out of Hell Valley and on to a steep hill. He couldn't hear any gunshots or shouts behind him, so when they got to the top of the hill he stopped to scan the landscape.

"Do you think we lost them?" she asked.

"Let's hope so," Bond said. "Come on, let's keep going this way. I want to put as much distance as possible between us and them before we stop to rest."

She sighed and followed him without complaining. She limped a little, not only because of the twisted ankle she had experienced a few minutes ago, but also because the gash in her calf was throbbing. Mayumi wondered if her stitches had loosened.

As they came over the hill, they saw a paved road at the bottom. Beyond that was an empty car park next to a small lake surrounded by a fence. The unusual thing about the lake was that it was emitting smoke.

"That's *Oyunuma*," Mayumi said. "It's always boiling. Another tourist attraction, like *Jigokudani*."

"Remind me to buy a postcard," was all that Bond could say.

They made their way down to the edge of it. Even though it was very dark, Bond could see that the pond's sickly, greenish surface was bubbling violently and producing an immense amount of steam. They could feel its heat from where they were standing.

"I can't go on," Mayumi said as she walked to a bench that was situated on a platform built near the pond. This time, Bond could see that she had no choice but to rest.

"At least we know the road goes back to Noboribetsu," she panted. "We're not lost."

Bond removed the mobile from his pocket and shook it. It rattled, useless. "So much for calling a taxi," Bond observed.

"You may have spoken too soon, James-san. Look."

She pointed to the end of the road. Headlamps came around the bend and headed towards the car park.

"Quick, hide!" he said as he pulled her behind the bench. He peered around to watch the vehicle approaching. Was there an available escape route? The only way out was back up the hill, but that was in full view of the car park. The boiling lake was behind them. They were trapped.

Once it was close enough, Bond saw that it was a Mazda Bongo Friendy, a conventional minivan with a camper pop-up roof. Not a typical yakuza mode of transportation.

Bond watched as it pulled to the edge of the car park and stopped. The driver got out and shone a torch over the area. There was something familiar about the figure.

It was Ikuo Yamamaru, his arm in a sling.

Bond jumped up and called to him. The Ainu jerked his head around.

"Bond-san!" he called. "I have been searching for you!"

"I should have guessed from that tin can of a car that it was you," Bond said. "We're very glad to see you."

"The homing device in your mobile led me to you," Ikuo said. "It works like a charm."

"I thought the damned thing was demolished."

Ikuo chuckled. "The police band has been going crazy. I heard someone ran across *Jigokudani*! Was that you?"

"I'm afraid so."

"Are you mad? You could have been killed!"

"We had no choice. Don't worry, we're all right. Just lightly char-grilled."

"Quick, get in the car," Ikuo said. "Ryujin-kai are all over the place. They have every road covered that the police don't. This is going to be tricky."

They piled into the van and Ikuo got behind the wheel.

"How's the bullet wound?" Bond asked.

"They took some metal out of me," the Ainu said. "I was very lucky. It just damaged some muscle. It didn't hit my collarbone or anything else important. I have to wear this sling for a few days, though."

Ikuo pulled out of the car park and got on the main road.

"Do you see the mobile mounted on the side there?" Ikuo asked Bond.

"Yes."

"Take it and punch Memory Zero."

Bond did as he was told and held it to Ikuo's ear. When the other party answered, Ikuo spoke a language into the phone that was unfamiliar to Bond, but it was similar to Japanese. When Ikuo was finished, he listened and then replied affirmatively. The Ainu nodded at Bond, who lowered the mobile and shut it off.

"My friends are expecting us," the Ainu said, smiling broadly. "Now if we can just make it through town without being seen. All day long I think I have been watched. They may know my affiliation with you, Bond-san, so before nightfall I changed cars with a friend. I hope they're not looking for a van like this one."

He turned the van onto the main street through Noboribetsu and said, "Perhaps you should keep down."

Bond and Mayumi got on the floor of the van as they drove past the Dai-ichi Takimotokan. A black Mercedes and a motorcycle were idling on the other side of the street.

"Enemy spotted," Ikuo reported. "One Mercedes and a Kawasaki . . . uhm . . . what *is* that . . . ? Oh, it's a Z400FX! Huh. I haven't seen one of those in a long time. Looks like two men in the car."

When the van passed them, the yakuza reacted and pointed. The man on the Kawasaki burst away from the curb and rode close behind the van.

"I was afraid of that," Ikuo said. "We have been seen, Bond-san."

The tyres screeched and the van lurched forward. Ikuo looked in the rearview mirror and saw the Mercedes pull out and join the chase. The biker was gaining on them easily.

Hoping to divert them, Ikuo swerved off the road towards the statues of *oni* that guarded the edge of town. The King of Hell, angry and demonic, loomed over them as they circled the display. The Mercedes and biker were right behind, but Ikuo made a sudden swerve and doubled back with a screech. When the Mercedes attempted to do the same, it collided with the statue. The *oni* toppled, landing on the bonnet of the car. The biker pulled around the wreckage and stayed on the Mazda's tail, not easily shaken off.

"I'm sure those fellows in the Mercedes are radioing for backup," Bond said. "And we still have company behind us."

"See if you can get rid of him," Ikuo suggested.

"I've lost my gun," Bond said, looking back at the rider.

"Ah. Look under the seat."

Bond reached beneath and felt a cloth bag containing something very hard. He pulled the bag out, opened it and removed a shiny new Walther PPK.

"Don't tell me," he said. "It's from Tiger."

Ikuo grinned and concentrated on driving. Meanwhile Bond checked the firearm, loaded a magazine and then leaned out of the window. The Walther recoiled with a familiar jolt and the rider was knocked off of the motorcycle as if he had been kicked in the chest. The bike ran on and crashed into the trees on the side of the road.

"Nice work, Bond-san!" Ikuo said. "You got him on the first shot."

Bond sat and holstered the gun. "Many thanks, Ikuo. I felt naked without one."

"No problem. Look, here we are."

The van drove into a car park and stopped in front of a sky-lift station. The signs indicated that visitors were at "Bear Park." The place was closed, but Ikuo got out and told the others to follow him. The three of them ran to the building, where Ikuo unlocked the door with a set of keys he had in his pocket. Then they made their way to the sky-lift port area. A gondola hung in front of them, inert. Ikuo unlocked a control panel on the wall and flipped a few switches. The sky lift powered up and the gondolas began to move.

Ikuo ran to the next gondola and said, "Hurry! Get in!" The three of them jumped inside and sat just as the automatic doors closed. The gondola lifted and began to glide along the cable across a deep ravine. The vista was a vast forest of darkness. In the distance they could see the glittering surface of Lake Kuttara as a black but starry sky enveloped them.

When the gondola reached the other side, a trip that took five minutes, the automatic door opened and they stepped out. Three of Ikuo's Ainu friends were there to greet them. They chatted in their language for a moment and then Ikuo turned to Bond.

"Another Mercedes followed us here. They just got in the sky lift. My friends saw them on television monitors." He pointed to small black-and-white screens on the wall that displayed a view of the lower station.

"Shut it off when they're over the ravine," Bond said.

"I have a better idea," Ikuo said. "Come on."

They followed Ikuo and the other men into Bear Park, a theme park run by and featuring the culture of the Ainu people. It consisted primarily of a zoo filled with Hokkaido brown bears, a small museum and a quaint reproduction of a *kotan*, an ancient Ainu village.

Ikuo explained as they rushed into the dark and quiet preserve, "The Ainu believe that the bear is a god from heaven, come to bring us fur and meat." He pointed to the centre of his forehead. "The god lives in between the bear's eyes, right here."

Mayumi looked over a rail into a deep pit and saw dozens of dark shapes.

"Are those bears?" she asked a little too loudly. One of the animals growled at her ferociously, breaking the silence of the night air. This caused her to cry out, which woke up most of the other bears.

"Mayumi!" Bond urged.

"Sorry!" She followed him into a building, where a few other men were waiting. Ikuo greeted them and issued some instructions, opened the shades on the window and shut off the lights. From there they had a good view of the main path through the park. It was just as they had left it—silent and still. But after a moment, two figures came walking up the path from the sky lift port.

"They look like yakuza, all right," Bond said.

The two men nervously crept forward, looking all around as they walked.

"The Ainu keep the bears, raise them and take care of them," Ikuo whispered. "We perform sacred rituals with them and we use them to attract tourists. We also *train* some of them. Watch."

The two yakuza had their pistols out, ready to fire at anything that moved.

The roars came suddenly and were tremendously loud. Everyone in the control room jumped except for Ikuo.

The two adult Hokkaido brown bears stood upright, six feet away from them, and began to bellow at the two men. Paralysed with fear, they both dropped their guns. Then the bears lunged forward on all fours. The men turned and fled, screaming for their lives.

The bears followed them to the gondola port and finally could no longer be seen; only the roars could be heard in the distance.

"Maybe they'll get away, maybe they won't," Ikuo said. He switched to a different camera so that the port station was on the monitor. The men jumped into the frame and scrambled into a gondola. The bears could be seen at the edge of the screen, frustrated that they couldn't catch their prey. As the sky lift pulled away from the station, the animals meekly turned and ambled back to the village.

25
G8 Eve

Naoshima Island is located in the Inland Sea, south of Osaka and Kobe, about halfway to Hiroshima. Most people reach the island from Okayama by taking a train to Uno and then hopping aboard a ferry that spirits visitors to the island on a twenty-minute ride. In full view is the extraordinary Seto-Ohashi Bridge, which links Honshu with Shikoku, the smallest of Japan's four major land-masses. Benesse House, a luxury hotel on the southern tip of the island, adjoins the Naoshima Contemporary Art Museum. Works collected and exhibited by the museum are not confined to the inside of the building but are also dispersed through its grounds, creating a superb contrast between nature and man-made art. Designed by world-renowned Japanese architect Tadao Ando, Benesse House is a symbiosis of nature, architecture and art striving to devise a space where people can reflect upon humanity. A perfect spot to hold a G8 summit conference.

James Bond arrived on the island the day after the escape from Noboribetsu. After a long and healing night's sleep at Ikuo's home in the Ainu village near Bear Park, Bond and Mayumi had flown back to Tokyo. By that time, Japan's National Police Agency, in a rare collaboration with the Koan-Chosa-Cho, had raided the Hokkaido Mosquito and Vector Control Centre and taken possession of the building and its contents. Everyone connected with the company was held for questioning. Simultaneously, the offices of CureLab Inc. in Tokyo were raided. By the end of the day, seventy-two people were under arrest. The merger with Yonai Enterprises was voided, and the authorities had launched an investigation into all of Yonai's business dealings.

Mayumi was ensconced at the Imperial Hotel with Bond in adjoining rooms until the morning of his departure. The plan was that she would stay there until after the summit conference and then she would face up to the legal wrangling over CureLab and the McMahon Estate. Before he had left the hotel, Mayumi made Bond promise that he would return in one piece and come back to see her.

"I hate to admit it, James-san," she had said, "but I like you. Just a little."

"Well, I like you too," Bond replied. He thought for a moment before adding, "You should try not to be so angry at the world. You're a lovely, clever girl and you don't need to be mixed up with deadbeats. You have a marvellous future ahead of you"—he smiled—"if you use your pretty little head."

"Don't patronise me."

"I'm serious. Look, I'll be away for two days, three at the most. When I come back, I will help you as much as I can with all of this family business. I'm not an expert, but I believe the lawyers are going to try to prove that the merger was illegal as it was done without your consent as the major shareholder and the power of attorney was a forgery. You will be meeting with lawyers over the next two days. Pay attention and consider everything they have to say."

Before he had left, she put her arms around him and

kissed him, then abruptly turned and went back to her room.

Bond's flight out of Tokyo flew southwest over magnificent Mount Fuji to Okayama, where a company car met him and took him to the small port town of Uno. There, he caught the ferry to the island, where Tanaka greeted him at the dock.

"Bondo-san, I am so happy to see you," Tiger said, giving him a warm embrace. "I see that you have survived your adventures in Hokkaido and are no wear for worse."

"Tiger, you're picking up too many Western colloquialisms," Bond said. "It's 'worse for wear.' "

"Whatever. Come, let's go to the site."

They got into a chauffeur-driven Toyota Celsior that had been provided by Benesse House's president for Tanaka's exclusive use. It was well equipped, complete with a bar, telephone and a television in the backseat.

To get from the ferry port to Benesse House, the car had to pass through Naoshima Cultural Village. Tiger pointed out items of interest along the way, including the recently built Town Hall and several traditional Japanese "homes" that were in fact works of art. Tanaka explained that the interiors of the homes contained multimedia pieces designed by Tadao Ando in collaboration with artists from other countries. In essence, the houses themselves became the art.

"Naoshima means 'honesty island.' The inhabitants of the island still live simply," Tiger said as they drove out of the village. "Much of the island is owned by Mitsubishi Materiel, and they run copper and gold factories that employ practically everyone."

The car soon entered the section of the island that had been purchased by Benesse Corporation and had been renamed Benesse Island. They went through the gates and drove up a steep hill to a magnificent modern building made of marble, concrete and steel. Benesse House was

designed to incorporate the three basic geometric shapes—
a square, a circle and a triangle—in an impressive, imposing structure that faced the Inland Sea. Farther up the
hill was the Annex, connected to the main house by monorail. The Annex contained more luxury hotel rooms surrounding a unique, continuously flowing "flat" fountain.
Bond was immediately taken with the place, not only
because of his appreciation for inventive architecture, but
for its serene and peaceful ambience, which was palpable
as soon as they got out of the car.

Tanaka accompanied Bond as he checked in and then
proceeded to show him around the building. There was already a flurry of activity. Amongst the caterers, Tanaka's
staff of twenty men from the Koan-Chosa-Cho was busy
making sure that the building was secure.

They walked through the first large gallery in the museum, which was cylindrical in shape and three storeys
tall. An inclined ramp circled the outer edge of the room,
allowing visitors to walk up to the other floors and still
view the artwork in the gallery. The main piece exhibited
there was a unique multimedia sculpture designed by
Bruce Nauman called *100 Live and Die*. It consisted of
one hundred idiomatic expressions written in neon light
that combined common human states, moods (sick, well,
fear, black, red) or activities (eat, touch, play, cry, love) with
the phrases "and live" or "and die." Phrases—"speak
and live," "smile and die," "think and live," "love and
die"—flashed randomly on and off, creating a collage of
contemplative ideas.

They continued into the large gallery on the basement
floor that extended upwards by staircase into the ground
floor. The staff were setting up tables for the conference
alongside the pieces of art that adorned the walls and occupied space on the floor.

"The opening breakfast reception will be held in here,"
Tanaka explained. "It's the largest room in the building, so

there is enough space to sit and eat or walk around and mingle. The more intense meetings will take place in the conference rooms upstairs on the first floor."

Tanaka got everyone's attention. "For those of you who have not met him, this is James Bond, a member of British Intelligence. He is to be my deputy in command during the conference. He is also my very good friend. Should he ask for anything, I expect you to oblige him to the best of your ability."

They all shouted, *"Hai!"* and bowed deeply to Bond.

A young man approached them and Tanaka said, "Bondo-san, I am pleased to introduce my personal assistant, Yoshi Nakayama. If ever you need something and cannot find me, please ask Nakayama."

Nakayama bowed and then shook Bond's hand.

The men returned to work, and Bond stood back to survey the gallery. It was a long, rectangular room with a staircase on one side that allowed visitors to go from the basement level to the ground floor. Sculptures and artwork adorned the walls. The far end of the room was made of plate glass windows that opened to the outside, where two marble sculptures were displayed in a concrete pit that could be viewed from the ground above or from below within the museum. The pieces in the pit were flat, smooth blobs of polished marble that gave the impression that they had been dropped from the sky. The entire display was designed by Kan Yasuda and was called *The Secret of the Sky*. Other artists represented in the gallery included Jackson Pollock, Andy Warhol, David Hockney, Frank Stella, Yukinori Yanagi and Alberto Giacometti.

A large anatomically correct plaster heart, complete with aortas and ventricles, dominated the centre of the room. It was exquisitely painted and sat on a pedestal that was electrically powered so that the object could rotate when it was turned on. What was particularly unusual was that a large stake pierced it at an angle. The heart was about six feet in diameter. Entitled *Love Hurts,* it was created by an artist named William Kanas and was part of a new temporary exhibit of sensational, controversial works by young British artists. Bond recognised the styles of some of them, like the one with six pieces of a llama suspended in formaldehyde solution in six separate tanks.

"Some of this stuff was brought in specially for the conference," Tanaka explained. "All of the flowers, the plants . . . The hotel management told me that the decorations were delivered a week ago by a florist and interior design firm that they always use. We have potted them up and checked the earth. We also made sure that the florist and design firm checks out."

Bond indicated the bonsai waterfall devices that had been lined up in a crate at the side of the room.

"Well, I don't like those things," he said. "We know about those."

"You are right. We are getting rid of them. We will smash them to pieces and burn the remains. We don't want anything in here to contain mosquito eggs."

Tanaka issued some orders to his men, who immediately began removing the crates from the gallery.

"What about all these pieces of art?" Bond asked. "Granted that might be too generous a description for some of it."

Tanaka sucked air through his teeth. "Much of it is part of a new exhibition that was brought in three days ago. That big heart, those weird things over there, they're all part of a touring private collection. The curators will not allow us to touch them or remove them. We've checked them out against insurance documents and catalogue details."

Bond frowned. "I'm not happy about that."

"Nor I. But there's nothing we can do about it. The insurance costs for the pieces are astronomical."

"Who owns the collection?"

"A wealthy Japanese patron of the arts who has a long association with Benesse, who insist he's OK."

Bond nodded and moved on. "What about pesticides? Do we have mosquito repellent?"

Again, Tiger inhaled through his teeth and replied, "Management of the museum would not allow us to use it. I did not want to alarm them by going into too much detail about what we were looking for, and they have forbidden the use of pesticides in here. But we have some other tricks up our sleeves."

Bond began to walk slowly around the room, inspecting the flowerpots and planters. They were filled with rich soil and contained all manner of exotic Japanese plants and flowers. He wasn't familiar with some of the species, but he recognised blue, plum, and white-coloured irises that originated in the Far East, as well as a variety of red and white lotus flowers.

Bond continued walking and took a look at the tables and settings. He examined the entrances and exits. A large object covered with a tablecloth was set to the side of the room.

"What's under here?" he asked.

"Ah, Bondo-san, that is our secret weapon. I will tell you about it later."

"In that case, Tiger, I'm afraid that I'm going to be superfluous and will be bored to death at this conference. You have everything under control," he said.

Tiger laughed. "Come, let's go see your room."

By late afternoon, delegates from the G8 countries began to arrive by helicopter from Osaka. Helicopters landed on the temporary wood and brick helipad that had been built on a clearing near the beach.

James Bond was assigned to watch over the arrivals, greet the delegates and send them on their way to Benesse House in specially hired cars. Bond met each of the representatives from the eight members of G8: the United States (the president himself had decided to attend), Britain (the prime minister, whom Bond already knew), Japan, Canada, France, Italy, Germany and the newest member, Russia. As was always the case with G8 summit conferences, one additional representative from the European community joined the meeting: in this instance the delegate was from Spain. Each representative brought along an entourage of aides and bodyguards so the hotel was at complete capacity.

The conference was to begin in the morning with a breakfast reception and an address by Benesse Corporation's president. The meetings were to proceed following that and would continue for two days. Bond wasn't privy to what was being discussed at the conference, and he frankly didn't care. His only concern was to make sure that everyone remained safe and healthy. As M had put it, this was a baby-sitting job, and such as it was, Bond was resolved to do it right.

That evening, he and Tanaka ate with some of the delegates in the restaurant. They were served a traditional *kaiseki* meal, but they both refrained from having sake since they were on duty. Bond was on the alert, so he ate very little. He was watching everyone in the room, looking for the slightest hint of something out of the ordinary. It was all going too smoothly. From what he had seen in Noboribetsu, he knew that the Ryujin-kai were clever. If they wanted to infiltrate this thing, then they would find a way to do so. But the hotel and restaurant staff had been thoroughly vetted, all vendors who had come and gone had been checked out, and the respective governments had verified the backgrounds of every man and woman on the guest list. Everything really did seem to be in order.

Bond noticed that Tanaka was breathing heavily and had a pained look on his face.

"Are you all right, Tiger?" he asked.

Tanaka nodded and held a hand to his chest. "Heart-burn. It will pass in a little while."

"When's the last time you saw your doctor?"

"Just before you arrived in Japan. Do not worry, Bondo-san. I know the difference between heartburn and a heart attack. What is the saying? I am a shell of my for-mer self. But as long as the brain still functions properly, I don't mind."

Tanaka held up his glass of water and waited for Bond to do the same. He then clinked the glasses together and said, *"Kampai."*

At three o'clock in the morning, the delegates were asleep, the building was completely silent and the night guard made his rounds throughout Benesse House for the fifth time that night. He started in the basement's main gallery, where the reception would be held in just a few hours.

Walking up and down the aisles formed by the cloth-covered tables and planters, he focused the beam of his torch over every object and surface. Nothing appeared to be amiss. He made a notation in his logbook, then climbed the stairs to the first floor. He would return in one hour to repeat the process.

The first indication that the gallery was not completely vacant was the slight scraping noise that came from the plaster heart in the centre of the gallery. An astute listener might have recognised the sound as the unscrewing of a panel from the inside of the hollow object, but no one was around to hear it.

The heart appeared seamless but in fact it was made of several panels that had been fitted and fastened together from the inside. Very slowly and quietly, one panel was removed and placed inside the object. After a moment, two small legs popped out of the opening, followed by the trunk, arms, and head of Junji Kon, the killer dwarf known as Kappa.

He had spent the last four days inside the heart, but he was used to confined quarters. He was equipped with everything he could possibly need: food, water, a portable toilet, even reading material and a light and the all-important clock. The inwardly curved bottom of the sphere was lined with cushions that a normal-sized man might find uncomfortable to sleep on, but it was perfect for one the size of Kappa.

The Koan-Chosa-Cho knew that the heart was owned by a wealthy patron of the arts. What they and the staff at Benesse House didn't know was that the collector was Yasutake Tsukamoto's *Saiko-komon,* or advisor, the equivalent of the Italian mafia's *consigliere.* The *Saiko-komon* had used his influence to dictate how the heart was built and delivered to Naoshima Island. Kappa was installed in the finished work of art and it was brought to the island in one piece. It only had to be fitted on its pedestal once it was inside the museum.

Kappa emerged from his lair, reached back inside and removed a case that he placed on the floor. He opened it and revealed a number of glass mosquito canisters exactly like the one he had used on the *Cassiopeia.* Each container had a timed hinge and was filled with water and recently hatched mosquitoes. The insects had been developing for a week, had become adults and would have dry shells within a few hours.

Diligently and meticulously, Kappa went around the room and, using his trowel, dug holes in the flowerpots and planters. He then buried one canister in the soil of each stationary pot and planter so that the containers were spread out over the entire room. When he was finished, he went back over his handiwork to make sure that the soil was flattened and did not appear to have been disturbed.

Glancing at his clock, Kappa saw that he had a little

more time before the guard returned. It felt good to be out of that heart for a while! He reached inside, pulled a raw cucumber out of a plastic bag and began to munch it. After he had eaten half of it, Kappa set the remains on the heart's pedestal and then proceeded to stretch his short legs, perform lifts on his toes and reach for the ceiling to exercise his back. He was about to repeat the regimen when he heard a door creak somewhere nearby, alerting him to the guard's imminent return. Carefully picking up his tools, Kappa crawled back inside the heart and replaced the panel. When it was screwed on tightly, he settled onto his cushions and went to sleep.

26
Red Widow Dawn

The dawn brought a beautiful clear day, although the forecast predicted that the temperature would rise considerably. Alone in his room, Bond was already feeling the heat and it was not yet seven o'clock.

The outfit that Tiger had provided him with was not exactly summer wear, either. Beneath his three-piece Ozwald Boateng suit Bond wore something that had been made exclusively for the situation at hand. Patterned after the full-bodied ninja suits, the garment was worn underneath the outer clothes like a complete body stocking and had extensions that could be rolled out to cover hands and head. In case of a mosquito attack, Bond could quickly protect his exposed skin. It wasn't foolproof, but it was better than nothing.

He took a moment in front of the mirror, examining his hard face. The scars and scabs from the beating were still present but looked much better. Nevertheless, Bond noticed that many of the people he had met the day before were nervous in his presence. Perhaps that was a bonus.

Zero hour!

Bond made sure that his headset was working, and then he left his room. He took the monorail down the hill to the main building, made his way down the stairs and into the main gallery, where Tanaka, Nakayama and the other men were already busy with last-minute preparations.

"Bondo-san, *ohayo gozaimasu*!" Tanaka said warmly. "Are you ready for another day of international espionage and combating terrorism?"

Bond laughed. "*Ohayo gozaimasu* to you too."

"This line of work beats going to an office every day, does it not?"

"Office or not, I've clocked on," Bond replied. "Are we on time?"

"Everything begins in an hour. So far everything is on schedule."

Bond squinted at his friend and said, "Tiger, you still look a little pale."

Tanaka frowned, rubbed his chest and said, "Do not worry, Bondo-san, I am all right. It's probably just nerves."

Bond nodded and then turned to inspect the room. He walked along the perimeter, paying special attention to the plants and flowers. He noted that the plaster heart was rotating on its pedestal, the motor emitting a low hum. The tables looked immaculate, as they were now dressed with fine china, chopsticks and silverware for those guests who were unaccustomed to using the sticks. Satisfied that Tanaka's men knew what they were doing, Bond stood out of the way beside three standing figures that were a part of the museum's permanent art collection. They were painted, flat silhouettes of men with mechanized jaws that moved up and down. The piece was appropriately named "Three Chattering Men." Bond surveyed the entire room one more time from this vantage point and then went to check on the British contingent to the conference.

By eight-fifteen the room was packed with people. The main delegates sat at the head table with Benesse Corporation's president, Soichiro Fukutake. Bodyguards stood behind the table looking particularly conspicuous while attempting to be the opposite. The aides and other conference attendees filled the other tables. Breakfast was part-Japanese, part-Western to accommodate everyone's tastes. Glasses of orange juice and champagne were served for toasting purposes and that duty was handled graciously by Mr. Fukutake, who welcomed the delegates to his museum and hotel. While people ate, conversation was lively and animated throughout the room. None of the guests had been informed of the possible terrorist threat. It had been decided early on that it was unnecessary to alarm anyone unless the Koan-Chosa-Cho had evidence of something concrete. Tanaka had made the decision to keep a low profile for the time being.

Bond, Tanaka and the other secret service men patrolled the perimeter of the room, keeping an eye out for anything unusual. Tanaka positioned himself near the plate glass window looking out at the pit containing the marble "Secret of the Sky" sculptures. He happened to glance at the planter full of lovely white irises that was sitting beside him.

Was the soil *moving*?

Tanaka leaned over to examine the dirt more closely. It *was* moving! Something was buried beneath the soil and was attempting to dig out, like a mole might do. *It was some kind of trap door—no, the lid of a jar,* Tanaka thought.

Then, the hinged top of the glass container opened fully, knocking aside the soil that was on top of it. Tanaka was horrified to see a swarm of mosquitoes fly out of the container and into the air.

He spoke into his headset, "Alert! Alert! There is—" but he found it difficult to continue speaking. He was seized with a sudden, sharp and excruciating pain in his left arm and chest.

No! he thought. *Not again!*

The iron crab clutched at his heart, paralysing him, squeezing the breath out of his lungs. He broke out in a sweat and the lights dimmed to black. He stumbled backwards and tried to catch something to hold on to, but it was useless.

He didn't feel the floor when he crashed headlong onto it.

Bond saw Tanaka fall and spoke rapidly into his headset. "May Day, May Day, Tanaka is down!" He and three other agents rushed to the end of the room and knelt beside the unconscious man.

"Call for medical help," Bond ordered Nakayama. "Quickly!"

The delegates and other personnel stopped chattering and craned their heads to see what was happening. Bond stood and addressed them.

"No cause for alarm," he said. "It appears we have a man with a heart condition. We have sent for help. Please, there is no cause for alarm."

Fukutake approached Bond and said that the helicopter was on its way. It would take Tanaka to Okayama immediately. After a moment, four members from the emergency medical team that was stationed outside the building entered with a stretcher. They spent a few minutes on the floor with Tanaka, trying to revive him but they quickly realised that they would do better in the ambulance. They capably loaded him onto the stretcher and carried it outside. Bond watched from the front door as his friend was loaded into the vehicle. Before long it sped away toward the beach and the helipad.

"You are in charge now, Bond-san," said Nakayama who was standing behind him. "This was Tanaka-san's order." Distracted, Bond nodded and turned to rejoin the breakfast meeting in the main gallery.

The commotion had served to distract everyone in the

room from what was happening around them. Operation Red Widow Dawn had commenced, silently and with meticulous timing. The rest of the mosquito containers had opened inside their respective planters and flowerpots, releasing the deadly insects into the air. No one noticed them at all; the insects were practically invisible, especially in the bright light of the morning sun that streamed in through the plate glass windows and the skylight.

Bond wiped his brow as he re-entered the room. He was concerned for his friend, but it was out of his hands; he had to hope and pray that the doctors could do enough.

Slap!

Bond whirled around to see one of the women from Italy with her hand on her bare arm. She then looked at her palm and made a face.

Bond's heart skipped a beat. He snapped his head up, turning his gaze to the space above the guests' heads.

Another slap on skin, this time from the British prime minister's aide.

"Someone let in a mosquito," the man said casually.

"Get everyone out, now!" Bond called into the headset.

His eyes darted back and forth as he felt a rush of adrenaline. Were they in the room? Was it happening?

And then he saw them. Sure enough, dozens of mosquitoes were flying above the guests' heads, gliding lightly and delicately and looking for targets on which to land.

The bodyguards and aides leapt into action. "Ladies and gentlemen, please come this way. Do not panic!" Nakayama called out. An evacuation had been rehearsed among Tanaka's staff and therefore was initiated smoothly and efficiently. The delegates, not at all sure what was going on, rose from their seats and began to file out of the room in an orderly fashion.

The prime minister addressed Bond, saying, "Double-O Seven, would you mind telling me what is happening?"

"Please, sir, just get out of the room," Bond said, his eyes still searching the space above their heads. "Nakayama-san, please make sure that door doesn't stay open for too long," he ordered. The men at the door acknowledged him by closing it after three people went through, then opening it again for three more.

As the evacuation progressed, Bond unrolled the extra pieces of his undersuit, put on gloves and unfolded the mask and hood that neatly covered his head. He reached into his pocket and pulled out goggles to wear. They were specially tinted to highlight objects that were in front of a light background. Once the goggles were in place, he could see the insects much more clearly. They were coming out of the planters!

Bond ran to the covered object in the corner of the room. He pulled off the cloth, exposing the strange contraption.

It was a Mosquito Magnet, a device originally created in America but adapted by the Japanese. It resembled the type of professional hair dryer that was found in a salon, only there was no chair. The device is commonly used by vector control organisations to attract and blow mosquitoes into a collection container so that their population density can be tested for viruses. Its operation is simple enough — a warm, moist carbon dioxide plume is produced from propane gas to attract the bloodsucking insects. Mosquitoes are naturally attracted to carbon dioxide, as well as to body heat and other chemicals present in the breath of warm-blooded hosts. As they approach the source, they are vacuumed into a net where they dehydrate and die. It is powerful enough to be effective outdoors in an area the size of nearly an acre.

As soon as Bond flipped the switch on, he could see many of the insects change their flight plan and head towards it. He watched in amazement as the mosquitoes flew straight into the container; they were trapped and had no escape route.

Another item sat on the floor next to the Mosquito Magnet—a large metal bucket full of machine oil, something that would come into play shortly.

Bond checked on the progress of the evacuation and was relieved to see that nearly everyone was out of the gallery. "Nakayama-san, after you have the conference attendees safely outside, get all of your men out. I don't want to take the chance of anyone getting bitten."

"Bond-san, some of us should stay and help you," Nakayama replied through the headset.

"That's an order, Nakayama-san."

"Hai!"

Bond immediately began to move from planter to planter, removing the glass containers from the soil. After he gathered an armful of them, he then went back to the table and dropped them into the bucket of oil, thereby immediately killing any remaining pupae and eggs. He continued this procedure until he had gone completely around the gallery.

Next he went back to the Mosquito Magnet to check on its progress. There were dozens of mosquitoes trapped in the can. He scanned the air around him and noted that there were a few insects still flying. He rotated the machine so that it faced towards the centre of the room and waited until he could see that more of the mosquitoes were gravitating towards the fan. Bond tapped his headset and said, "Nakayama-san, I think I've done all that I can do in here. I'm coming out. Let's seal the room and wait a while. These bugs will either be caught in the trap or they'll die in a few hours. I just hope that none got out of the gallery."

"Me too, Bond-san."

"How are things out there?"

"Fine. Some of the delegates are demanding to know what has happened and why they weren't told about it beforehand."

"I'll let your government handle that one."

"I believe that three people were bitten," Nakayama said. "A bodyguard for the German diplomat, an Italian woman and an aide to the British Prime Minister."

"Bad luck. Perhaps if we get them to the hospital before symptoms occur, they might have a chance."

"They're on their way."

Bond moved away from the table and walked past the plaster heart in the centre of the room. He reached down to switch off the rotation motor and noticed something peculiar.

Half a raw cucumber was lying on the edge of the pedestal.

Bond picked it up and studied it. Why were alarm bells going off in his head?

Then he remembered.

He turned his attention to the plaster heart and tapped it. Hearing the hollow sound was the catalyst that he needed. Bond picked up a chair and swung it as hard as he could at the heart, shattering its shell. He struck the object again, this time enlarging the hole he had made. He kept at it, striking the heart as if it were a Mexican *piñata*. But no sweets or prizes fell out of the object when he was done — there was just a big hole.

Could his hunch have been wrong?

He carefully moved closer to the heart so that he could peer inside.

Nothing.

Kappa leaped out of the object, grabbed hold of Bond's upper body and wrestled him to the floor. Bond grappled with the dwarf and felt a sharp pain on his left shoulder. Kappa held a Balisong and had managed to slash through Bond's suit and cut him. Bond put all of his energy into blocking the dwarf's jabs, but the assassin was fast and stronger than he looked. Bond didn't want a repeat of what had happened in the Seikan Tunnel, so he locked both of his hands on Kappa's wrist. He dug his thumbs *hard* into the soft spot, causing the dwarf to yelp in pain and drop the butterfly knife. Bond let go of the wrist and backhanded the killer with a sharp, surprising blow that knocked Kappa completely off of him and onto the floor.

The dwarf used his uncanny ability to bounce back to his feet, but instead of attacking Bond, he ran toward the exit. By the time Bond had got up, the dwarf was already at the door that led into the circular gallery at the front of the museum. Bond chased him into it but when he got there, the dwarf was nowhere to be seen.

Damn! The trickster had used his freakish skill to hide.

"Nakayama-san," he said into his headset. "Be on the lookout for a dwarf."

"A dwarf?" Nakayama asked.

The "100 Live and Die" sculpture blinked randomly at Bond . . . *Speak and Die . . . Kill and Live . . . Stand and Die . . . Sick and Live . . . Yellow and Die . . . Smell and Live . . .*

The stone staircase curved around the room to the top floor. The dwarf couldn't have made it up that far. Nakayama and his men were beyond the front entrance and reception area, so the killer couldn't have gone that way either. There was only one place he could be.

Bond stepped around the sculpture and pulled his enemy up by the neck. He slammed Kappa against the stone wall and clutched his throat, holding him several feet off the ground.

"Please!" Kappa choked, his voice a high-pitched whine. "Spare my life . . . and I will tell you . . . our secrets!"

"Shut up," Bond spat. "You're going to answer for Reiko Tamura."

The dwarf could hardly breathe. "Wait!" he gasped. "There is a major . . . attack . . . in progress . . . on . . . the West . . ."

Bond loosened his grip—a little.

"This had better not be a trick."

"Spare me . . . please! I know where . . . Yoshida is . . . ! You . . . can . . . stop . . . Red . . . Widow . . . Dawn . . . !"

Bond was suddenly reminded of the folklore legend about the supernatural kappa. The creature supposedly had an honourable nature and would bargain for his life.

"Then talk." Bond relaxed his grip enough to allow the dwarf to speak clearly.

Kappa looked at him with surprise. "You are an honourable man, Bond-san. I will tell you what I know. Twenty men, carrying deadly mosquito eggs, are on their way to America. Some are travelling to the West Coast, some to the central states, and some to the East Coast. They will distribute the eggs in major cities. I can provide you with their exact destinations."

"How do you know this?"

"I am part of the Ryujin-kai's inner circle. There is one other thing that you should know."

"Go on."

"The mosquito eggs that they carry . . . they are different from these. The ones they have are samples of the new version—the mosquitoes that can pass the virus on to their own eggs"

Bond felt a flicker of fear.

Nakayama and several men ran into the room, guns drawn. Bond let the dwarf down and turned him over to them.

"Nakayama-san," he said. "Take him into a conference room, and fast. He has some things to tell us." Bond looked at Kappa and added, "And they had better not be folk tales."

27

Quick Response

After the discoveries at the Hokkaido Mosquito and Vector Control Centre were presented along with Junji Kon's statement to the Japanese government, the Koan-Chosa-Cho and the National Police Agency's report was taken seriously. A quick response was ordered against what was unanimously agreed to be a threat to Japan's national security, not to mention the rest of the world.

Kappa's statement claimed that Goro Yoshida's private army, with the help of the Ryujin-kai, was about to attack the United States with a biological weapon, namely the mutated, fast-acting West Nile disease, using genetically engineered mosquitoes capable of transferring the virus to their eggs. Twenty carriers had taken off from Tokyo that very morning on various flights that would arrive in the U.S. several hours later. Eight men were to arrive in Los Angeles, six men would be in Chicago shortly after that and the remaining six would land in New York. Each courier held dried mosquito eggs attached to ordinary laboratory filter paper hidden in a modest envelope inside a jacket pocket. Neither the eggs nor the filter paper were detectable by airport X ray. Since dried mosquito eggs could still hatch once they were soaked, they were the ideal conduits for smuggling a biological weapon into the country. Each carrier had a specific assignment that directed him to a public place with standing water present—a pond, a lake or a pool. The eggs would be released into the water where, during the course of about seven days, the deadly mosquitoes would hatch, bite hosts, lay eggs and die. The new eggs would hatch a week later and another swarm of mosquitoes would repeat the deadly cycle. In another week, a full-blown epidemic would be sweeping the country.

The Japanese decided to contact the American government immediately and at the same time turned the case over to the Japan Ground Self-Defence Force (JGSDF). Launching an air strike on what was essentially Russian territory was obviously a diplomatic challenge but clearly necessary. Goro Yoshida had shown that he had committed treason against Japan, had taken steps to attack the country and was an enemy to world peace. The Russian government, which may or may not have known that Yoshida had resided on the island of Etorofu for years, reluctantly gave Japan permission to bomb the terrorist camp, provided that the air force did not travel beyond the coordinates that Junji Kon had provided.

James Bond and Nakayama insisted on flying in one of the six combat helicopters that was to take part in the raid on the Kuril Islands. They sat in a Boeing CH-47J Chinook, a large chopper that transports personnel and vehicles. Accompanying them were three Bell AH-1S Huey Cobras, helicopters that were capable of antitank combat, and two Bell UH-1J Hueys, medium-sized choppers that carried personnel or equipment. Bond and Nakayama had flown to Osaka, where they caught a shuttle flight to Hokkaido. They arrived just in time to join the attack force. M, alert to international protocol, had warned Bond that his official capacity was as an "observer," and that he was not to use any weapons. Of course, they both knew that in self-defence he could cancel that particular directive.

About the time that the task force was leaving Hokkaido, the first wave of carriers arrived in California. FBI and Customs officials immediately arrested the incoming passengers at the gate, confiscated their luggage and took them into custody.

The JGSDF force flew over Etorofu and reached the target site not long after the events in California. They were expected. Yoshida's ground forces met the helicopters with heavy resistance. His army was in possession of a Stinger and a 30mm automatic cannon with a radar fire-control system in a revolving turret that was mounted on an AMX 13–type tracked chassis. Yoshida had purchased the weapons from the Russian mafia.

The AA gun, perched in a well-protected dugout, was successful in knocking down one of the Cobras within the first two minutes of the attack. The aircraft exploded and hurtled to the ground, where it burst into a gigantic ball of black smoke.

"Take out that cannon!" the commander in charge ordered.

The remaining five choppers were armed with SNIA BPD HL-12-70 rocket launchers, Bofors Bantam antitank missiles, AS.12 attack missiles and other weapons capable of obliterating an entire village. The teams directed this immense firepower at the AA gun, blowing it to pieces in the space of ten seconds. When the smoke cleared, there was nothing left of the dugout.

Before the five choppers could reposition themselves for a full strike on the entire complex, a stinger missile shot out of nowhere and sliced through the Huey that was flying only sixty metres away from Bond's. As that chopper went down in a heartbreaking trail of fire and smoke, Bond spotted the soldier with the stinger and pointed him out to Nakayama. The man was perched behind sandbags covered in camouflage netting. Nakayama passed the news on to the door gunner, who walked his fire onto the stinger's position. The rounds kicked up dirt and dust, taking out the enemy just before two Hellfire rockets from one of the Cobras completely obliterated the area.

The remaining four helicopters unleashed an inferno on the terrorist camp. Bond felt a surge of adrenaline as he watched the landscape torn apart by the bombardment. The entire operation took thirteen minutes and forty-two seconds before the officer in charge made the "cease-fire" call.

A blow-by-blow replay of the events that had occurred a few hours earlier in Los Angeles interrupted normal service at Chicago's O'Hare Airport. Two hours later, FBI and Customs agents met the arrivals into JFK in New York.

The confiscated mosquito eggs were sent to the Centers for Disease Control in Atlanta, Georgia, for analysis. All of the agencies concerned agreed that if it hadn't been for the British Intelligence agent who had delivered the information to the Japanese government so quickly, America would have had a disaster on her hands. No one wanted to think about what might have occurred had the carriers dispersed after arriving in the country.

Back in Etorofu, more than thirty of Yoshida's soldiers were waiting to surrender when the helicopters set down on the camp's airstrip. Bond was forced to take a secondary position as the troops went on to search through the remains of the bunkers for survivors. The Japanese government, still embarrassed by the prominent role a British Intelligence *gaijin* had played in bringing Yoshida's plans to light, were at least able to save face by claiming sole responsibility for the success of the raid.

The only disconcerting thing was that Goro Yoshida, dead or alive, was never found.

•   •   •

Shortly before sunset on the day after the successful raid on Goro Yoshida's camp, Yoshi Nakayama delivered a package to the suite in the Imperial Hotel.

"I hope I am not interrupting anything?" he asked politely.

Bond was dressed in a *yukata* but held the door open for him. "Not at all. Come on in."

"Thank you." Nakayama entered, carrying a large, elongated package wrapped in brown paper.

"What is the latest news on Tanaka-san?" Bond asked.

"As you know, the bypass repair was successful," Nakayama said. "Even Tanaka-san will need to rest now. But he is fine. I spoke to him an hour ago. He sounded weak and tired, but in good spirits. He said to give you his best wishes and to thank you for everything you have done."

Bond waved away the words and said, "I'm just happy that he's going to be all right. Now what's that you're carrying?"

Nakayama handed the package to Bond and said, "This is for you, in gratitude from the Koan-Chosa-Cho." He bowed.

Bond returned the bow and said, "Nakayama-san, this was not necessary."

Nakayama held up a hand and said, "Please. You have done a wonderful service for Japan. That is for you, and you are cleared to take it through Customs back to England."

"I'm intrigued," Bond said as he began to open it. Mayumi came in from the bedroom, also wearing a *yukata*. Nakayama's eyes widened at the sight.

"What's going on?" she asked. "Is it your birthday?"

"No, but I feel like it is," Bond said. He tore the wrapper off and opened the box. Inside was a beautiful black and gold *katana*. The *saya*, or scabbard, was inlaid with an intricate red and yellow floral design. The *kashira* was black with a firm leather grip.

"It's beautiful," Bond said with reverence in his voice.

"James-san!" Mayumi said. "That's a rare antique!"

"It is from the twelfth century, Bond-san," Nakayama said. "It was originally owned by a samurai who had been in service to the emperor."

Bond unsheathed the blade and noted the temper line pattern on the border of the cutting edge.

"It was made by Masamune, the greatest Japanese swordsmith," Nakayama said, interpreting the symbols etched on the *tang,* which was hidden inside the grip.

"I am deeply honoured," Bond said. "*Domo arigato.*" He bowed again.

"You are welcome."

Bond placed the sword on the table near the large picture window that looked out on the city of Tokyo. The sun had become a blazing red sliver that was quickly dipping behind the cityscape.

"So tell me, Yoshi, what has happened? I've been looking at spreadsheets with Mayumi today, as promised, and I haven't been able to watch the news." Mayumi put her hand to her lips to stifle a giggle.

"There has been a flurry of activity with regard to Cure-Lab and Yonai Enterprises. The whole plot has been exposed. Masuzo Kano, the chairman and president of Yonai Enterprises, committed suicide by jumping out of a twenty-seventh-floor window. The merger is declared void."

"As we had guessed." Bond looked at Mayumi. "This means that you're a very wealthy lady, Mayumi."

She shook her head in disbelief.

Nakayama handed Bond a packet of papers. "These are copies of documents that we found in a hidden safe in McMahon-san's office at CureLab. Not too much that is very interesting, I'm afraid, but we also found an envelope addressed to Mayumi-san, to be delivered in case of her father's death. I give it to you now." He handed it to her and she held it in her hands as if it were something dreadful. Her name was written in her father's script in both English and Japanese.

"Do you want to open it?" Bond asked.

"Not yet," she said, a little shaken.

Bond turned back to Nakayama. "What about the Ryujin-kai? Their boss, the *oyabun*—Tsukamoto. What of him?"

"He has disappeared. No one knows where he is, but there is a warrant out for his arrest. A team is also still going through the destroyed bunkers on Etorofu in an attempt to locate Goro Yoshida's body. We are afraid that he may have left the island before the raid."

"So he's probably still out there somewhere," Bond said. "That's not a very comforting thought."

"It's one of the reasons why I am here. We need to provide you with twenty-four-hour protection until you leave the country."

"Thank you, Nakayama-san," Bond said, "but I have never needed 'protection.' I can take care of myself."

"Famous last words," Mayumi said.

"Nevertheless, Bond-san," Nakayama said, "we will have a man posted outside your room." On his way out, Nakayama introduced Bond to the guard who sat in a chair in the corridor, then he shook hands, bowed and said good-bye.

When Bond came back to the room, he found Mayumi lost in thought with the envelope in her hand.

"This has been a very strange few days," she said. Her eyes welled up. "The only good thing about them was meeting you."

"You've left one line of business and must now run another. That's much more important," Bond replied.

She shook her head sadly. "How do you know I won't go back to a life on the dark side? I can't see myself running the company. I never asked for this. I keep thinking about my poor sisters. Kyoko had spent her whole short life preparing to take over the business. All I can do is wish I was not my father's daughter." A few tears ran down her smooth, beautiful face.

"What is it that happened between you and your father that caused you to hate him so?"

"He deceived the family. He was one of them, James-san, he was part of the Ryujin-kai."

Bond blinked. "What are you talking about?"

"It's true. He did business with Yasutake Tsukamoto. When Tsukamoto-san said that there was someone besides my great uncle who provided the Ryujin-kai with what they wanted, he was talking about my father. I saw him once . . . at the soaplands where my boyfriend worked in Tokyo. I was hanging round there with my friends."

"Are you serious?"

"He was Tsukamoto's guest. The two of them came one night. Tsukamoto apparently didn't know that I was there. He brought my father and we saw each other. Needless to say, we were both shocked beyond words. From that moment on, he could never look me in the eye. He knew that I saw through him. So I ran away from home."

"Then what happened?"

"I went to Sapporo, got in deeper with the yakuza. I heard through various sources that he continued to work with the Ryujin-kai. He did things for them."

"Provided them with trade secrets?"

"Yes. Now . . . now I think I was doing all that to spite him. To throw it all back into his face."

"Mayumi, you should have told me this earlier."

She held her hand over her face. Bond pitied her, knowing full well how much pain she was in. But perhaps this pain was necessary.

"Why don't you open the envelope?" he suggested quietly.

Mayumi sniffed and nodded. She tore it open and pulled out a single page covered in her father's handwriting. Mayumi read it silently, and then handed it to Bond. The letterhead bore the name "Peter McMahon" and the handwriting was neat and legible.

Darling Mayumi—

I know that you believe I let you down. I want you to know that my involvement with the yakuza was an inheritance from your grandfather, who had been doing business with them ever since Fujimoto Lab Inc. was founded. I was in the process of trying to break relations with them when the disastrous incident at the soaplands occurred. For that I am truly sorry. It is the greatest regret of my life. After you left home, the only way I could keep track of you and make sure that you were safe was by continuing to cooperate with them. They told me that you were working for the Ryujin-kai in Sapporo and that you would remain safe and would be taken care of as long as I helped them with what they wanted. I didn't feel I had a choice. Please understand that your parents both love you very much. I only wish I could have held you in my arms, my darling daughter, and told you all of this myself. Your poor mother knows nothing of this.

Dad

Mayumi looked lost and bewildered.

Bond handed the note back to her. "Your father provided those trade secrets because it was the only way he could receive news of your well-being. Don't you see? That's exactly the way the yakuza works. They gave assurances to your father that you were safe, working in Sapporo, and as long as he helped them, then you would continue to be safe. Mayumi, he did it to protect you."

Mayumi's lip quivered a moment, and then the tears flowed freely.

"I'm sorry," she managed to say.

Bond sighed and then held her close. She clung to his chest. "I don't know what to do, James-san. I don't know whether to grieve or to be happy."

"Hush," he said. "You are free to do anything you want. You can sell your shares for billions of yen."

She sniffed and was quiet for a while.

"You have a way of making me feel better," she said. "Are you sure that you have to leave tomorrow?"

"I'm afraid so. How shall we spend the time?"

"In bed. Come on."

28
The Final Action

They had made love into the night. Mayumi finally declared that she wanted to relax with a bath and invited Bond to join her. He thought it sounded like a terrific idea but suggested that he fetch a bottle of sake to enjoy while they soaked. She began to sing the traditional Japanese folk song *Sakura* as she went off to the bathroom to fill the tub and light a few scented candles in order to create a more romantic atmosphere while Bond put on a *yukata*.

He could still hear her singing and the sound of the water running as he went into the other room, opened the fridge and removed the bottle of Ginjo sake that they had opened earlier in the day. He grabbed two glasses, turned and started to head back towards the bathroom when he noticed that the door to the suite was ajar.

Bond's senses became alive, activated to full alert.

The front room of the suite was empty. The cupboards were closed. How and when did the door get opened?

He set the bottle and glasses on the counter and crept to the door. When he peered into the corridor, he saw that the guard that had been posted outside was lying on the carpet in a pool of blood. From the severity of the wound on the man's neck, Bond could see that whoever had done this had attempted to behead his victim.

Bond shut the door, locked it, whirled around, and scanned the room again. Mayumi was still singing in the bathroom. Should he use the telephone on the desk? His mobile was in the bedroom.

He had moved four steps into the room when the voice halted him.

"Forget the telephone, Mr. Bond. It cannot save you."

Goro Yoshida was standing in the open doorway of the large walk-in wardrobe, the door of which had been closed earlier when Bond passed through the room. Yoshida was dressed in a kimono that included the *montsuki hakama* half-coat emblazoned with the wearer's family crest of a dragon and a *hakama,* a culotte-like garment worn over the kimono. The edges of the hot red tattoo on his skin threatened to leap out of his clothing. He wore a magnificent *katana* sword at his side, along with the shorter, dagger-like *wakizashi.*

Yoshida stepped into the room, followed by Yasutake Tsukamoto, who had been standing behind his friend and master. Tsukamoto was wearing ordinary clothes, which created a skewed contrast to the *Yami Shogun,* and he was pointing a Glock at Bond.

Bond said, "Yoshida-san, I was wondering if you would turn up. *Konban wa,* Tsukamoto-san, it's good to see you again." Bond bowed, keeping his eyes glued to Yoshida's.

"Shall I get the girl?" Tsukamoto asked Yoshida.

"Not yet," Yoshida said. "By the time she is aware of our presence it will be too late. You can deal with her next." He stepped forward and addressed Bond. "We are both men of action, Mr. Bond. The great writer Yukio Mishima once said that 'a man of action is destined to endure a long period of strain and concentration until the last moment when he completes his life by his final action:

death.' That moment has come for you, Mr. Bond. I have risked my safety coming into the country like this and had it not been for the efforts of the Ryujin-kai I would not be here to personally see you destroyed."

He drew the sword and assumed a *Gedan no kamae,* the stance of holding the *katana* at middle height but with the tip dipped down, inviting the opponent to attack.

"I'm afraid you have me at a disadvantage, Yoshida, I don't have my sword with me," Bond said. He started to walk casually to the desk on the other side of the room, where he had left the gift Nakayama had given him.

Keep calm! he willed himself. He concentrated on keeping levity in the situation to throw them off guard. "I was just about to pour some sake," he said. "Would you like some?"

"Stop where you are!" Yoshida lunged with a perfectly executed *Morote uchi,* a two-handed cut intended to slice deeply into a man's trunk, but Bond's agility saved him. He leapt forward and performed a forward roll on the floor. The sword nearly struck the carpet. As a trained swordsman, Yoshida did not allow the blade to swing past the intended point.

Once he was on his feet, Bond's momentum catapulted him to the desk. He grasped the scabbard and pulled it toward him as he fell to the floor.

The sword came at him again with a *swish!* Bond rolled to the side and pushed himself to a standing position. Bond unsheathed his *katana* and tossed the scabbard behind him. He too smoothly adopted the more traditional stance, the *Chudan no kamae.*

Yoshida pulled back and froze in a *Haso no kamae,* a stance in which the sword was held vertically, with the hands by the right shoulder. At first his face revealed surprise that Bond could arm himself so quickly, but he slowly smiled and projected a powerful self-confidence.

"Very well," Yoshida said with a glint in his eye. "You

have shown your resourcefulness. Tsukamoto, put away the gun. Mister Bond and I shall fight honourably."

"No, Yoshida," Tsukamoto said, lowering the gun but keeping it in his hand. "I will shoot him if I have to."

"You will not have to," Yoshida said.

What had he got himself into? Bond suddenly thought. Just as he had thought when he had faced Ichihara back-stage at the Kabuki theatre, Bond was not sure if he could best his opponent. He had gone through a short, inadequate course in *kenjutsu* during his general training. He knew a few basic moves, but he was no match for Goro Yoshida, an experienced *kenjutsu* disciple. Bond feared that he didn't stand a chance.

The two men silently faced each other for what seemed like an eternity. Yoshida stood like a statue, the smile never wavering. He exuded a calmness that was frighten-ing. Bond could easily see how the man's charisma had seduced an entire yakuza gang.

Behind him, Tsukamoto sweated heavily.

Yoshida was waiting. Bond remembered a maxim of Japanese swordfighting: that whoever attacked first, lost. The better swordsman almost never attacked first. Franti-cally, Bond attempted to recall everything his instructor had taught him, but there wasn't much to draw upon. Bond did remember a technique called *enzen no metsuke,* or "gaze at the far mountains." This was a way to watch an opponent so that you saw all of him simultaneously. It was not wise to concentrate on one part to the exclusion of another. The technique helped to avoid falling for a feint or move meant to distract or mislead.

Bond reminded himself about breath control. That was one thing the instructor had drilled into them. One's *kokyu,* the ability to manage one's breath, was vital to maintaining control. By breathing deeply and slowly, a good swordsman fought against the body's natural ten-dency to become agitated under the stress of combat.

And then there was the most important concept of swordsmanship: *zanshin.* Awareness. Watchfulness. A "lingering heart." Without *zanshin,* a swordsman could never hope to vanquish an opponent.

It was Bond's *zanshin* that saved his life. Keeping his eyes locked with Yoshida's, Bond foresaw the attack. Yoshida's eyes betrayed him: his pupils dilated the split second before he acted.

Yoshida jumped forward and attempted a *kesa giri,* a diagonal cut that could open the victim from his upper left to lower right. It was called this because it followed the same line of a Buddhist monk's *kesa,* the sash hanging from the left shoulder to the right hip. Bond, however, flashed the *katana* in front of him just in time, warding off the strike. The metal blades clashed with a harshness that reverberated throughout the suite. Once the swords were swinging, they didn't stop. Yoshida and Bond slashed at each other repeatedly.

Yoshida was toying with him, Bond thought. He had reached his limit and Yoshida was blocking his blows effortlessly.

When the terrorist went on the offensive, all Bond could do was back away and keep his sword in front of him, warding off the powerful swipes. He collided with the sofa and fell back onto it; the worst thing that could possibly happen. Yoshida raised the sword above his head and brought it down hard, hoping for a *kiri kudashi,* the finishing cut. But Bond rolled and crashed onto the table, shattering the glass top. The sword stopped short of chopping through the sofa cushions, giving Bond time to get up. His own sword had never left his hand, so he took the opportunity to swing it backhanded at Yoshida. The blade struck the terrorist's left arm, embedding into his flesh.

Yoshida cried out and recoiled. He let go of his sword and fell on the floor. Tsukamoto pointed his pistol at Bond but Yoshida shouted, "No!" Clutching his bleeding arm,

Yoshida got to his feet, retrieved his sword and assumed the *Gedan no kamae* stance. Bond, much of his body cut and scraped by the broken glass, stepped back and resumed his own position.

The staring contest resumed. No one noticed that the sounds coming from the bathroom in the back of the suite had ceased. The only thing that could be heard was the breathing of the two men.

Then, the blades flashed once again, striking each other in a firestorm of metal and sparks.

Bond concentrated on the basic moves. Give and take. Receive and deflect. The two men executed these manoeuvres repeatedly as they danced around the room, smashing into furniture, stamping on glass and creating a shambles.

Blood gushed out of Yoshida's arm. Bond had severely damaged a major artery and part of a muscle, but the madman kept attacking as if it had been a mere flesh wound. He swung the sword with the speed of a demon, keeping Bond on the edge of disaster. Bond parlayed the blows, creating a *clish-clash, clish-clash* clamour that made Tsukamoto flinch.

When Bond saw the glint of metal spark off of his own sword and felt a sting on his neck, he knew that he'd been hit but not badly. Yoshida's blade had touched his skin but Bond had deflected the cut just in time to prevent serious damage. The conflict halted momentarily as Bond stepped back and resumed his stance. He slowly put his hand to his neck and felt the blood.

The staring recommenced. Again, the lunge of metal and the ferocious colliding of blades. Again, they waltzed around the room in a macabre ballet, each man intent on ending the life of his opponent.

Bond shouted a *kiai* then lunged with a *gyaku kesa giri*, a diagonal upward cut. Unfortunately, Yoshida had somehow anticipated the manoeuvre and blocked Bond's *katana* hard with a downward strike. Bond's sword flew out of his hand and slid across the room. He was defenceless.

Yoshida stopped, held the sword pointed forward in *Chudan no kamae* and prepared to pierce Bond's chest. He lunged quickly, forcing Bond to propel himself backward onto the floor to avoid being stabbed. The *Yami Shogun* stepped over Bond and raised the sword high above his head, ready to bring it down on his victim.

A shot rang out. Yoshida froze with the sword in the air. Everyone in the room turned their heads to see Mayumi, standing in the doorway to the bedroom. She was wearing a *yukata* and she was holding her Browning. She had fired it at Yoshida and now swung it toward Tsukamoto.

"Drop it," she commanded. "Next time I won't miss."

Tsukamoto tossed the Glock away. Mayumi then trained the gun on Yoshida.

"I called the Koan-Chosa-Cho and they have alerted the police," she said. "Drop the sword and give up."

Sirens could be heard on the streets below, but it would take the authorities several minutes before they could make it up the tower to the thirty-first floor.

Yoshida smiled, then slowly lowered the *katana*. He dropped it on the floor and turned to Bond. "Mr. Bond, I could have killed you just now, but I suppose she would have shot me."

"I certainly would have," Mayumi said. "One of the things I've learned in the last few days is to keep a gun in the bedroom." She moved next to Bond.

Yoshida looked at Tsukamoto and said, "Did I not tell you that our actions tonight might result in our deaths? This is not the way I want to die. It would not be honourable." From the inner folds of his kimono, he produced jar that looked frighteningly familiar to Bond.

It was a container full of mosquitoes just like the one Kappa had on the train.

The madman said, "All I have to do is release the top and dozens of hungry, infected mosquitoes will fly out into this room, into the ventilation ducts, and all over the hotel."

Bond took the gun from Mayumi and pointed it at Yoshida. "Come on, Yoshida, you don't want to do that."

"Why not? It would vanquish you, my enemy, and I would die like the kamikaze, honourably and with courage."

"Your death would be futile."

"Futile? No death can be called futile," he said. "Mishima-san said, 'If we value so highly the dignity of life, how can we not also value the dignity of death?' " He turned to his compatriot and said, "Tsukamoto, prepare for the ritual. It is time." He handed the *katana* to the head of the Ryujin-kai, who had a look of abject terror on his face.

"Yoshida, please, do not do this," he whispered.

"Do you want to go to prison?" Yoshida asked. "You know as well as I that in a few minutes there will be no escape from this hotel except through death. You should follow me after you have performed your duty as my second." He looked at Bond and Mayumi. "You two, stand back," he said. "Or I will unleash the insects. Mr. Bond, you can put away your gun. If you stand back and do not interfere, I will give you the jar unopened. I am no longer a threat to you."

Bond suddenly realised what Yoshida intended to do. He felt himself to be in a situation that defied the normal laws of sense and self-preservation—a world where rules of conduct and a notion of honour had been laid down centuries before. Slowly, Bond lowered the gun.

Yoshida knelt on the floor. He reached up to the collar of his *montsuki hakama* and tore it off of his shoulders. He then pulled it down so that he was bare to the waist. His entire chest, arms and back were covered in the blinding crimson tattoos, and the deep wound Bond had inflicted upon his left arm was bleeding heavily.

While holding the insect jar in one hand, Yoshida pulled the *wakizashi* from his belt. He put the scabbard between his teeth and unsheathed the blade, then dropped the scabbard.

The sound of voices and running feet outside the suite grew louder. The authorities had arrived.

"Are you ready, Tsukamoto?" Yoshida asked as he turned the point of the dagger toward himself, resting the tip gently against his exposed abdomen.

Tsukamoto was shaking. "Goro. *Sensei.* Can I at last call you *sensei*? You have always been a *sensei* to me. Please, do not do this."

Yoshida replied, "Yasutake, you have always been my friend. I thank you for your loyalty. Now perform your duty."

Tsukamoto paused a moment and quietly said, "Yes, *sensei*." He took a position behind Yoshida and raised the sword high.

Yoshida whispered a brief, silent prayer, then he carefully placed the insect container on the floor beside him.

The police banged on the door and called out. In a few seconds they would bash it down.

The man with the red tattoo glared at Bond and then thrust the *wakazashi* deeply into his flesh. Yoshida's eyes bulged and watered, but he was determined to go through with the *seppuku*. He tugged on the blade until it moved along his trunk horizontally, splitting his gut. As the entrails began to gush out of the open red crevasse, Tsukamoto brought the sword down quickly and cleanly.

Goro Yoshida's head flew off of his torso, hit the floor and rolled to where Bond was standing. Mayumi screamed and hid her face in Bond's arms.

The door burst open, and in seconds the place was swarming with armed officers. Yoshi Nakayama entered, took one look at the room and then ordered that Tsukamoto be arrested. The officers immediately relieved the Ryujin-kai's *oyabun* of his sword and handcuffed him.

Bond reached for the mosquito container and carefully picked it up. He gingerly handed it to one of the men, who promptly placed it in a reinforced container made for transporting bombs.

As they started to take him out of the room, Tsukamoto said, "Wait." The escorts stopped, allowing Tsukamoto to turn to Bond and say, "The *Yami Shogun* died the way he wanted, as Mishima did. He sacrificed his life in an honourable way rather than go through the humiliation of the courts. As for me, well, we shall see what my lawyers can do. If they are unsuccessful in freeing me, then my destiny is sealed. I have been aware of this for some time now and I am ready. I did not always approve of what the *Yami Shogun* wanted to do, but I must take responsibility for my part in it. Instead of shame, I feel pride. As for you, Bond-san: your victory is empty. Goro Yoshida robbed you of the finishing blow, the *kiri kudashi*. This was *his* victory."

Bond stared at the man coldly and said, "You know something, Tsukamoto? I don't give a damn. He's bloody *dead,* and that's all I care about."

Tsukamoto's eyes flared, but the men pushed him out of the room before he could say anything else.

It seemed like hours later, but in fact Nakayama and his men finished with them in forty-five minutes. Bond and Mayumi were moved to a different suite. The minor cuts Bond had suffered were treated. The couple answered questions and signed statements, and then they were alone again.

For a while, they sat together in silence. Neither of them could forget what they had witnessed. Mayumi knew that it was something that would haunt her forever.

"I'm going to sell my shares," she said, breaking the stillness. "And I am going to start something new. Something I like. I don't know what that is yet, but it will be something with a future."

Bond squeezed her arm in encouragement. "You have strength, ingenuity and courage. You should be all right. Beauty helps, of course."

"James-san, I think that's the first nice thing you've said to me. But I suppose it is safe to say such things when you are flying back to London tomorrow."

"Have you heard my flight has been delayed? I have some unfinished business here. Rather more than I thought."

She broke into a smile. "James-san, you really are most diligent."

Bond allowed himself a slight bow. Mayumi laughed, then stretched out sensuously on the bed. Bond marvelled again at her beauty. He moved down beside her and gazed admiringly along the length of her body at her soft translucent skin. He murmured softly into her neck, "My researches into some of the — finer — details of this case are incomplete. Perhaps you might be able to help."

"Cooperate with your enquiries?" she suggested with a wicked smile.

"I hoped you might understand," he whispered as he began to lay the ghosts of the past to rest once more.

Sources

For readers interested in the works of Yukio Mishima, the following were used as sources for this book:

Chapter 12: *Patriotism* (New York: New Directions, 1995)

Chapter 15: *Runaway Horses* (New York: Knopf, 1973)

Chapter 15: *Kyoko's House* (1959), as quoted in John Nathan, *Mishima* (Boston: Little, Brown, 1974)

Chapter 23: *The Sailor Who Fell from Grace with the Sea* (New York: Knopf, 1965)

Chapter 28: *The Hagakure: A Code to the Way of Samurai* (Tokyo: Hokuseido, 1980)